Bill standing there in the middle of the street with his long cinnamon curls hanging from under his hat to down past his broad shoulders, a pistol in each elegant hand, hardly appeared the nasty foe he could be when riled, aroused, or threatened.

Alice heard his somewhat lilting voice call to the cowboys:

"You fellers not able to read?"

One of them stepped forward, a man taller than Bill and clearly a cowboy by the way he was dressed: dusty Stetson with the front brim pinned back, bib shirt that looked like it was stained with blood and a few other things, and of course those greasy chaps.

The cowboy said, "Read? Why, you some sort of schoolmarm come to teach us?"

"Signs posted either end of town," Bill said calmly, "says firearms prohibited. You fellers know what that word means—prohibited?"

"Why of course we do, we ain't some ignorant trash!"

Bill said, "You must be the mouth for this lot."

"I'm Phil Goddamn Coe, you must know. And what's it to you?"

"You don't check your weapons, Phil *Goddamn* Coe," Bill said, "I'll sure as damn hell show you what's it to me."

Also by Bill Brooks

Forthcoming
LAW FOR HIRE: DEFENDING CODY

BILL BROOKS

LAW FOR HIRE:

PROTECTING

HICKOK

HarperTorch
An Imprint of HarperCollinsPublishers

This is a work of fiction. Names, characters, places, and incidents are products of the author's imagination or are used fictitiously and are not to be construed as real. Any resemblance to actual events, locales, organizations, or persons, living or dead, is entirely coincidental.

HARPERTORCH
An Imprint of HarperCollins*Publishers*
10 East 53rd Street
New York, New York 10022-5299

First HarperTorch paperback printing: July 2003

HarperCollins®, HarperTorch™, and ♥™ are trademarks of Harper-Collins Publishers Inc.

Printed in the United States of America

Visit HarperTorch on the World Wide Web at www.harpercollins.com

10 9 8 7 6 5 4 3 2 1

For Michael Shohl,
who still believes there are books
yet to be written.

LAW FOR HIRE:

PROTECTING

HICKOK

Prologue

———————————————

Wild Bill was down to just his socks when the commotion started.

"Lord God almighty," said Squirrel Tooth Alice, who was lying on the bed with a rose between her teeth. One of the thorns pricked her lip, and a drop of blood bright red as a ruby formed upon the small sweet mouth Bill had intended on kissing.

Bill went to the window and looked down onto Main Street, his bare hams pale in the glow of a dozen candles Alice had lighted to set the mood. Bill was her favorite customer, and she only charged him half the going rate because he was the most famous man in all of Kansas, and because he was handsome as a racehorse, and because he was the city marshal.

"It's a bunch of knothead cowboys shooting off their pistols," Bill said. "I'll have to go down and tame them before they kill some innocent."

"Couldn't it wait just a little until you and me finished our business, honey?"

"Why, those yahoos could kill half the decent citizens of Abilene in the time it would take us to derive our pleasure, Alice. The town fathers don't pay me to fornicate."

Bill tugged on his drawers, then his checkered pants and silk shirt, the whole while half regretting he had taken the job of Abilene's peace officer because it could be mighty inconvenient at such times. And the pay sure wasn't up to the standards of a man of his talents or tastes. If it wasn't for poker games and getting paid two bits each for shooting stray dogs, he'd practically be penniless.

Bill pulled both his revolvers from out of his boots, where he liked to keep them when undressed; otherwise he wore them tied to his waist by a red sash. But he did not deem it necessary to wear the red sash just to go tame a few knothead cowboys.

A stray bullet *wanged* off the metal sign of the bicycle shop next door and shattered the window glass where Bill had been standing seconds earlier. Alice noticed that Bill never even ducked, or showed any sign of excitement other than his member having deflated when he first looked out and saw trouble brewing on the street.

Bill stomped his feet down inside his boots and threw Alice a forlorn look.

"If it ain't one damn thing, it's another," he said, and went out the door, an ivory-handled pistol in each hand—the Navy Colts given him by the citizens of Hays for cleaning up their town just before they fired him. Even had his name inscribed on the backstraps: *J. B. Hickok*.

Alice quickly wrapped herself in a midnight-blue silk kimono and rushed to the window. It would prove to be the best seat in the house. She was careful not to step on any of the broken glass that had fallen into the room from the exploded window and cut her pretty feet. She always felt a certain erotic thrill when she saw men fighting or shooting off their guns at one another. She couldn't explain it, not even to Bill. There was just something about all that masculine violence that got her feeling feverish.

In a few moments she saw Bill stroll out the front door of her bawdy house and stalk across the street toward the rowdy cowboys. They were laughing and firing off their pistols and shoving one another, and some were swearing like they didn't know how not to. Alice felt her blood ripple with intrigue and figured by the time Bill finished his business with the bunch of yahoos, she'd be about ready to ride him all night. And Bill could take it too. Not like a lot of those young bucks who came swinging in her door wearing their greasy chaps and big hats and crowing like banty roosters about what great lovers they were and how long it had been since they'd been with a woman and how the fairer gals should stand aside so as not to suffer heart attacks. Some of those waddies would barely get it in a gal before they popped off like a cheap firecracker. Some she barely had to get undressed for—just a kiss and a touch often did the trick.

The cowboys as a lot weren't worth a tinker's damn as lovers, but they sure were easy money. And as long as she had a lover like Bill to take care of her more womanly nature, there was no need to be niggardly in her attitude toward the cowboys.

Buttery light lay on the street from all the rowdy establishments along Texas Street: saloons and gambling halls and the opera house, bordellos and dope dens. That section of Abilene known as the Devil's Addition turned into a regular Sodom and Gomorrah once the sun set, which it did every night.

Alice could hear the *rinky-tink-tink* of a piano being played badly. It had to be the professor—Three Finger Karl, a Dutchman who'd arrived the year previous claiming he'd been a concert pianist in Vienna until he lost a couple of fingers to a jealous ax-wielding husband of one of his female students.

The town was full up with folks like the professor: gamblers, pimps, drummers, buffalo hunters, cowboys, and charlatans of every ilk. Castouts from regular society: fortune seekers and dreamers. Abilene had become a regular circus, and Alice loved every second of the wicked nights and the loose life she'd chosen.

She saw Bill stroll to within about twenty paces of the collected cowboys. He looked like a prince—in fact, the dime novels written by that drunken hack Ned Buntline had labeled him *Prince of the Pistoleers*—a nom de plume he abhorred when sober.

"Makes me sound like some sort of prissy fool," Bill complained on several occasions. "Those cowboys will think I've come to kiss them rather than arrest them . . ."

Bill standing there in the middle of the street with his long cinnamon curls hanging from under his hat to down past his broad shoulders, a pistol in each elegant hand, hardly appeared the nasty foe he could be when riled, aroused, or threatened.

Alice heard his somewhat lilting voice call to the cowboys:

"You fellers not able to read?"

One of them stepped forward, a man taller than Bill and clearly a cowboy by the way he was dressed: dusty Stetson with the front brim pinned back, bib shirt that looked like it was stained with blood and a few other things, and of course those greasy chaps.

The cowboy said, "Read? Why, you some sort of schoolmarm come to teach us?"

"Signs posted either end of town," Bill said calmly, "says firearms prohibited. You fellers know what that word means—prohibited?"

"Why of course we do, we ain't some ignorant trash!"

Bill said, "You must be the mouth for this lot."

"I'm Phil Goddamn Coe, you must know. And what's it to you?"

Alice could feel that familiar tingling sensation just above her knees, and it was moving upward to that special place Bill liked to call her beaver pelt.

"You don't check your weapons, Phil *Goddamn* Coe," Bill said, "I'll sure as damn hell show you what's it to me."

The cowboys surged a few steps toward Bill, but he didn't so much as flinch.

Then Phil Coe did a stupid thing: he drew his pistol and snapped off a shot in Bill's direction. Alice felt herself get all squirmy. Bill simply turned his body sideways to his adversary and brought his arm straight out—the Navy Colt aimed like an accusatory finger at the cowboy—and *bang! bang!* shot him twice through his body.

Even from as far away as she was, Squirrel Tooth Alice could see the dust fly out of the cowboy's shirt—or what looked like dust but probably was more Phil's innards along with some bone and blood.

"There's two pills for you," Bill said calmly. "Take your medicine Mr. Phil Goddamn Coe."

It was like Bill had shot them all—for they all fell a step or two backward and watched their leader twist around like a fish dangling at the end of a line, then fall facedown in the street.

"I still got plenty of doctoring left in me, any of you other fellers want an appointment!" Bill said, his voice rising like that of an opera singer. His blood was up, and Alice knew when his blood was up, whether it was because of fornicating or fighting, Bill's voice could get as high as a girl's.

A shadow came running up from Bill's right. He spun and shot the shadow as easily as he had the cowboy, and the shadow dropped like a stone even as the echo of Bill's pistol carried out onto the prairie.

Then it got so quiet you could almost hear the stars moving around in the night sky.

Bill stood there, arms out wide, a Navy pistol in each hand, the one in his right still curling smoke. The other, he swept back and forth, and the crowd of cowboys shrank into the shadows until there was only Bill and two corpses on the street.

Alice was pretty sure she'd had a screaming meemy.

Bill walked over to the last man he shot and turned him over. He lay nearly directly under Alice's window.

She saw Bill bend and look closer then stand again, and something seemed to cause him to sag—some invisible weight like the hand of God pressing down on him.

"Oh," she heard him say. "Oh."

In a few moments he came into the room. Alice had already removed her kimono in anticipation that Bill would be as ready as she was. But he wasn't. The lamplight flickered across his face, creating deep shadows and making his nose look longer than it was. Bill sat on the edge of the bed and did not say anything.

Alice said, "Well, they had it coming, Bill. No use to fret. The world is full of cowboys, and the loss of two is hardly a great disaster."

"No," Bill said. "Mike didn't have it coming."

"Mike?"

"Williams," he said.

Mike Williams had been Bill's deputy until a few minutes ago. Now he was a cooling corpse.

"I didn't know," Bill said several times. "I didn't know it was him."

Alice tried her best to console him, but Bill had lost his lust, and after a few minutes of uncomfortable silence, he patted her shoulder and said, "I guess I'll go to the chink's," and stood and left.

The only amusement Alice would find this night was her pet squirrel, Henry. It was hardly what she'd hoped for.

* * *

And while Bill went off to the chink's to dance with
the harlot, opium, the late Phil *Goddamn* Coe did get
delivered down in Texas in a fairly ripened state of de-
composition, in spite of the ice put inside his lead-
lined coffin at every opportunity. From Abilene to
anyplace in Texas by wagon was a hell of a long way
to go.

And once delivered thus by an unhappy old vaquero who could no longer earn his trade aback a
horse, and thus resigned to errands and chores grin-
gos would pay him to do—including the transporta-
tion of dead cowboys—a certain woman whose heart
lay broke within her bosom took delivery and paid
the vaquero fifty dollars upon demand and a handbill.

"*Gracias*," said he, feeling now ready for a few
drinks in the local saloons of El Paso.

"Oh, Phil. I will avenge you," said she, "even if it
takes all the rest of my life to do it."

For she was a woman wronged, in her mind—
short-changed in the arena of love by one Wild Bill,
Prince of the Pistoleers—and far past her prime to
find another she loved as much as Mr. Coe.

Chapter 1

His name was Teddy Blue and he was cut from the cloth of wanderer. Born of breeding, his father was a Chicago lawyer and personal friend of the late President Lincoln. His brother had become a captain in the Chicago Police Department on his way up the ladder of success, as they say, until gunned down in a seedy bordello on that city's South Side. The murder broke a certain resolve in the younger man's heart. He told his father he was dropping out of law school.

"I forbid it," the patriarch said. "It's foolish and uncalled for."

"I want to go away for a while. Find out who I am, where I belong."

"You belong here."

But he was his own man now and they both knew it.

"Finish law school then go find out who you are," the father urged, for he was a man who had known such feelings in his own youth, had sailed the seas to China and fell in love with a dark-skinned woman in Marrakesh. He understood the urgency of youth, but

hoped now that his only surviving son would take the
more direct route to his ultimate destiny.

But instead, the boy walked the streets at night feeling lost, angry. He stood outside the house with its
many windows and watched his parents move about
like shadows within and felt their sense of loss as
well. He wasn't sure where he would go when he
went. He half wished the war was still going on so he
could join the battle. He stayed aimless throughout
the winter, tasted snow on his tongue, got drunk, con-
sorted with the low crowd in the harbor bars, fought
and lost his virginity to a woman named Sadie. Then
one evening he went on a lark to Nixon's Amphi-
theater and saw three of the West's most famous frontiersmen performing badly—Buffalo Bill Cody, Texas
Jack Omohundro, and Wild Bill Hickok—and it
stirred something deep and primeval in him and he
began thinking about the West. By the spring he'd
gone to Texas. And by the end of the next summer
he'd helped take a thousand longhorn cattle north to
Kansas.

The letter of his father's suicide came General Delivery, at the end of his last cattle drive to Ellsworth,
Kansas. He read it and it filled him with a sorrow that
surprised him. The news had come too late for him to
do much but get pie-eyed drunk with an old saddle
tramp named John Sears who had taught him to shoot
a pistol well enough to make men cautious of him.

"You going back, or what?" Sears said. They were
in copper bathtubs big as small boats, full to sloshing
over with soapy water and two fat whores.

"I don't know," Teddy said. "I feel like an outlaw."

"You ain't done nothing to be ashamed of."

"I went country on 'em, John."

"Shit, you did what anybody with hot red blood would have done."

"The old man wanted me to stay and become a lawyer. I already had two years in college."

John shifted his stogie, spoke around it as one of the fat whores washed his hair then rubbed her big bosoms all around his head.

"Which one?" he said.

"Which one what?"

"Which college did you go to?"

"Harvard."

"No shit."

"No shit."

"I heard of it."

"You have?"

"Hell, I ain't ignorant, in spite of what you might think."

"I never said you were—I just figured you were always out here in this country."

"I still got family . . . well, some anyway, back in Boston and that area."

"You from there?"

"No, I'm from Ohio originally. Farm kid too lazy to pick corn and milk cows. Came out to this country when I was fourteen. Liked it well enough to stay."

"You ever going back?"

"This country's ruined me on anything East."

"Look at us . . ."

"Honey, you want to do that some more," John

said to the fat whore, and she giggled, and he said, "By God, a man could fall in love easy enough if he let himself."

Then Hide Walker, their ramrod, came in and said that the grangers had gone to the city fathers and the city fathers had come straight to him and said they didn't want no more Texas cattle coming into Empire next season and that he could just forget about it if that was what his plans were.

Hide stomped around saying goddamn this and goddamn them sonsabitches and they could all kiss his sorry ass, and he was nearly as drunk as they were but wasn't enjoying it half as much.

"I guess I'm going to pay you boys off and let you catch on with whatever you can catch on with."

John Sears said, "I'll take mine in silver, I like the weight of it in my pockets." Hide went and got him his money in silver and gave it to him. Then, still angry, he said, "You know what those sonsabitches said to me? Said, we wasn't welcome no more and they was going to run all the whores out and turn all the saloons into churches and schools and put up fences to keep us out, and I said, 'Shit I wouldn't come back here if you was to give me a elephant to ride.'"

John damn near drowned laughing, and Teddy ached with a bittersweet sorrow of having learned of the death of his father and the death of a part of the West he'd come to love.

"You want my whore?" he said to Hide, stepping out of the tub, soap running off his lean frame.

Hide looked at the whore and said, "I reckon it beats falling off my horse" and stripped down and got into the tub, then said, "I guess this is the end of something I don't understand no more" and sat there glum in just his hat, pulled down so tight his ears bent over. John Sears couldn't stop laughing.

"What're you going to do?" Teddy said to him, "now that there isn't going to be any more drives north?"

"Well, I'm going to fuck this whore till one of us is about ruined, then I'm going out to New Mexico, I reckon."

"You heard of something good down that way?"

"There's always something good somewheres. That country is about as good as any, I reckon."

Teddy shook their hands, John's and Hide's, and said, "I guess I'll take the train home to Chicago, even though it's too late for me to do much but see my mother."

"You finish up your business back there, come look me up," John said. "Maybe I'll have something going by then."

"What about you?" Teddy said to Hide.

"Shit, I don't have a Chinaman's clue. Horses and cows is about all I know. I guess I'll drift back down to Texas and catch on with some outfit or other."

"You could go with me down to New Mexico," John said.

"Why, there ain't nothing but bandits and Mexicans down there, what I heard."

"All the better . . . Hard for a feller to get in trouble in a place like that."

"I don't know nothing about it. I don't know nothing about much these days."

"She's been paid for already," Teddy said. "Enjoy . . ." And he left the place and went and sold his saddle and bought himself a train ticket to Chicago.

He sat waiting in the wind for the rest of what was left of that night and the first light of morning, which, like the color of unpolished silver, crawled silently over the grasslands. Then the sun rose above the horizon and the land all changed with the light on it so that it looked new again, with the dying grass heaving its death song against the wind.

He could see the shanties and the new buildings that had grown up beside them, and remembered the places where tents had once stood. And down at the end of the street he saw the steeple of a church that wasn't there the year before. Neither was the bank across the street built of brick and limestone, with large plate-glass windows that reflected the morning sun so that the glass looked like liquid gold.

Then before he knew it, the whole land seemed set afire and things began to stir to life. Folks appeared on the street, wagons pulled by horses rambled in off the prairies, dogs set to barking, and shopkeepers swept the sidewalks in front of their establishments.

He sat there on the bench looking at it all, looking down the long twin tracks of steel that would eventually bring the morning flier that would carry him away from this place, and he wasn't sure how he felt about it all. It seemed strange to him to be leaving the country—like he'd been in it all his life and never anyplace other.

He felt like he'd come to this country one way and

was leaving it another. Then he could hear the flier's whistle a mile out, and watched it turn from being a black dot on the horizon to what it was. Its big cowcatcher engine pulled a dozen cars behind it and screeched to a stop there in front of the station. It shuddered and huffed clouds of steam like a dragon and he could smell cinder on its breath. The engineer leaned out the window of his cab, his face sooty, and looked down at Teddy and nodded.

"Brought her in on time," he said, a wrinkle of pride across his brow.

Teddy climbed aboard one of the cars, handed the conductor his ticket, and found himself a seat next to the window. He thought he might even change his mind, go find John Sears and tell him he wanted to go to New Mexico with him. But he'd been gone three years into that country already, and in that time he'd lost half his family, so it seemed he should at least go home out of respect—even if it proved temporary. The West wasn't going anywhere, he told himself. It would still be there if he decided to return. He just knew it would be different than what it had been. It was changing, and would change some more by the time he got back to it.

He crossed one leg over the other and noticed how worn were his boot heels, then caught a glimpse of himself in the window's reflection. It looked like the face of a stranger staring back at him. He hardly recognized himself sitting there under his old Stetson as he swiped at his black moustaches. He looked like John Sears and a whole lot of other waddies and saddle tramps looked when they were yet young, before they got wind-whipped and horse-thrown and drank too much liquor and whored too much and got blooded by maybe killing a man or three. He looked innocent yet, but not as innocent as before.

The train jerked and shuddered, and soon enough Ellsworth, Kansas, fell away from the windows and there was little to see but a sea of grass. Here and there a few scattered trees that looked like they had wandered onto the plains and gotten lost stood lonely vigil. Occasional thin streams wiggled through the grass, the water clean and clear, and he remembered what it was to drink it. He saw an occasional soddy standing off by itself, a wisp of dark smoke curling from its stovepipe. It could be a mean empty land with a loneliness to it he understood. But it was a free land too. A land where a man didn't have to answer to anyone's calling but his own most of the time. If ten million folks moved on it tomorrow, there'd still be free places to wander.

John Sears said it was the goddamnedest most uninteresting place he'd ever seen.

"I'd never want to die here, would you?"

He could see old cattle trails—a wide swath of beaten earth through the grass—trails that no longer would be used. The cattle would stop coming now, and the grass would reclaim the scarred earth for its own. He could see fences where there didn't used to be any, and it broke his heart a little to see them.

Two hours of watching the same thing, he grew weary of looking at it. Sleep begged for his attention. A cowboy never got enough sleep once a drive began. He felt like now it was all catching up to him because it could, and he settled his heels on the seat across from him and slept under his hat and dreamed of horses he'd known and women he'd known and old John Sears and the dust of a thousand cattle and not much else.

Chapter 2

———⋄———

With a worried hand she wrote the letter:
Pinkerton's Detective Agency, Chicago, Illinois . . .

Three weeks he'd been gone—a week longer than they had been married. Some dark dread troubled her days and troubled her dreams at night, and once she awoke and heard an owl hooting and realized she'd never before in her whole life heard an owl hooting in Cincinnati. But this time she had, and it sent a chill into her and she sat up the rest of the night thinking about it and the last time she'd seen him.

Nibbling at her lower lip, she debated again whether to go ahead and send the letter once she finished writing it. What would James think of her if she did send it? He was such a proud haughty man, and if he learned of the letter, of its intent, he might grow angry with her—angry enough to ask for a divorce. She couldn't bear to think of him leaving her. Their courtship had lasted years, but their marriage had hardly a life of its own yet.

It was she who had eventually proposed marriage.

James knew his way around women—of that she had little doubt. But he'd been reticent to utter the words she so wanted to hear. So finally she put her cards on the table one evening and asked him if he would marry her after a prolonged kiss. To her mild surprise and joy, he'd said, "I guess we oughter."

She did not want to ruin everything now by causing him to think she doubted his abilities.

Dear Sir,

I write to you with all great haste and would much appreciate a fast reply as to whether you will accept assignment . . .

She remembered the first time she had looked upon him—there in dusty Abilene when he came to inquire about the huge circus tents of her Hippo-Olympiad & Mammoth Circus. She'd been practicing her tightrope walking, and he stood holding open the flap of the tent, watching her. The outside light gathered around him in such a way that it caused him to verily glow, to seem surreal, ghostly, a heavenly creature. She nearly fell off the tightrope at the sight of his handsome stature.

My husband is the famed Wild Bill Hickok and I fear lately for his life . . .

The first words he said to her as she balanced on the rope were: "That's a clever way of getting around."

He appeared the perfect specimen in every respect.

Normally, I would not worry about my husband,

*for he is generally quite capable of protecting himself.
But lately he has been having much trouble with his
eyesight and I fear he might even be going blind . . .*

He stood a full head and a half taller than her—
which for her was not unusual since she was a petite
woman. He was, she guessed, six feet tall. Cinnamon
curls spilled from beneath the broad brim of his sombrero and cascaded down onto his broad shoulders.
He had matching moustaches, and he made no apologies for the length of his hair or his beauty. He wore a
brace of silver pistols with ivory handles inside a red
sash wrapped round his waist. Over this he wore a
Prince Albert coat unbuttoned and free of dust and
prairie dirt. She would come to learn of his fastidious-
ness on the train from Abilene to Cincinnati while
honeymooning. He wore a white silk shirt, which she
would also learn he ordered by the dozen from a St.
Louis mail-order house. His voice was light and airy,
his hands graceful—the fingers long and tapered. He
seemed hardly the blood-lusting shootist that appeared on the covers of Beadle's and DeWitt's *Dime
Novels.*

*. . . and now he has returned West to seek new for-
tune so that I may soon join him to live in wedded
bliss. His destination is Cheyenne, Wyoming Territory, for the coming winter—then on to Deadwood
Gulch in Dakota in the spring . . .*

He had invited her to join him for supper that evening, and they dined on oysters and calves livers, and
James—he told her his Christian name was James
Butler—mesmerized her with his stories, some of
which she was sure he made up. She had to admit to

herself that she was quite taken with the fact of how well-known and respected a man he was. Their meal was interrupted several times by gentlemen stopping by their table to make his acquaintance. The men verily ingratiated themselves, and the wives on their arms were unabashedly adoring.

He seemed to take all the attention with a certain passive interest, fobbing off such adoration as little more than gratitude for his services as city marshal.

Bill made mention, before he left, that there were those out to assassinate him. I in fact begged him not to journey West but to stay here in Cincinnati with me. But he maintained his belief that while many might want him dead, few were capable of such a deed . . .

She was surprised by her sense of jealousy whenever a woman approached their table and introduced herself to him, even those who were in the presence of their husbands. For it was quite plain to see that such women tried not at all to hide their desire for Wild Bill to take special notice of them. And sometimes, depending on their beauty, he did not make any effort to dissuade such attention, and he often flirted outrageously.

She was further surprised to find herself immediately formulating a plan to nurture their budding friendship into something much more. And when he at last walked her back to the circus grounds that evening, the large tents luminous and billowy as clouds under a full prairie moon, her heart was beating as rapidly as the hooves of a runaway horse.

Like the true gentleman she thought of him as, he bent low and kissed her gloved hand. Only a self-imposed modesty prevented her from inviting him into her wagon for a nightcap. For she knew it would hardly take anything at all to give herself to him completely. But widowhood and wisdom had taught her to play a close hand in matters of the heart, and so she did not give away so easily or quickly the prize most men sought of women on moonlit nights. That would come later and a lot more often than even she was prepared for. She sighed, thinking of how efficient and voracious a lover Wild Bill could be.

. . . but I fear James is being incautious and vain about his skills to think that he is invincible. I've been to the woolly West, and I know the sort of men who inhabit that part of the country. I know that some of them would not hesitate to kill my husband if only for the entitlement of "Killer of Wild Bill." And I know too that such men are always observant for weakness in their adversaries. It would not take long for such men to see that my husband suffers from a weakness of the eyes and take full advantage of that fact. He is most vulnerable . . .

"I know we will meet again, Mr. Hickok," she'd said to him that evening, the moon's light giving his features the whiteness of bone.

"Do you really think so?" he said.

"Yes, I believe that we are fated toward a greater destiny than simply this one night together, as lovely a night as it has been. Do you believe in such things as destiny Mr. Hickok?"

He confessed that he had come to believe in things of the "spirit nature." And when she asked him what he meant exactly, he stuttered a bit—from shyness, she supposed—then confessed, "I don't know how to explain it."

She said there would be plenty more times when he would have the opportunity to try and explain it to her, and she gave him a quick kiss on the lips. Her boldness seemed to please him. When he smiled, his long blond moustaches lifted and she thought he was going to say something that would hardly be considered temperate. But instead he touched the brim of his sombrero and went whistling off toward the town's lights. She waited until his happy whistling faded, and went to sleep that night still formulating plans for their future.

Whatever the fees to send a man to protect my husband until he once again returns to me safely— and it would have to most certainly be without his knowledge—I am willing to pay. I will eagerly await your response, dear sir. Most sincerely, Agnes Lake Hickok, General Delivery, Cincinnati, Ohio.

The question still nagged her even as she sealed the letter inside the envelope and addressed it: should she actually send it and risk the wrath of her husband and his possible humiliation if he found out?

He had left only the week previous, but his absence seemed like months already. Theirs had been a whirl-wind honeymoon, traveling with the circus wherein she exhibited her equestrian and tightrope walking skills and James put on shooting exhibitions and talked about forming his own Wild West Combination to take East, where "the dudes would pay plenty to see some buffalo and savage *Induns*."

It was one of the things she adored about him, his ability to dream of a greater world than the one in which he lived. He was fearless and bold in every way. And he was quite aware of his celebrity. Yet he still managed to maintain a certain dignity and did not take unfair advantage of any man. Sure, if there were those who wanted to buy him drinks and offer him free meals and the best tables in restaurants because of who he was, he did not turn them down. And if some men let him win at poker for the privilege to say they'd gambled with Wild Bill, he did not leave their money on the table. And if lovely women wanted to introduce themselves to him and brazenly show off their physical attributes, he did not avert his eyes. She did not want to think of what else such women might offer him and that he might accept.

But in spite of everything, he had confessed one evening: "I have reached my prime, Aggie. I've seen and done things most men can only dream about. And now I want to settle down and live a quiet life. My wild days are over. I want to die in bed, not in some saloon with my face down in the sawdust." This, merely a month before he said he had gotten the itch to go west again one last time and make his fortune and bring her to him so that they might live in comfort all the rest of their days. He spoke of a gold strike in Deadwood Gulch.

It was her dream as well, for them to live out their lives in a quiet comfortable fashion. But their separation seemed now a rent in the fabric of that particular dream and, ominously, she felt troubled by the rather sad countenance she'd seen when he waved good-bye to her there on the train platform.

She dressed and hurried to the post office, hesitated only an instant more before dropping the letter into the mail slot, wishing it had wings so it might fly to Chicago and be there by morning so Mr. Pinkerton might send her a reply affirming that her fears were justified and send a man straightaway to watch after her darling James.

But something most unexpected occurred when the letter slipped from her fingers: it felt as though the last thread connecting her and James Butler Hickok had been snapped. An odd empty feeling rippled through her very spirit, and tears flooded her eyes. She could only pray that such a feeling was nothing more than the mad imaginings of a worried wife.

Chapter 3

It had risen from the ashes of a terrible fire that swept over it during the time he'd been in the West. He'd read about it in Leslie's *Harper's Weekly* and sent a telegram asking if his family was okay, and his father sent one in return saying, yes, they were, and everyone was determined to rebuild, for that was the strength and will of the people.

He hardly recognized this risen city when he stepped off the train under a cold rain that pelted his Stetson.

A hooking wind brought with it the stench of the stockyards and slaughterhouses, and it wasn't the same stench as in the feedlots of Kansas and Texas. No, this was a smell that had blood mixed into it, and he didn't care for it much.

Rain stippled the gray waters of the Chicago River, and later, when the hansom drove along the curve of Lake Michigan, he could see the rain dimpling its flat calm surface. He went straightaway to the great house and stood out front for a time trying to decide whether to go in or turn around and head back to the train station. The house seemed to leer down at him like a stranger, and he thought he saw movement behind one of the curtains on the second floor. He went up and lifted the brass knocker and let it fall against the heavy oak door.

His mother's name was Mary. She greeted him wearing a wreath of dried flowers round her head, and he could see she had become slender and that her cheeks were rouged and her eyes happy.

"I can't believe it," she said.

"I know I must look a sight," he said.

She hugged him and wept. The rain chased them inside. Flames danced in the parlor's fireplace, and a man stood up from an armchair, a book in his hand, a piece of red ribbon marking the page he'd been reading. He came forward and said in a English accent, "My name is Fletcher Devonshire."

The man offered him a hand as smooth and delicate as his mother's.

Her dress of lace was beaded with pearls. Wearing it, she seemed soft and airy and hardly a woman in mourning.

"Fletcher is a poet friend of mine," she said.

He wore a velvet jacket and trousers.

They had lunch in the atrium toward the rear of the house, and even the rainy gray light seemed somehow less gray there. Fletcher asked him to tell them about the West.

"I'd someday like to go there myself," he said. "They've all sorts of wild Indians and things, I hear."

Teddy felt disinclined to tell them much, but Mary begged him and so he told them stories, but none of them true.

The true stories he kept to himself. He did not tell them about Ed Ferguson, who accidentally walked his horse into quicksand on the Canadian River then drowned trying to save the screaming creature. He did not tell them about the charred body of Jack Beck they'd found after he'd been struck by lightning, his spurs fused together. And he did not tell them about Pedro Garcia—the one they called Pretty Pete because he was so handsome even the whores would give themselves to him for free—who was killed with a pitchfork by a jealous mush head.

No, such stories were not for dinner conversation or, as he could see by their stolen glances, lovers still freshly in their love.

He was given his old room to sleep in, but could not sleep because the night sounds of the city were different than those of the cowtowns and the prairies. And down the hall he could hear laughter followed by closing doors, and it wasn't his father who was causing her to laugh but an English poet in a velvet suit.

He took a hansom next morning to the cemetery and found the graves of his brother and father. A pair of ornate marble headstones the color of evening light along the Pecos marked their resting place.

He sat cross-legged on the ground the way he'd learned to on the plains whenever he ate or palavered with his pards.

"Well, boys, I've been to see the elephant and back," he said.

But the dead never answer, nor tell their secrets, and did not with him.

"It's about ruined me on this place."

A crow hopped along the ground, its curious black bead of an eye fixed upon him. The bird cawed once and hopped atop a small stone obelisk with the name CHARLES carved into its base.

"I'm different now," he said, then pulled a silver flask that had once been his father's and took a swallow of the finest bonded whiskey money could buy. "I guess you're different too . . ."

He poured a bit of the whiskey over each headstone and watched it run down their names like two small lost rivers seeking refuge.

"To old pards," he said, then took another swallow.

The sky was like a dome of pewter. The air had in it the taste of coming winter. The crow, satisfied the obelisk wasn't something to eat, flew off to the upper branches of a robust elm whose limbs the wind had gleaned bare as old bones.

"I'd sure like to know the whole story," he said. "Who it was killed you . . . killed us all. Did you know she's in love with an Englishman? Wears velvet pants. A poet, of all goddamn things. Calls herself a libertine. Shit, I don't hardly know what that means other than she wears her hair cut short like a man's and smokes cigarettes and . . ."

He finished off the last of the liquor, thinking it was about the only thing better here than out there where he'd spent the last three years, where the only whiskey he'd ever drunk was the busthead in the rowdy frontier saloons and the kind they made from cactus called *tiswin*.

"Well, boys, she's all changing. Nothing's what it once was, but I guess you already know that, don't you."

He set the empty flask against the old man's stone, and it looked like some sort of fancy canteen. Instead of some precious *objet d'art*.

Then he left and wandered the streets that seemed now foreign to him from everything he knew. He felt lost and empty and without reason, and such a feeling was foreign to him too.

His mother told him the evening before about the discovery of his father, how she'd come home to find him in the carriage house, hanging. She told him that Horace's death had left him irretrievably depressed and how he had hired the Pinkerton Detective Agency to investigate Horace's murder because he did not trust "the crooked Chicago police."

"They were friends, you know, Mr. Pinkerton and your father," she said. "Through their mutual friend the late Mr. Lincoln."

No, he didn't know.

She explained that his father had gone every day to the detective agency to check on the progress of the investigation, but that clues were scant and led nowhere, and his father had grown more and more morose.

"It was as though the bullet that killed your brother passed through his flesh and bone and into your father's very soul," she said. "If he had loved me like he once did, love might have saved him. But he gave up on life after Horace's death and your leaving. He gave up on me and himself and everything else."

He resisted spilling his heart to her. She was, after all, now a *libertine*.

He wandered the city streets without thought or direction. And as if by some fated plan, he ended up standing outside a three-story building over whose edifice hung a sign that read: PINKERTON'S NATIONAL DETECTIVE AGENCY—WE NEVER SLEEP. There was a large eye painted in the center.

He went in and asked to see Mr. Pinkerton, and was told that Mr. Pinkerton was at his New York office. He explained why he had come, and the fey young man sitting at the desk directed him to a door down the hall, saying, "Mr. Bangs is Mr. Pinkerton's associate."

George Bangs rose to greet him. A short stocky man of middle age, with a black beard wired with gray and dark suspicious eyes. Teddy told him who he was and how he'd come to be there.

"So you are the prodigal son," Bangs said. "Your father talked about you a great deal."

"I don't know about being a prodigal. I've been three years gone to the West, and if that makes a prodigal then I guess I am."

"I guess it does. How may I help you, Mr. Blue?"

Teddy asked about the progress on the investigation into his brother's death, and Bangs offered him a wary look beneath a broad furrowed brow.

"We've made some progress, I can tell you that, sir."

"I'd like to know what exactly."

Bangs sat in his chair and said, "Why not have a seat" and when Teddy sat in the oak chair opposite, the detective checked the time on his pocket watch before responding to Teddy's inquiry.

"It's all somewhat complicated by the fact that the police did their own investigation, of course, since Horace was one of theirs. They've been quite close-mouthed about it and won't let us have access to their reports. But we have our own methods of gaining information . . ."

"I didn't come all this way to dosey-do, Mr. Bangs."

"No, I don't suspect you have. But you must understand this as well, Mr. Blue. That what makes our operatives—and therefore our entire operation—as efficient as it is, is dependent on keeping confidences. I understand quite well your position and desire to know the facts, but until we have things nailed down, I can't risk our investigation by showing you what we have. You can understand that, I hope."

"No, I can't. My father paid for this investigation, it would seem—"

The detective cut him off with a wave of a meaty hand.

"Were you to take some piece of information I might show you and go off half cocked in search of some sort of justice, you could jeopardize the entire investigation and possibly forewarn your brother's killer, allowing him to slip the net of justice."

"Can you at least tell me what he was doing in a cathouse in the first place?"

"What men usually do in such places, I assume."

"He wasn't that way."

George Bangs arched an eyebrow. "You mean he was more saintly than to visit a whore? Perhaps he was, perhaps he'd gone there on official business of some kind or another. I can tell you if that was the case, we've not learned of it yet. But I'll make no effort to besmirch the memory of your brother, sir. My only obligation is to find the truth. Isn't that what you want as well?"

"Horace was the most decent man I ever knew. He wouldn't need to visit a whore if he needed a woman's company."

"That's all I can tell you about the matter, I'm afraid."

"Then I've wasted my time, and obviously my father wasted his money hiring your agency."

Teddy started to stand, feeling as he did a bit dizzy.

"Perhaps you've not wasted your time at all. There's a matter I'd like to discuss with you. Please," Bangs said, indicating Teddy retake his chair.

When he did, Bangs said, "Do you mind if I ask you if you found the West to your liking?"

"Good enough, I suppose."

"As I recall, your father said that you were attending law school before you went out to that country?"

"Yes."

"And have you made plans to return to law school?"

"I don't think so. That country has a way of ruining a man on doing any sort of inside work."

"Does it ruin him as well on the law?"

"Not necessarily. But I admit it alters your thinking some about the law. Most men in that country have to become their own law. Out there, laws aren't so much written down as carried on a man's hip. He either abides by a code of conduct, or he doesn't. He either enforces the law or breaks it. Pretty simple stuff."

"Do you think you'll go west again?"

"I'm seriously considering it. Thing is, some of it is getting about like it is around here: tamed, run by men with paper collars and paper contracts. Cowboying is a dying business. I'd have to catch on with some outfit. That, or rob banks, maybe." Teddy thought wryly of old John Sears. Laid up maybe in some hotel in Las Vegas, New Mexico—a place John often talked fondly of—with maybe a bank bag of cash and a couple of señoritas.

George handed Teddy a cigar and a cutter. Instead of taking the cutter, Teddy bit the end off the stogie and spat it into the spittoon by the desk, then struck a match with his thumbnail and lit the cigar.

George Bangs lit his own after cutting off its end, then took an envelope out of his desk drawer. "If you had something to catch on to, would you go?"

"It could be."

"I might have a proposition for you then," George said, pushing the envelope across the desk toward him. "Read this."

"This genuine?" Teddy said upon reading the letter.

"I sent Mrs. Hickok a telegram, and she confirmed it was indeed genuine and she's quite desperate to hire us. Did you ever meet her husband out in that country?"

"No."

"Do you think you could locate him?"

"A man with Wild Bill's reputation wouldn't be all that hard to find."

"I'll be honest with you, Teddy, you possess the qualities we look for in our operatives. You know that country and you know the people in it. I'd like to hire you for this assignment. Would you be interested?"

"In becoming a Pinkerton?"

"There are worse things you could do."

"I'm not interested."

He got up to leave. The liquor was wearing off and the world was starting to feel too real and he could hear the trolleys clanging their bells out on Michigan Avenue, and he didn't care for it much.

But before he could open the door, George Bangs made him a proposal that stopped him dead.

"If you were a Pinkerton, I'd be able to show you the file on your brother's case. You'd know everything we know. I'm also sure that Allan himself would take a special and personal interest in finding your brother's killer. He's the best detective in the country and he is a genuine bulldog when it comes to family—something that you'd be considered as, were you one of us."

"Sounds like blackmail," Teddy said.

"No. If I knew who the murderer was, I'd tell you. But not until I was sure who that person was would I show you the file. Unless of course you take the job and sign the usual confidential disclosure clauses and so forth."

"Why not offer me the job of finding my brother's killer then? Why assign me out West to another case?"

"Because I need you there and not here. Once I tell Allan the situation, you can be sure he'll get directly involved—and frankly, he's a lot better at being a detective than you are. Trust me, I know what I'm doing here, Mr. Blue. You'd be better served taking the Hickok assignment."

"You mean you would?"

"Yes, as would the Pinkerton Agency."

Teddy felt anger, felt like he was being manipulated, unnecessarily so. He wanted to reach across the desk and show this fellow what it felt like to be hit by a cottonwood fence post—something old John had said that time they got into a scrap with a few cowboys from the Lazy H one drunken night in Hays. Teddy had swung on this lanky fellow and missed and hit old John by accident. John went down but got back up and said, "Feels like you hit me with a cottonwood fence post." Teddy asked John why he was so specific on the type of wood, and John said, " 'Cause cottonwood's about the hardest goddamn wood there is."

He wanted George Bangs to know what it felt like to be hit by a cottonwood fence.

"Let me ask you something else," Bangs said, taking advantage of Teddy's hesitation. "What if your mother had written this letter instead of Agnes Hickok? What if it was Horace that needed protec-

tion and I could have sent somebody to save him but
the man I could have sent refused me, and that fellow
was you?"

"From what I've heard of Bill Hickok," Teddy said,
some of his anger tempered now, "he can well take
care of himself."

"As was Horace such a man, but it didn't save him
from assassins, and it won't save Bill Hickok from
them either. Not if he's going blind, as his wife states
he is. You've a chance to do something worth doing
here, and help yourself in the process."

"I don't care for your politics, Mr. Bangs."

"Of course you don't. Nobody on the other side of
that desk ever does. But I'll apply any politics I need
to in order to see the job done we're hired to do. Including finding your brother's killer and protecting
the likes of one Wild Bill Hickok. I make no apologies
for my politics, sir."

Teddy remained silent, running the possibilities
through his mind.

"Ask yourself, Mr. Blue, what do you really have to
lose by accepting the position? And then compare
that with what you have to gain."

"Let me see the file."

"I'll consider your handshake as your bond."

Bangs held forth a hand. Teddy shook it.

As Teddy looked over the retrieved file, George
commented: "Our informant has him visiting a lady
named Desiree Drake. Most likely an alias, of course.
But she's since disappeared out of the city. That is
where the trail runs cold. Unless we could locate her,
of course, which we haven't been able to so far."

There in the file was a photograph of Horace in his police uniform. Below it, a description of Desiree Drake:

> 5 feet 2 inches tall. Weight approximately 110 pounds. Raven hair. Green eyes. Strawberry birthmark in the shape of a star on left hip. Prior arrests for solicitation and prostitution. No known address.

Teddy stared into the eyes of his brother, then closed the file.

So it was that he found himself on the train the next morning heading west again. Only this time he wasn't so sure of himself as he had been the first time. He told himself a dozen times he was wrong to take the job, that he could do nothing to protect a man like Wild Bill. But George Bangs had played to his sense of guilt about Horace, and to his vanity as well, by making it seem like Teddy was his last recourse. Of course that wasn't true, but Bangs made him feel that way, for Bangs understood about the ways of men—it was his job and he was good at it.

Bangs had given him a hundred dollars cash money for expenses, a dossier on James Butler "Wild Bill" Hickok, and instructions on how and when to stay in contact with the home office to file reports.

"Keep good record of your expenses," Bangs said. "Allan's a real stickler."

Then, when he was set to go, Bangs said, "I'm assuming you carry a pistol," and Teddy showed him the double action Colt Lightning, with its bird's head grips, he'd bought in Abilene—just like the one old John Sears carried, but without the same history to it as old John's had.

Bangs smiled and said, "Good. Let's pray you'll not have to employ it."

"Employ it?" Teddy said. John would have laughed his ass off and probably said that the only thing that would be getting employed if he pulled his gun would be the undertaker.

The train would take him first to Denver, where he'd switch and take one up to Cheyenne, a place he heard, now that Abilene had been tamed, was about the wickedest place a man could spill some blood— his own or somebody else's.

He couldn't do any good in this place, he told himself; he might just as well go back out there to that country where it felt like he'd left his soul.

An hour outside of Chicago it started feeling a lot like freedom again, and he watched out the window as the shadow of the train moved across empty harvest fields as though it were chasing the sun. And he liked the feeling it gave him.

Chapter 4

Colorado Charley Utter felt fateful the day he met Wild Bill. Charley's wife had sent him atop the roof to shovel snow, afraid the early autumn storm would cave in the ceilings and kill her and the children. She was a nervous woman to begin with, and took on a regular basis Doc Johnson's Bitters, which always left her a little more listless than Charley would have liked on certain occasions when he was feeling most romantic. Such was the case when she sent him up on the roof to shovel snow.

"Heights make me nervous," he said halfway up the ladder. But she held no compassion in her glazed eyes.

"Would you have the roof cave in and kill us all in our beds?"

"No dear."

It was while shoveling and looking off toward Pike's Peak and thinking of the gold that had at one time been discovered up there that a hansom pulled up out front of Charley's Denver house. He heard the horses snort and saw emerging from within the cab a rather tall, handsome cuss with ringlets of russet hair falling from under his big sombrero. This feller wore a fur cap and a cape and checkered trousers stuffed down inside his boots. Charley had paused to catch his breath anyway—forgetting how hard real work could be, and how heavy the first snow always was.

"Howdy," he called down to the stranger.

The man looked around, and Charley noticed that he right away let one of his hands go under his woolen coat, where Charley suspected there might be a pistol or three.

"Up here," Charley said, and the feller looked up, shading his eyes with his free hand—the one not going under his coat.

"What are you doing on the roof, there?" the feller said.

"Shoveling snow off it so it don't cave in and kill my family."

"You reckon it might?"

"No, but my wife does."

The feller looked around, then back up. "She must be the nervous type," the feller said.

Charley knew right away he and this feller had some common ways of thinking about life and those in it. "Might I ask your business, sir?"

"You might. I'm looking for one Colorado Charley Utter. I heard this is his house."

"Might I ask why you'd be looking for him?"

"Might you be him?"

"I might be if I knew the reason you're looking for him. Or I might not be."

"I reckon you are him or you wouldn't be up on

that roof shoveling snow down off it to keep your kin from getting killed by the weight."

Charley climbed down, and the feller stuck forth his hand and said, "Name's Hickok. James Butler, but most call me Wild Bill. You ever heard of me?"

"I'd be the only one in this country that hadn't and a liar if I was to say no."

"I've heard of you too. I heard you were an enterprising fellow."

"I don't like grass to grow under my feet, if that's what you mean."

"I don't either. You a drinking man?" And when Charley acknowledged that he was, Bill invited him to take a drink or three with him at the nearest, nicest saloon.

"It's not so much I'm particular about my whiskey as I am where I swally it," Bill said.

"I have been known to hold a particular notion or two myself," Charley replied, before going in the house to tell his wife he was off to the Rocky Mountain Oyster Club with one Wild Bill Hickok himself.

"He's a thoroughly dangerous sort," she said. "You be careful, Charley."

"Oh," said he, giving her a kiss on the cheek. "I'd never put myself in harm's way for fear of missing your sweet warmth in my bed at night. I'm feeling kinda tangy, if you must know."

She blushed at such bold talk but took no real offense when Charley patted her haunch through the many folds of her skirts.

"I shall be back," he said with a wink. "I hope you're feeling a bit tangy too."

* * *

So that's how they became pards—deciding they'd
take a wagon train of adventurers up to Cheyenne before winter set in hard. And then when spring broke,
take 'em on up to Deadwood, where they could all
make their fortunes in the goldfields. Them that
didn't get shot or stabbed in card games, kilt over
some prostitute, had their heads bashed in for their
poke or wagon, or got themselves scalped by the Indians Custer and his bunch failed to corral.

Charley was a natural organizer with a good business sense, the way Bill heard it. And of course having
a chap with Wild Bill's reputation signed on for protection would naturally make the pilgrims feel safe.
Some might even feel safe enough to take a wife or a
consort of the feminine variety along for company in
a place that was likely not to have many decent free
women available to them.

After several hours of coming to agreements on exactly how and when they'd form the intended wagon
train, how much they'd charge, and how long it would
take getting from Denver to Cheyenne—considering
the possible vagaries of weather that time of year,
what sort of supplies they'd need, and how they were
going to advertise the expedition—the two shook
hands.

All this took place near the middle of September.
And by the time Charley got everything organized and
sojourners signed up, it was almost the end of September and he was getting restless, and Bill was too.

"I wish you'd not go off to such a godforsaken

place," his wife said the night before their scheduled departure.

"Oh dear, everything will be just fine. I've a good feeling about it all. I feel like we're headed for glory, Bill and me."

"What if it snows while you're gone and the roof falls in and kills me and the children?"

"I've hired old Ned to come and shovel the roof whenever it snows," Charley said soothingly. "Why, you know I'd never let anything bad befall you or the children."

She felt his cold searching fingers there under the blankets and knew Charley was feeling tangy again, as he always felt whenever he was about to leave off for somewhere for an extended period of time, or whenever he worked at something overly hard, or whenever he drank too much champagne, or whenever the sunset, or a hundred other things that would put him in such a mood. Still, she couldn't think of herself of ever loving anybody but Colorado Charley Utter.

And they left that very next morning, and now had been in Cheyenne for the better part of yet another month.

Charley was taking his morning bath when Bill walked in out of the sun.

First it was hard to tell who it was. Then when he came closer, Charley could make out that it was his pard under that broad sweep of a hat with those near reddish curls hanging down to his shoulders.

Bill took off his hat and combed his hair with his fingers. The air was cold yet in that high country, and Charley could see Bill's breath, just as he could the steam rising from the hot water the chink had filled his tub with.

"Awful cold to be bathing," Bill said.

"Never start my day without a bath," Charley said, scrubbing his shoulders with a horse brush.

"I guess someone wanted to assassinate you, it'd be easy. Like shooting one big fish in a barrel."

Charley noted how much Bill seemed to dwell on somebody always getting assassinated. Usually it was Bill himself that Bill referred to.

"I doubt anybody with an ounce of decency would shoot an unarmed man in a tub of water," Charley said.

"I've known some that would. . . ."

Charley preferred not talking about death before breakfast. "I been thinking," he said.

"About what?"

"About we oughter go up to Deadwood Gulch and strike it rich, like we said."

"I been thinking the same thing," Bill said. "In the spring."

Charley lathered the soap through his hair; he too had long hair, though not as curly as Bill's and several shades darker.

"Just one thing you oughter know before we throw in together," Bill said.

"What's that?"

"I'm married."

The soap ran down into Charley's eyes and he did

his best to knuckle out the sting. "When'd you get married?" he said.

"About a month before I saw you on that rooftop, shoveling snow. Me and Agnes Lake."

"The circus lady you tole me about?"

"That's the one."

The chink came over with another bucket of water and poured it over Charley's head, washing out most of the soap and clearing his eyes.

"You want more water Mr. Charley?" the chink asked.

"No, that'll do."

Bill sat passively on the upturned pail, watching the traffic that ran past the barbershop—miners and gamblers, whores and gun artists, all of them waking up from whatever hell they'd fallen into the night before. Charley's camp was just one of a few dozen or so tents and wagons set up on the outskirts of Cheyenne—a place everyone referred to as Tent City. The hotels were full up with men waiting for the weather to break so they could head to Deadwood and up into the Black Hills. Some had already gone— to what end or fate, nobody knew. The Army patrolled the hills—Custer and the Seventh. They'd warned the whites to stay out, that the Indians were more than willing to take whatever white scalps they were offered. Reports had come back daily of some miner being found shot so full of arrows he looked like a porcupine, or found with his skull bashed in, a bloody patch where his hair had once grown.

But it didn't stop those who wanted to get an early jump on the gold rumored to be in those Black Hills.

"She wanted me to run the circus with her," Bill said. "I told her my show business days were over with. Cody about ruined me on all that."

Charley stepped out of the tub. He looked white as fish belly except for his hands and face, which had been permanently chafed umber by wind and sun.

Bill averted his eyes. He didn't care to look at another man without clothes on. Charley didn't seem to care if the whole town saw him naked. He sometimes walked around camp that way saying how it was good for the constitution to let all his parts air dry, how natural it was for a man to go naked in the world the same way he'd arrived in it. Some of the whores coming out of their nearby tents would see him and giggle and call to him, "Hey, Charley." He was plump and round as a fat hen. He didn't care.

Finally he crawled into a fresh set of buckskins, ran a Mexican comb decorated with abalone shell through his hair, and trimmed his moustaches with a pair of dainty scissors in one hand and a small mirror held in the other.

"Wasn't you already married?" Charley asked.

"No," Bill said. "I never was—leastways legal."

"The stories you tole—I thought you was married to Squirrel Tooth Alice . . . or was it Indian Annie?"

"Neither one," Bill said. "I never married nobody officially until I married Agnes."

"Calamity is going all over the camps saying how you and her got married . . ."

"You know that's about a dang lie and a half."

"I know it."

"You want to go get some breakfast?"

"I could eat me a whole entire buffalo hump, couldn't you?"

"Say, did you ever eat dog?" Bill said as they left the barbershop and headed for one of the cafés.

"No. You?"

"No, I never could even consider it after Abilene. I used to shoot them for two bits a piece to keep the population down—just the strays, though, nobody's pets or anything."

"I know it," Charley said. "You've mentioned it a time or two."

"Oh, I guess I forgot I told you already."

"I ate turtle once. You?"

"No," Bill said. "I never did think I'd care much for it."

Over breakfast of Spanish eggs and antelope steaks they talked about all the things they ate and all the things they didn't eat over the years. Bill said he once ate a blue heron out on the plains when he'd gotten lost in that country and nearly starved.

"I never thought I'd eat anything nearly as tall as I was, but you'd be surprised what you will eat if you get hungry enough."

"I once ate a garter snake on a dare. It wasn't but about this long," Charley said, holding his fingers apart six inches.

"I don't think I never would eat a snake of no kind for no reason," Bill said.

"I wouldn't eat another," Charley said, ordering another glass of buttermilk.

Charley could see Bill's eyes were troubling him.

He could see how red they were around the edges and how often Bill swiped at them with his forefinger and how often he blinked.

"You know, I seen a pair of glasses over at the mercantile is made to keep the sun out of your eyes," Charley said somewhat casually, for he knew Bill to be vain about his appearance and reputation.

"I wonder how a fellow would look wearing dark glasses if he didn't need them for reading?" Bill said.

"I think he'd look all right wearing 'em."

Bill dabbed at his eyes again. "You don't think nobody would see it as some sort of a weakness or being prissy, would you?"

"I think it might set some sort of new style or something. I seen folks wearing 'em down in Denver already."

Several people stopped at their table and introduced themselves to Bill and said what a pleasure it was to meet him and how they'd read about his exploits in DeWitt's *Dime Novels* and *Harper's Weekly.*

Bill took it all in stride, glad-handed them and didn't shy from the attention.

"You and Cody are about two of the most famous men in America," Charley said.

"It's kindy nice in a way," Bill said. "But it brings with it problems too. There's a goodly number of fellers that would be happy to make their reputation off me. Shoot out my lights and say there were the one who killed old Wild Bill."

"Ah, you oughter not think in them terms."

"Sometimes when I to the chink's I experience what

death is like," Bill said. Charley could see how forlorn the look in his eyes was.

"You can't know nothing from smoking that opium, Bill. It's its own kind of madness. Hell, I've known fellers that smoked it then went and laid out and stared at the sun till they went stone blind thinking they were looking into the face of God. I know one feller who rode his horse off a cliff from smoking it and another who shot his mother."

"I don't know, Charley. What I seen wasn't all that bad."

Wanting to change the subject because he knew it would make Bill more morose, Charley said, "What's the most interesting thing you ever ate?"

Bill smiled, said, "Beaver pelt."

"Beaver pelt?"

"Belonged to that gal I knew back in Abilene named Squirrel Tooth Alice."

"Oh, that, you mean . . ." Charley laughed, and Bill did too.

It was later that very week when Charley got the letter from Agnes, who obviously knew of him through Bill. She said she wanted him to promise not to mention it to Bill or nobody else. She went on to write about how she'd hired Allan Pinkerton's detective agency and that they were sending a man to protect Bill from would-be assassins. Charley felt a bit pie-eyed stunned by such revelations. Bill would be ashamed to learn his new bride had taken such measures.

I hear you are Bill's best pard, she wrote. *He's told*

me a lot about you. Don't let vanity, his or yours, blind the eyes I pray will watch over him. Please telegraph me your promise. Mrs. Agnes Hickok.

It troubled him a great deal she would do such a thing, and he wished she hadn't done it, but understood in a way why she had. By now he loved old Bill Hickok like a brother and he'd do anything for him. But he sure hated keeping secrets from him, even if the secret was meant to protect him.

Agnes had included the man's name Pinkerton was sending. Teddy Blue.

Charley ran the name through his mind.

He concluded he never had met or heard of anyone named Teddy Blue.

Later that evening in the Gold Room he said to Bill, "You ever heard of a fellow named Teddy Blue?"

"No, I never did hear that name. Why do you mention it?"

"No reason."

Bill didn't seem concerned about it one way or the other, and won fifty dollars that night playing poker while Charley was upstairs with a girl named Lilly Rose, getting what he liked to call "waxed."

Charley, in his postcoital reverie, thought every day should end in a night like the one he'd just had, and that every man should have him a pard like Wild Bill, and every man should be free to go about the world as he pleased.

Then Charley thought about his wife and daughters and felt a little ashamed of himself.

Chapter 5

————◆————

It was near evening and snowing when the train pulled into Denver. It was a soft easy snow that fell from the sky with near laziness though not much of it was sticking, for it was late in the season for snow to stick. Teddy felt stiff from being on the train for five days.

He asked for directions to the nearest hotel from the stationmaster and bought himself a ticket to Cheyenne at the same time. The hotel was about ten blocks up the street toward the center of town. He decided to walk.

It felt good to be West again in a way he couldn't have explained to anybody if they had asked. And even though Denver wasn't exactly a larger version of Abilene or Ellsworth or San Antonio, it still had the feel of the West to it.

He found the hotel and was registering his name in the book when the clerk said, "Would you like some companionship for the evening, sir?"

He looked at the man, guessed him to be in his

fifties, nearly bald except for a few strands of hair combed over from one ear to the other. Freckled hands.

"Do I look like that sort to you?"

"Oh, no sir, I didn't mean me, I meant that if you were interested, I could arrange, for a slight price above the hotel rate, of course, to have a young lady sent up to your room. Anything you wanted—even Oriental."

"Oriental, huh?"

The clerk nodded.

"Sure, why not . . ." It was impulsive, but the feeling of emptiness was in him.

The room was comfortable with an iron bed, carpet, a washstand with a round mirror above it, and a window that looked out onto Colfax Avenue. The flier to Cheyenne wasn't due to leave until the morning. He set his valise on the bed, undid the shoulder holster with the Colt Lightning and placed it atop the washstand, then put his coat on again and went out for a walk.

He found a steakhouse and oyster bar and went in, and it was warm and cheerful and well-appointed. The thought of a good meal piqued his senses. Teddy ate with gusto and then went to the bar drinking a cocktail and listening to a diva on the stage set up at one end of the bar who sang a bittersweet song about love that couldn't last. Men were wiping their eyes by the time she finished, raising their glasses and shouting requests for other songs, which she gladly accommodated.

It was all very entertaining, but Teddy was bone-tired and still had to face another extensive journey by train tomorrow. He headed back toward the hotel.

He had gone only a block or so, noticing as he went how deserted the streets seemed. The snow was beginning to pile up now that the sun had gone down. It was a pretty sight, snow falling against the glow of the gas street lamps.

He caught a movement out of the corner of his eye—a shadow—then two men were in front of him. They wore caps with the bills pulled down low over their eyes and short coats. One stepped close to him, said, "Say, we were just wondering—"

He hit the man with a short straight jab to the point of his chin and turned his attention immediately to the other one. But too late. Something hard and mean struck him across his collarbone and buckled his knees. He knew it was a lead sap from the way it felt, the snapping sound his bone made when it broke and sent a wall of fire through his chest, numbing his left arm.

They were quick and fast with their fists and kicks, like a pair of fighting dogs attacking him as he tried to resist, the three of them dancing shadows, moving in and out of the street lamp's glow, the snow falling so prettily.

For the first time in his life he felt real fear. He hit and was hit. He could taste blood in the back of his throat.

The thought of what Horace might have felt in those last dying seconds of his life flashed through his mind with every punch and kick.

One said, "Get him off his goddamn feet. Let's take him into that alley and finish him . . ."

He felt the world tilt, saw the glow of street lamps swirling overhead as they pulled and lifted him, the darkness closing in.

Then he saw Horace—his face peering from the shadows, his mouth moving wordlessly, the form of a man holding a smoking pistol, the naked hip of a woman with a star-shaped birthmark fading in and out.

Don't let's all die like this.

He wasn't sure if he'd actually heard the words, but they were like hot steel touching his skin, burning into his blood and bone. The words produced a fury in him, unexpected and unabated, and he twisted free of the clawing hands. He lashed out at the nearest face with a flurry of punches, striking hard over and over again until he felt flesh and cartilage give way, turn to something sticky and soft under his knuckles, and saw the man sink to his knees and topple over.

The other climbed on his back and was trying to rake his face, but Teddy swung him around into a brick wall, drove his shoulder into chest and ribs and heard them distinctly popping. The man's yelps did not save him as Teddy drove a knee into his face, then took the small skull with its greasy hair and slammed it hard into the wall, knowing it was quite possible it had cracked like an egg, but no longer caring.

He stood bent with his hands on his knees, trying to breathe through his blood-clogged nostrils—his attackers silent now, curled shapes in the darkened alley. He regained enough air into his lungs to stagger toward the light. Once on the street again, he saw that the hotel was only a block away. He realized he was no longer scared, no longer filled with that same dread Horace must have known as he drew his final breath.

He went up the back stairs of the hotel and into his room.

He shucked himself out of his coat, and in doing so felt the deep aching pain of his broken collarbone. His eye fell on the holstered Lightning and he wondered if he had been armed whether he would have shot and killed the two men. He realized in that moment that he had never shot a living thing. Would he have done it? Could he do it the next time? And would he stand a bullet for Hickok, or deliver one, if it came to that?

The world seemed full of hard edges. He spat blood into the basin, then filled it with water and washed his face. There was a nick above his eye, and he stanched the blood with the cuff of his shirt. His cheek was scraped but to no great damage.

There was a knock at the door.

He slid the pistol from its holster and held it down along his leg as he opened the door.

She was small and pretty, with coffee-brown skin and black hair that gleamed under the hall's gaslights.

"Mr. Tom say you want company."

Teddy had forgotten the agreement he'd made with the desk clerk.

"No, not tonight," he said.

"You hurt," she said, touching his face. It was such a delicate touch he nearly wept.

"I'm afraid there's been a mistake," he said. "But let me pay you for your trouble . . ."

She followed him into the room when he turned to get his wallet out of his coat.

"I'm Kiko," she said.

He took ten dollars from his wallet and handed it to her.

"No," she said. "I don't want. You don't like me. It's okay. I go."

He stopped her. "Don't go," he said.

"Okay," she said.

She was there on the bed next to him when he awoke. Morning light fell through the window. He sat up and almost fell back again from the pain of his collarbone, remembered the way the pain felt lost during the night each time she kissed him there. She slept as silently as a child.

He dressed, strung his fingers through his hair, and set his hat down on his head. He slipped into the shoulder holster rig, tightening it like a binding around him to ease some of the pain. The weight of the pistol lent some comfort.

He took the money he'd offered her last night, placed it on the bed next to her and kissed her cheek, and she did not stir. He said her name and she did not answer. She was the kind of woman that could make a man change his plans.

He left and walked to the train station, passing the

very alley of his attack. Curiosity caused him to look. The alley was empty. He was just as glad he didn't see two dead men lying there.

It had stopped snowing.

Chapter 6

———————

Bill went to see the fortune-teller, Madam Moustache. She had big bosoms and claimed the ability to speak to the dead.

She looked at his muddy boots. He removed them. She nodded and led him into her séance room at the back of her tent.

"You have something for me?" she said.

He handed her five silver dollars, which she placed in a tin box under a red scarf.

"For the gods," she said, smiling.

She sat across from him at a small round table covered with a black cloth.

"Who do you want to visit today?" she said.

"Mike Williams," he said.

"Someone who is related to you?"

"A feller I killed by accident."

"I see," she said, taking his hands in hers and closing her eyes.

He followed suit.

She began an incantation. He felt a bit spooked.

But that was the way the netherworld was—spooky.

She called Mike's name. Her voice changed. Sure enough, the wind blew against the walls of her tent.

"He's here," she said.

Bill opened his eyes. "Don't see him."

She opened her eyes and looked into his. "You cannot see in that way."

"Oh," he said, and closed his eyes again.

"What do you want to tell him?" she said.

Bill hesitated, feeling a bit foolish. The wind stopped, everything became quiet.

"He's waiting," she said.

"Tell him I'm sorry, I never meant to shoot him that night . . ."

"He says he understands, that you shouldn't be troubled, that where he is now is a wonderful place and that he is very happy."

Bill opened his eyes and looked around, then looked directly at Madam Moustache.

He felt himself sweating.

"I could stand a drink . . ."

The wind began to beat the sides of the tent again. Madam Moustache shuddered and her hands shook inside his.

"He's gone," she said.

"Read the cards for me."

"Let's have a drink first."

She reached into a cabinet, took out a small decanter and two glasses and poured them each a brandy. He looked surprised when he tasted it.

"This is fine stuff."

"It doesn't pay to drink cheap liquor," she said.

"The wind up in this country never seems to let up. It makes me nervous."

She took out a pack of picture cards and began laying them out. "You will soon find great fortune," she said after turning up the second card.

"Me and Charley's going to the goldfields soon as the weather breaks."

She turned up another card. "Love will also be yours—a great love," she said.

"Already know as much," he said.

She poured them each another brandy.

She turned over the next card. Bill saw the way her face changed.

"What is it?" The card she'd overturned had an illustration of a dancing skeleton on it.

"It's nothing. A mistake. Do not worry . . ."

"It's the death card, ain't it?"

"Yes," she said. "But I don't think it signifies anything in your case. All the other cards indicate—"

"Shit, I knew it."

Charley found Bill drinking at the Gold Room. Charley could tell Bill was in the doldrums by the look he wore. He might have been drunk as well. Drunk, or carrying a head full of opium.

"You been to the chink's," Charley said.

"I went to see the fortune-teller . . ."

"That Gypsy with hair on her lip?"

"She foretold it," Bill said.

"Foretold what?"

"You know, don't you, Charley? It's coming for me, death is."

Bill always made even the air around him morose when he talked of death and assassination.

"She say how, when, where?"

Bill shook his head. "Could be any minute. Why, somebody could walk right through that door and blow my brains out all over this bar."

"You'd spot them a mile off, Bill. You're good at spotting danger."

Bill waggled his head again. "I've lost my feel for it, old pard."

"No you ain't, Bill. No you ain't."

They stood in silence for a time, then Bill said, "Listen."

Charley listened but he didn't hear anything other than men talking in low voices, the click of the roulette wheel, the scrape of a chair, the clink of glasses.

"What am I listening for, Bill?"

"Hear it?"

Charley shook his head. "Don't hear nothing unusual. Hear what?"

"The wind," Bill said.

Charley tried to hear it.

"I had her contact Mike. I told her to tell him I was sorry about shooting him. He said he forgave me."

Bill was maudlin, and there wasn't nothing worse Charley could have seen than a maudlin Wild Bill.

"Why don't you let me buy you a girl," Charley said. "How about Lilly? She's from San Francisco and does this neat little trick with her—"

Bill cut him off with a wave of his hand. "I'm married now, Charley. I put all that aside . . ."

"Hell, Bill, ain't nobody'd know."

"I'd know. I'd know. I got to get myself right with him."

"With who?"

Bill pointed toward the ceiling. Charley looked up, but all he saw was the painting of a near naked lady with a flimsy scarf draped over her bosoms and wrapped discreetly between her thighs. Then Charley realized that Bill wasn't pointing at the nude but beyond the ceiling, beyond the cloudy sky with snow still falling out of it. Bill was pointing toward heaven and where God kept house.

It gave Charley the shivers to hear Bill say things like that. Bill never did before profess any great faith in godly matters. As far as he knew, Bill never started talking about such things until after he shot Mike Williams. From what he'd been told, Bill hadn't visited a dope den till after the shooting either.

"Maybe you could just let Lilly rub your feet," Charley said. "It might make you feel better."

Bill shook his head. "I am going back to our camp and write Agnes a letter. I don't want her worrying about me."

Charley felt a twinge of guilt about not telling Bill about the letter he'd received. What was a pard supposed to do? Bill straightened from leaning on the bar and adjusted his pancake hat so the brim swooped low on one side. He threw Charley a final look with those mournful eyes before turning and heading for the door. Charley wished the weather broke so he and

Bill could go up to Deadwood and make their fortunes. That's all it would take to put Bill back in good spirits again—a nice fortune. Money was a happy thing; the weight of it in a man's pocket made a feller smile.

Charley saw Lilly sitting with a broken-nosed miner drinking the watered liquor the girls drank. Lilly was about the best of the girls working the club, young and petite and not too ugly, and gave a man his money's worth. Some of the girls had been plying their trade so long they'd became dispirited and were like rag dolls in a man's arms. But not Lilly, who showed unusual exuberance, probably because of her youth. Charley had a yen for Lilly in a way he had not for any of the other working girls he'd ever been with. He went over to the table where she and the miner sat and said to the miner, "I'll flip you for her."

"What's that supposed to mean?" the miner said.

"I'll toss this gold piece and you call it. You win, you get Lilly and the gold piece. I win, I get Lilly."

The miner had three or four places in his mouth where teeth should have been when he smiled.

Of course, Charley won. He never knew why he had such good luck, but he did. They climbed the stairs arm in arm, and Lilly didn't disappoint, just like Charley knew she wouldn't.

"I sure am going to miss you when me and Bill head off for the hills," he said, all winded, lying there next to her.

"You know the thing about you I like best?" she said.

"No, what?"

"The fact you wash."

"Cleanliness is next to godliness, darling."

"I didn't know you were a Christian, Charley."

"I ain't exactly. But I am a little."

Lilly gave him the next one free because he was such a sweet little fellow. Charley didn't object.

Chapter 7

———◆———

Cheyenne seemed like a cruel place flung up at the end of nowhere, like the wind had swept it away from the rest of civilization then petered out. Off to the distant west were mountains, but little in between. Cheyenne was a crossroads to other places—a jumping-off spot to the goldfields in the Black Hills. It was a holding place for miners, gamblers, pimps, prostitutes, and shootists, all feeding off one another: opportunists, predators, and prey.

Teddy figured he could empty his pistol into the middle of the entire population and not hit a preacher or a virgin.

Snow lay melting on tin roofs, dripped off eaves when the sun struck, but froze again when it retreated. The streets were wide and muddy. Now that it was nearing spring, the population had swollen to nearly busting out the seams. The town was built around the Inter-Ocean Hotel and the Union Pacific Railroad Hotel. Most everything else was a collection of raw lumber false-fronted buildings where a man could buy mining equipment, get a haircut, purchase a pocket watch, or buy a woman if he was willing to wait in line.

Gathered at the edge of the town proper was a collection of tents and wagons where most of the transient types set up camp, waiting for the weather to break and allow them to make it to the Black Hills— to Deadwood Gulch and Lead.

Among these denizens rode Sheriff Jeff Carr. Tall, broad-chested, and mustachioed, he looked like a man who could kill you for the slightest provocation and probably would. He rode a dapple-gray gelding, and his rump settled down in a Texas double rig and tapaderos on the stirrups to keep the toes of his boots from getting muddy.

He was there astride his horse as the passengers of the train debarked. It was his custom to look over new arrivals, trying as he might to spot the gun artists and those who might bring with them trouble to his town. Jeff Carr didn't care for trouble, and he made sure those departing the train saw the badge pinned to his coat and the double-barrel Whitney shotgun balanced across the pommel of his saddle.

Teddy Blue didn't fail to notice the lawman, and the lawman didn't fail to notice him.

It was late afternoon and plates of ice were reforming in the large puddles of the street. The sun was sunk low enough to throw its light along the ground, and where it struck ice, it turned it blue. A sharp wind chased in from the north. Teddy pulled his collar up. Even though it was close to the end of March, it wasn't close enough yet by a long shot to being spring to that country.

The cold nibbled at the cut above his eye, stung the swollen places of his face, and troubled the broken bone in his chest.

He entered an establishment called Allen's Variety Theater and asked the bartender if he'd ever heard of hot toddies. The man said of course he had, he was from New Jersey, and asked did he want a single or a double, and Teddy said, double.

It was amazing what a hot drink could do for a man's disposition.

He looked around thinking there was an off-chance he might see Wild Bill among the club's denizens. Then he realized a man of Wild Bill's disposition probably didn't engage in business much before noon.

He finished his drink and asked where the telegraph office was, then went there to send a telegram to George Bangs.

HAVE ARRIVED IN CHEYENNE THIS DAY. WILL MAKE CONTACT WITH SUBJECT AT FIRST OPPORTUNITY. SEND MORE EXPENSE MONEY—ANOTHER ONE-HUNDRED DOLLARS—THE DOVES HERE ARE A LOT MORE EXPENSIVE THAN YOU CAN IMAGINE. T. BLUE.

The clerk looked at him when he got to the last part. "A joke," Teddy said. "Where can a man get a decent room in this town?"

The clerk expressed his doubts that a man could get a decent room at any of the hotels.

"About every yahoo that can carry a pick and shovel is in town waiting for the weather to break to go north. Most of 'em brought their own tents, some wagons."

"Surely must be some place a man can lay his head."

The clerk shook his head.

Teddy made the rounds at the hotels anyway in hopes he might find something, but soon learned there wasn't a room to be had. He was beginning to think that taking the job with Pinkerton's had been a mistake. After all, what could he truly expect to accomplish, given the circumstances? The last of the sunlight winked out beyond a treeless shelf of land, and a cool, black silver night came creeping in. If it had had teeth it would have eaten them all.

He went back to the Gold Room in the Variety and ordered a meal after finding a table off in one corner.

"You want the special?" the waiter asked.

"What is the special?"

"It's the same as it always is—elk steaks and beans."

"Why is it called a special if it's always the same?"

The waiter simply looked at him.

"Okay," he said. "Bring me an iced beer as well."

He ate without enthusiasm and studied the crowd. Rowdy men in close quarters drinking liquor and gambling. It was like a match waiting to be struck. Sure enough, a fight broke out, and he wasn't surprised. It was quelled by a thickset barkeep with a hickory club who knocked the combatants senseless and threw them out the door. It wasn't just the liquor that put men in such a quarrelsome mind-set. It was also a handful of rather homely women those men vied for. The men were lonely, far from home and wives and girlfriends, so far in fact that the women didn't look nearly as homely as they were, and so were prized. The upper part of the establishment contained rooms divided off by nothing more than red curtains—nests for quick and cheap love, a place a miner could work off his liquor and loneliness and the girls could support themselves.

A kid selling newspapers came up to this table. "You want to buy a *Leader*?"

"Sure," he said, and handed the kid a nickel.

"How about buying me a beer," the kid said.

"You're too young to drink beer."

"No I ain't."

He was a spunky brat, buck-toothed, about five feet tall and eighty pounds.

"Tell you what, I'll buy you a meal, you look like you could use it."

"I'll have what you just had," the kid said, looking at Teddy's half-eaten supper.

The waiter came over and asked Teddy if the kid was bothering him, said, "Goddamn you, Bonney, how many times I have to tell you to leave my customers alone."

"He's not bothering me," Teddy said. "Bring him the special."

The kid ate like a wolf.

"It must be hard having a girl's name," Teddy said as a way to make conversation.

The kid glared at him. "It's my last name, not my first."

"My apologies."

"You see that fat bastard standing over there at the bar?"

Teddy looked around, saw a tall man with a big belly hanging over his belt, sooty features. "What about him?"

"Someday I'm going to blow a hole through that fat gut of his."

"What for?"

"None of your business."

"You're a feisty little monkey."

"I ain't no monkey, and if you ain't careful, I'm liable to blow a hole in you as well."

"Where's your folks to let you hang out in saloons this time of night and make threats on people you don't know?"

"What's it to you?"

"Nothing. You done with that meal, you can say so long. You're starting to wear out your welcome."

"Thanks for nothing, mister."

Teddy watched the kid work his way through the crowd, trying to sell the last of his newspapers, saw the waiter go over and berate him and chase him out of the place.

"What's with that kid?" he asked the waiter when he returned to his table.

"Pain in the ass. He's headed for a rope if anybody

ever was. Bad kid. You check your wallet to see if it's missing?"

Out on the streets again, Teddy wasn't sure exactly what he should do about accommodations. The air had become colder, the wind a song of bitterness. The moon now shone through shattered clouds but there wasn't any warmth or comfort in it. He walked up the street toward the railroad hotel thinking if worse came to worse, he could possibly camp out in the hotel lobby.

He hadn't gone a block when he saw several people scuffling, heard their grunts and curses. Judging by the size of them, they were kids. He stepped in close, grabbed one by the collar, flung him aside and snatched another.

"Break it up!"

They scattered except for one—the kid with the buckteeth and what remained of his newspapers, some torn and others being whipped down the streets before the wind.

"Jesus, you look for trouble or does it just find you?"

The kid had a bloody nose, wiped at it with the sleeve of his coat. "You didn't have to butt in, I had 'em about whipped."

"Yeah, it looks like you did."

"Shit, they stole my money," the kid said, looking at his ripped pocket.

"You best get on home."

The kid stood there watching the last of his papers blow away. "She won't believe me," he said.

"Who won't?"

"My ma."

He seemed in that moment simply a boy who'd gotten into trouble, but Teddy reckoned he had enough of his own problems to get involved.

"She'll think I gambled it away or drunk it up or spent it on some dove."

"You're what, all of twelve years old?"

"Near fifteen . . ."

"I hardly think your ma will believe you spent your money on liquor and doves."

"She knows me, knows I'm wild. We need every cent I make. She's a widow runs a boardinghouse."

Maybe it was fate, or just plain luck.

"She wouldn't happen to have a room for rent, would she?"

The kid looked at him. "Tell you what, mister. You vouch for me those tramps beat me and took my money, and I'll see she rents you a room."

It was a simple house, nothing fancy, just on the edge of the town's limits, set off by itself. One story, flat roof, unpainted walls. A broken picket fence with dead vines strung through it.

The kid called her name, letting Teddy follow him into the front door.

She came from another room and stood there looking at the two of them.

"Man needs a room, Ma."

She was pretty, with light red hair, a sprinkling of freckles across her nose, eyes full of tired.

"What happened to you, William?"

"Some tramps jumped me, took my money."

She looked skeptical.

"It's true," Teddy said. "I came along and broke it up. And it's also true I could stand to rent a room if you have one available."

She shifted her attention to him. "It's a very small room at the rear. It might not suit you well."

"I'll take it."

"It's ten dollars a week. In advance."

He took the money out of his wallet and handed it to her.

"Breakfast is included if you get to the table before eight o'clock."

"Thank you," he said. He looked at the kid.

He could hear her talking to the boy through the thin walls, hear her coughing, the boy saying how he didn't do anything wrong, how he was tired of this dunghill of a town, how he was going to run away. He heard her later in the night crying, but the tired had closed on him fast and he fell into a sleep pounded with dreams, none of them good.

Chapter 8

"I am the woman who loved Phil Coe," she said.

The man reading the Bible looked up. "What's that to me?" he said.

"You are the Preacher, the one I've heard about?"

She was taller than most women. Taller than most men. He guessed her to be well over six feet and slender as a reed. And not what generally would be considered a beauty.

"My lover was killed in Texas by Wild Bill," she said.

"I'm sorry to hear."

"It's been six years ago this month. I thought I could get over it, but I can't."

"You must have loved him terribly."

"We were to be married."

"Again, my condolences."

"Your condolences are not what I've come to ask for."

He closed his Bible and set it next to him on the bench there in front of the hotel. El Paso held onto its heat like a miser to dimes. Sun baked the street, and

everything moved slow that time of day. The wiser
men were inside the saloons drinking, decent women
did not venture out, and even dogs found shade and
stayed in it.

"Would you care to have a seat?" he said, and she
sat next to him. He could smell that good clean smell
of freshly washed skin and hair.

"It has taken me this entire time to save up the
money," she said.

"Money for what?"

"For you, if you'll take it."

"And why would I take your money, Miss . . ."

"Just call me Olive," she said. "That and the fact I
can pay you is all you really need to know about me."

"Olive," he said, testing the sound of the name.

She took from her reticule a small sack weighted
with what he saw as twenty-dollar double eagles
when she opened it.

"Five-hundred dollars," she said. "It's all I have."

"Again, I'd ask you for what purpose would I take
your money."

"To kill Wild Bill, of course."

He smiled and watched a lone rider trot a big
piebald stallion down the street, rein it in front of the
Coney Island Saloon, dismount and go inside.

"May I ask why you come to me with such a proposal?"

"Because you're the Preacher, the one they say kills
men for money."

He laughed, but not very hard nor very loudly.
"You are an innocent, Olive. What makes you think I

won't just take your money and disappear and not
shoot anyone?"

"I'm not so innocent as you might think," she said.
"Still . . ."

She pulled the drawstring tight around the purse of
coins and dropped it back inside her reticule, stood
and said, "I am going to go to my house now. No one
lives there but me. If you change your mind, you can
follow me home, or find me later on your own. And if
not, then I've wasted our time and come out into this
dreadful heat for nothing. Good-bye, sir."

He watched her walk away, took out his Bible and
began reading again in the book of Ecclesiastes: *To
everything there is a season . . . A time to kill . . . a
time to embrace . . . a time to dance.*

She opened the door for him on the first knock, stood
away, and he entered. A hundred candles burned in
the room she led him into. They looked like fireflies in
the otherwise darkness.

"You took your time deciding," she said, "it's
nearly midnight."

"I'm a careful man, Olive."

"You will take the job then?"

"Yes," he said. "But it will take more than five hundred dollars in gold eagles for me to kill the likes of
Wild Bill."

"I figured as much. Do you like wine?"

She undressed slowly as he sat and watched, the light
of the candles flickering soft arabesque shadows over

her milk white flesh. He wondered if Heaven offered as much pleasure for a man's eyes, doubted he'd ever find out.

Finally she stood in a simple cotton chemise. Her hair unpinned gave her an attractiveness he'd not noticed before. She came and stood before him, and he undid the chemise and let it fall away.

"Are you sure you want to pay such a price to see a man dead?" he said.

"For every time there is a season," she said. It spooked him a little.

He awoke sometime during the night. All but a few of the candles had guttered out, and he thought they were eyes staring at him. Olive was asleep next to him on the pallet. Earlier she had whispered the name "Phil" then apologized for the faux pas. It didn't matter to him, really. She was a curiosity, a strange creature full of sorrow with wounded eyes. And afterward she'd said to him, "I give myself gladly to you in payment of revenge."

He fell back asleep, then awoke to see her staring at him.

He said, "You should forget this nasty business and let what has happened here this night be left at that. I understand the business of desperation and hatred and death. It is something you'll have to live with forever."

"Do you think I care?"

"No."

She clung to him. "Tell me your name before you go," she said.

"Does it matter?"

"Perhaps, a little, it does . . ."

"Paris Bass," he said.

"You can have me again, if you want."

So he took her, and she gave herself to him in a straightforward way and did not speak Phil Coe's name again but seemed rather to suffer in silence because he could feel her tears falling on his skin as she lay against him.

As he was dressing she said, "Have you killed many men?"

"I've killed enough to know how it's done," he said. "And I will kill Wild Bill."

"How will you find him?"

"Men like him aren't hard to find. They dote on the notoriety. They are vain, and in their vanity lies their weakness. They think everyone is an admirer and everyone is afraid. It is why they are easy."

"Why do they call you the Preacher?" she said.

He knotted his tie, then shook out his jacket and put it on. She noticed the pockets sewn into the inner lining were heavy with small pistols.

"It's a long story," he said, and held out his hand. She took it, moved in close to him. "That's not what I want. The five hundred, remember?"

"Oh," she said, and went and got the purse and gave it to him.

"You didn't think . . ."

"No."

"There surely must be plenty of men who would be interested in you, Olive."

"I'm sure there are, if that is what I wanted."

"You know how to pleasure a man."

"Do I?"

"Yes."

He settled his hat on his head and turned to go.

"How will I know when it is done?" she said.

"Everyone will hear about it when it's done. After all, how many are there like him?"

"Will you come back this way afterward?"

"No, Olive, I won't."

"I trust you won't take advantage of me . . ."

"I already have." He saw the look on her face and added, "But I'm a man of my word when it comes to these things. Do you think your Phil Coe went to his heavenly home?"

"I hardly would think so."

"Then he'll be there with the Devil to welcome our William."

As he made preparations to leave in search of Wild Bill, the Preacher did not concern himself with matters of time. If it took him weeks or even months to find Wild Bill, eventually he would, as he always did, find his man. And if someone else were to kill the gunfighter before he found him, well, either way, Olive would have her revenge. And when the wind shuffled just right, he could still smell that washed hair of hers, and he would, at least until the next one like her came along and struck a new bargain with him.

He rode along the El Paso road at a leisurely pace,

reading his Bible, this time opening to the book of James.

. . . each one is tempted when he is drawn away by his own desires and enticed. Then, when desire has conceived, it gives birth to sin; and sin, when it is full grown, brings forth death.

"Oh, what sins have you committed, sweet William, that this nearly innocent woman would see you dead, dead, dead?"

He felt fresh as the new day, ready to raise some hell and feed mother earth a feast of fresh bones.

Chapter 9

———◆◆◆———

He found her there in the kitchen, the morning light streaming through the window above her head as she sat drinking a cup of coffee alone. She looked up when he came in.

"You're too late for breakfast, Mr. Blue."

"Yes, I realize that."

Their eyes met, held for a moment, then she looked away.

"Would it be possible for me to have some of that?" he said.

Again she looked at him, saw that he meant the coffee and started to rise to get him a cup, but he waved for her not to and went instead and poured his own.

"Mind if I sit with you for a few moments?"

She didn't say anything, and so he took the seat across from her, saw that she had spread before her an aged copy of the *Police Gazette*.

"Anything interesting?" he said, sipping the steaming coffee—it was good.

"I was just reading about our town's famous visitor," she said. "Wild Bill. Do you know him?"

"I know of him."

"They've published a letter of his warning those who would try and assassinate him that he will be 'riding through your prairie dog towns and wear my hair long and am not hard to find by any who would try and corral William.'"

She looked up and across the table at Teddy.

"He seems like a strange man," she said. "Almost as if inviting trouble."

"I'm sure that is not his intent," Teddy said.

Her eyes were as green as the sea, and he thought of the land that gave up this Irish girl and wanted to ask her about herself but held off.

"That boy of yours—" he started to say.

"Another William that is hard to corral," she said in direct reference to the article. "Perhaps there is something to names. I've tried my best with him. His father died early. I suppose that has something to do with his wildness."

"Well, I won't trouble you further," he said, and stood and carried the cup to a sideboard.

"I suppose I was a bit short with you last evening when my son brought you home, Mr. Blue. I'm Kathleen Bonney."

"Teddy," he said.

She smiled. She was pretty.

He nearly bumped into the boy as he was going out, and the boy coming in with an armload of wood for the stove.

"You shoot a hole in anybody since I seen you last?" Teddy said, jibing the boy.

"Not yet, but it's still early."

"I'll keep an eye out."

"Would be a good idea."

"There a place in town a man could rent himself a horse?"

"Tut's," the kid said.

The kid was wearing a battered stovepipe hat. Teddy would see him wearing the same hat years later in a tintype that would be circulated after a New Mexican sheriff named Pat Garrett killed him. But right at that moment, he looked simply like an Irish urchin.

He found a café and ate breakfast, then walked the town to get the lay of it. He found the livery the kid had told him about and approached the man mucking stalls.

"You rent horses?"

The man straightened, eyed him down the length of a long oft-broken nose.

"You Jim Miller?" the man asked Teddy.

"No, I am not."

"You look a lot like him."

"What has that got to do with my renting a horse?"

"He's a known horse thief."

"I told you, I'm not him."

"Well, you look enough like him to be his twin."

"Forget about it, I'll find another livery."

"No, that's okay. I just thought you was him. I'll rent you a horse."

"Might need to rent two in a day or so."

"Two?"

"You have a policy against renting more than one horse at a time?"

"No, hell, you can rent 'em all if you want."

"I'll just need two."

"Dollar fifty a day each."

"That'll be fine."

He walked down to the telegraph office and asked if there were any messages for him. The clerk took a sheet of yellow paper from a pigeonhole and handed it to him. It was from George Bangs:

MONEY ON ITS WAY. KEEP EXACT ACCOUNTS. MR. P IS A STICKLER. BONAFIDE EXPENSES DO NOT INCLUDE EXPENDITURES FOR DOVES, AS YOU CALL THEM. KEEP ME INFORMED OF YOUR PROGRESS. IF UNTOWARD EVENTS OCCUR, INFORM IMMEDIATELY. G. BANGS.

Teddy folded the telegram and slipped it into his pocket, a bit of a smile playing at his lips thinking about expenditures for doves. He decided his next job was to locate Wild Bill and try to establish some sort of contact. He wasn't sure exactly how he was going to go about it, but as it turned out, the event would take care of itself.

He walked back to the boardinghouse under a glaucous sky, the clouds bellied in so low he could slap them with his hat. It would probably snow or rain. He wasn't in any mood for either. He figured Hickok would make his appearance on the streets of Cheyenne later in the day. He'd wait it out in his room, maybe get a little reading in.

* * *

She was there when he returned, doing wash now in a large metal tub full of steaming soapy water, stirring what looked like men's denims with a wood paddle. Sprigs of her hair clung to her forehead.

He paused, thought about what he was going to ask her, decided it was better if he waited a bit and went to his room.

It was a small room, barely large enough to hold the bed, a small bureau. A single window looked out onto the open prairies. He removed his coat and boots, the shoulder holster rig, and hung it over the head of the bed frame. He took a small red book from his coat pocket and sat on the bed where light from the window fell over his shoulder.

The book was a collection of Shakespeare. He had a fondness for such words; he liked to think that such words could preserve a man's civility even in the most uncivilized climes. The print was small. He put on a pair of spectacles and began to read where he last left off: *Sap check'd with frost, and lusty leaves quite gone, Beauty o'er snow'd, and bareness everywhere . . .*

He closed his eyes to absorb the image the words created. It struck him as being an apt description of this place—this frontier that was Cheyenne being re-born out of winter.

There was a knock at the door. He did not bother to take the revolver from its holster but instead went and opened the door to whoever was on the other side. Before him stood a short rotund man under a big-brimmed hat, dressed in fringed buckskin with fancy beadwork and porcupine quills needled into the leather.

"Charley Utter," the man said. "Some call me Colorado Charley. My mammy calls me Charles. It's all the same thing to me. How do you do, Mr. Blue? Mind I come in so we can talk in private?"

Without waiting for an answer, the man stepped into the room and looked around, then took up the chair Teddy had been sitting in by the window and noticed immediately the book. Picking it up, he held it close to his face then said, "Aha . . . Shakespeare. I know I'm in good company, sir."

"How may I help you, Mr. Utter?"

Charley waved a pudgy paw.

"Call me Charley or Colorado. No need for formalities in this dung heap of a place. Weren't for Bill, I'd be back in Denver dining on mountain oysters. But Bill, he's a wandering fool. Can't stay in one place more than a week. Always got to move on. Me too. He says soon as the weather breaks, we're off to Deadwood. *Deadwood!* I say that's the most rooting tooting son of a bitch of a place on God's green earth. Bill says, 'That's why we're going, Charley. Civilization's crawling up our asses like bed bugs in a fat lady's hair.' Old Bill . . ." Charley laughed, and when he did, his belly shook.

"Somewhere I must have missed something," Teddy said, a bit intrigued with a man who talked so much and so fast. All the westerners he'd ever known were taciturn men who, when they spoke at all, spoke in bits and pieces, like conversation was just some rags coming out of their mouths. But Colorado

Charley Utter did not utter so much as keep a running stream of words pouring forth.

"Why I'm here because of Billy Hickok," Charley said. "Me and him are pards, and I got a telegram recent from his wife, Agnes, down in Cincinnati. Though strictly between you and me, I ain't so sure Billy ain't made himself a bigamist. For he told me once he was married to a half-breed woman down in Hays name of Indian Annie. Billy gets sometimes potted and does things when he ain't always in his right mind, and women favor him greatly, so I can't say for sure if he was married legal or not, nor more than once. Then too, there's that crazy witch Calamity Jane who claims Bill married her in Abilene, but if he did, he must have been doped out of his gourd . . ."

Charley paused long enough to look at the passage Teddy had marked in the book and rub his chin. "That feller could sure enough write."

"You care to state your case, Mr. Utter?"

"Just call me Charley, old son. I don't hardly answer to much else. Promise me now."

Charley was as jerky restless as a fish out of water.

"How do you find the widow Bonney? Quite a lovely package, don't you think?"

"Should I just wait till you run out of wind?"

Charley grinned until his mouth looked full of horse teeth.

"All business, eh? Well, I don't mind getting down to it. But to me, there's always too plenty of time for business and too little for pleasure."

Teddy waited in silence.

"Like I said, it's about Billy the reason I come.

Agnes—er, Missus Hickok—told me she'd hired
Pinkerton's to watch Billy's backside . . . Begged me
to check out their man—which I figure to be you because you don't look like no miner, nor no gambler or
pimp either. I know the breed, and you ain't one. Fact
is, I've been observing you since you stepped off the
UP flier yesterday. And now I see that Colt Lightning
hanging there in that shoulder rig, I figure I am right
that you're a man makes his living with a gun, but not
one of them wandering itinerate types like Clay Allison or any of 'em."

"I'm not at liberty to state my business here in
Cheyenne, Mr. Utter."

Charley swept the hat off his head and ran his fingers through his thick knotted hair, paused and dug at
his scalp, then plunked the hat back down again as he
examined what it was he plucked from his hair, then
squeezed it.

"Well, the old lady . . . er, Missus Hickok, said in a
letter that she wanted me to put up some cash money
for Billy's protection, since she herself, is a bit low on
funds currently. I wired her I'd do it, but I'd have to
meet the fellow was going to do the protecting. So I
come to see what my money is a buying."

"I might not be your man."

"Oh, I think you are."

"You don't trust Mrs. Hickok?"

"It's a lot of money."

"I thought Hickok was your friend."

"He is. Best pard a man could want. I just don't
want to be throwing my money down a sand hole on

some weak sister ain't got the grit to protect old Billy, it comes down to a row."

"I won't state my business to you, Mr. Utter. You'll have to decide for yourself if the information you received is accurate or not. I will say this, though, if Hickok is a friend of yours, you'll keep such information as you've carried here today to yourself."

"Well, you're a sly devil, I'll give you that. Close-mouthed. That's a good thing. But can you sneak up on a fellow and blow his brains out if he's about to lay poor Billy low? Can you face down the tiger, Mr. Blue?"

Charley paced back and forth waving his hands about as he talked, questioned, and did his best to cajole Teddy into giving himself up.

"Let me ask you something," Teddy said. "If you're his friend, why does Mrs. Hickok feel the need to hire someone to protect her husband from getting back-shot? Why not just ask you to do it?"

"Well, for one thing, she don't know me all that well, except what Bill might've wrote to her about me. But then, for another thing, she probably knows from what he wrote that I ain't reliable. Oh, I love Billy like he was my own flesh and blood, and I would take a bullet in the mouth for him. Hell, I'd even shoot out old Calamity Jane's lights if he asked me to. But I got itchier feet than Billy does. I can't stand to be one place too long. Even if it is to ride out of town just to shoot me a prairie dog or three. I got the hankering to go to Chiney and South America and a lot of other places, and I can't be relied on to be any one place for any certain time. Billy knows it and he don't count on me . . . Just like I don't him."

Charley stopped abruptly and put his hand over his heart. Teddy watched with interest.

"Sometimes I get palpitations. Doctors say I got a hole in my heart. I say shit, how can that be? Wouldn't my blood all leak out? They don't have no answers, those medicos. I know Sioux shaman that got more sense. But sometimes it gets feeling funny in there and I have to take a extry breath or two. That's the other thing, don't you see? I could drop over dead as Caesar at a critical time, then who'd look after Billy? Say, you don't have nothing to drink, do you, it's about the cocktail hour."

Teddy shook his head.

"Most men don't drink before noon—leastways the civilized ones such as yourself don't. Well, you going to do it, or do I have to wire the old lady back and tell her she's been bamboozled?"

"Go and rest assured Mr. Utter that your friend won't have to worry about getting back-shot. But in return for such assurances, I'll need you to introduce us. If I'm going to guard him, I'll need to be in his confidence. You'll be the one who needs to be sly. If he suspects what's going on, well, you might be out of a friend, and I might be out of a job."

"Oh hey, old son, don't you worry none. Just be down at the Gold Room tonight and I'll get you set up with a meeting." Charley scratched his belly, said, "Damn graybacks. A man could wash all day and lay down just once with the wrong whore and come up with a head full of lice."

"This evening, then," Teddy said, holding open the door.

"Say around ten, eleven. Billy ain't much social before then."

"Remember, Mr. Utter. His life may depend on your discretion."

"You'd get more out of a dead man than you would me on this thing. See you later."

And with that, Colorado Charley Utter was gone, even though his presence seemed to linger on, as though his voice was still bouncing around the room.

Chapter 10

———◆———

Teddy paused briefly before heading toward town. Kathleen Bonney was there in the parlor reading a book. The angle of her head, the color of her hair, the lace of her collar—something about her, maybe everything about her, inclined him to speak.

"I was wondering, do you ride?" he said.

She looked up. "Yes," she said.

"I was wondering if you'd care to go riding with me, perhaps tomorrow, or the day after . . . if you've the time, of course. I know you're probably very busy running the house . . ."

She waited a long moment before answering. "Is that what you're asking me, Mr. Blue? If I want to go riding with you?"

"I suppose it is," he said.

"Then the answer is yes."

"I'll call on you in the morning to see where you're at with your business," he said.

"That will be fine."

Their eyes held for a moment longer, and he went out feeling quite good about the way she was.

There on the wide broad streets of Cheyenne, the evening light had fallen: a golden glow from the setting sun bouncing light off the face of the earth. It seemed a beacon to all the gold hunters gathered waiting for the last breath of winter to abate. It seemed a gruesome wait to men starved for riches, fraying some men's nerves and turning them violent and making them ill. So they waited in the saloons and gambling halls and bordellos, and some silently prayed they wouldn't have to kill anybody or that nobody would kill them in the waiting.

Teddy made his way to Allan's Variety to take his evening meal, perhaps play a hand or two of cards while waiting for the arrival of Charley Utter and Wild Bill.

The place was full of miners, gamblers, and about every other form of humanity imaginable, including the pistoleers who were a breed apart. You could spot them easily enough: men with watchful eyes and a certain tension in the way they stood or sat. Bill had it, so did the two standing at the end of the bar when he went into the Gold Room: Hank Rain and Ned Loyal.

He knew them from that time in Ellsworth. Old John Sears had pointed them out.

"Them's two bad actors," Sears had said.

"How do you know?" Teddy asked.

"Let's just say I've had me some wild times and run with a pretty bad crowd once."

Teddy had noticed how old John rubbed that place on his hand where his thumb was missing and in its place a scar of skin stretched over bone.

"They the ones who shot you?"

John simply looked at him and said, "Drink your beer, kid, and don't get me pissed off."

Now, he wondered if old John had made it to New Mexico. He wished he'd kept track of him.

Teddy found a table near the back, away from the gaming tables and long bar, away from the boisterous men who cussed and argued about everything, from which were the best whorehouse west of the Mississippi to who was the deadliest gunfighter. Some said it was Squirrel Tooth Alice's place in Abilene, and that it wasn't Wild Bill but Clay Allison who was the deadliest with a gun.

It all got lost in the noise of the hour, and Teddy didn't much concern himself with the opinions of miners—that lonely, restless breed of men who followed rumor and hope into the icy creeks and rock hills to muck out dreams.

The same waiter who had served him the night before made his way through the pack, a tray of empty beer mugs balanced in his right hand.

"What can I get you?"

"Whiskey, an ice beer to chase it. Bring me the special too."

Teddy ate and drank with deliberateness, meanwhile studying the activity around him. He noticed perhaps as many as a half-dozen working girls—cyprians, frail sisters, brides of the multitudes, doves, whatever you chose to call them—mingling with the miners, leading them off to the cribs that bordered the upper level of the saloon. He remembered his own initiation into the flesh trade that time in Abilene and the confession of his act to old John Sears, who simply smiled and spat and said, "You had Betsy too, huh?" It still sort of slid around in his belly to think of it. Those were happy times, though, maybe the happiest he ever spent.

He saw one of the doves, a dark-haired wisp of a woman who approached Hank Rain and Ned Loyal. They spoke for a moment, then she took them each by the hand and led them upstairs to one of the cribs. It seemed like a mean life for anyone, much less a girl barely a woman.

He tossed back the last of the whiskey, then took his beer and wandered over to the gaming tables where men were playing chuck-a-luck and buck the tiger. He waited until a spot came open at one of the card tables and bought his way in. The man dealing cards had hands like a debutante: smooth and well-cared-for. He was cleanly dressed in a cutaway coat, brocade vest, and was obviously a professional gambler.

They played several hands, and Teddy won two small pots then lost them back again. An hour into the game a lantern-jawed miner pushed back his chair and said to the gambler, "I think you're double-dealing me."

Barely looking up from his smooth hands and the cards they held, the gambler said, "You're not a good enough cardplayer I'd have to double deal you. You just ain't worth a shit at this game."

The miner stood suddenly and said, "I want to see what's up that sleeve of yours, and by God I want to see it right this fucking minute!"

It was as though the gambler did little more than flick his wrist, and one of the smooth hands held a derringer aimed at the large head of the miner.

"This what you're looking for? You want me to deal you this ace?"

The miner swallowed hard, like he was trying to swallow his teeth. "I guess . . . I guess I had it wrong."

"You in or out?" the gambler said.

"In, I reckon."

And like that, it was over with. Teddy cashed in and went to the bar.

It was palpable when Wild Bill entered the room. There were others with him—namely Charley Utter, who stood a head and half shorter. The path through the crowd seemed to clear of its own volition, and Wild Bill seemed to know exactly the status of his celebrity as he walked among them.

He's like the Jesus Christ of the West, Teddy thought somewhat humorously.

Wild Bill took up residence at one of the card tables. One man offered him his seat, but Bill shook his head, nodded toward another man sitting with his back to the wall.

The man stood, and Bill took his place. Charley whispered something in Bill's ear, then moved to the bar where Teddy stood.

Charley slapped a pair of silver dollars on the hardwood and ordered him and Bill each a cocktail.

"Look at him," Charley said. *The Prince of the Pistoleers.*

"I have to admit, he commands your attention."

Bill was dressed in a black frock coat with satin trim, a white silk shirt and matching white cravat. His long moustaches looked golden under the glow of the oil lamp hanging over the table—golden, like the light at sunset.

Teddy saw Bill remove his pistols from his sash and lay them on the table—one within reach of either hand. He had a broad, smooth forehead with a red line from the band of his sombrero when he thumbed it back.

The way the cigar smoke floated around him like a cloud, he could have been St. Hickok.

"Let me take him over his cocktail and I'll be back," Charley said.

Teddy watched Charley work his way through the crowd without spilling so much as a drop of the liquor in either glass. Wild Bill's head went up as Charley came within range of the table. Teddy could see the eyes narrow then relax as Charley extended him the cocktail glass, which he took almost demurely and sipped from, then swiped the liquor dew from his moustaches with a forefinger—left, then right.

Teddy saw Hank Rain and Ned Loyal exit the dove's room on the second floor. Hank was tucking in his shirt and Ned was combing his hair with his fingers. The dove came out seconds later, looking the worse for wear, but descended the stairs and immediately began to ply the crowd of miners again, and was soon leading one off on that familiar trek back up to her crib. Teddy wondered how many times exactly she'd climbed those stairs in her life.

Old John Sears had told him that time on the trail up to Abilene that he'd once been in love with a dove and that she'd taken her own life by drinking mercury.

"Saddest goddamn thing I ever experienced," the old man said.

"Why'd she do it?" Teddy asked.

"You tell me, we'll both know. It's the life, I guess is what it was. She sent me a letter right before. Said the life was wearing her out, wanted to know if I'd come for her and take her out of it. Hell, by the time I got there, she was gone and buried. Some of her working sisters told me what she did. I never did let myself love nobody again. Loving somebody is a sad goddamn thing to do."

Charley made his way back to the bar, his cocktail drunk down, and he ordered another.

"Soon's Billy's finished with his card game I'll get you two introduced. Say, have you tried any of the flesh here?"

"No."

"It ain't what you'd call first-rate like it is in Denver. But this is the frontier, and what can you expect, anyway? Most of the girls that come to these piss pot frontier towns have reached the end of the line—down to dimes instead of dollars. But miners ain't the choosiest souls that ever lived when it comes to female flesh, and I can't say I'm too choosey either unless I got a choice in the matter. Now old Billy, he's somewhat particular of the company he keeps. It's mostly because he can have his pick of the ladies. But I have to say, it seems since him and the old woman— er, I mean Agnes—got hitched, he's been about as faithful as you could imagine. It's like he just lost all interest in other gals."

Charley took a breath in order to swallow down half the second cocktail, licked his lips and said, "Pard, that's pretty good damn drinking, that is."

In between telling Teddy about Bill and their exploits together, Charley greeted every other patron with a howdy and a handshake and bought some of them drinks, and some of them bought him drinks.

"Seems like you know everybody," Teddy said.

"I'm just friendly. You have to be a friend to make a friend, is what my daddy always said—he was a drummer of stoves."

"Looks like some of it rubbed off."

"Some of what?"

"The gift of gab."

"Oh, that. I guess maybe so."

"You see those two men down at the end of the bar?"

Charley looked around the shoulders of a six-foot miner. "Yea'r."

"You know who they are?"

"No."

"One is Hank Rain, and the other one in the blanket coat is Ned Loyal."

"What about 'em?"

"They're gunfighters."

"I see."

"They were in Ellsworth when I was there. I can't

say for sure, but rumor had it they were on the scout for Bill, but Bill had already left town."

"You think they're here because he is?"

"Anything's possible. Thing is, they haven't acted like they've even noticed him."

"Well, you make sure you keep an eye on them suckers," Charley said. "Just give me the signal if you think they're going to move on Billy and I'll help you plug 'em."

"You any good with that?" Teddy asked, nodding to the long-barreled revolver hanging from the concho-studded holster on Charley's hip.

"This?" Charley said, looking down at it. "Hell, old Ned Buntline gave me it. You ever seen a barrel so long? He had it special made—one for me and one for Billy, only Billy won't pack his—says it's not practical, says time he pulled and cleared all that barrel, some-body would have him shot dead. He could be right. But don't be mistaken, I could kill anything that walked or crawled with this. It's just like a little rifle, is the way you have to think about it."

"Jesus, are you long-winded on everything, Charley?"

Charley just grinned and ordered himself another cocktail.

Chapter 11

———•◦•———

Teddy watched the dove take half a dozen more miners and cowboys one at a time up the stairs to her crib as he waited for Bill to finish his round of cards. Charley chattered away like a squirrel to anyone who would listen as he downed cocktail after cocktail.

Teddy felt a little more than weary of the assignment and wondered again if maybe it had been a mistake taking it in the first place. But then Bill threw in his last hand, rose from the table and came toward where Charley and he stood at the bar. The crowd parted like the sea for Moses.

"Just go along with whatever I say," Charley said to Teddy.

Bill paused before the two men, said, "I never had such a bad run of luck as I've had lately. I lost my poke."

"You know I'll stake you, charming Billy," Charley said in his jovial manner. He was well drunk now, but you could hardly tell it from when he wasn't.

"I'm hoping this weather breaks and we can go

north to the gulch," Hickok said. "I think there is a future for me there."

He hardly took any notice of Teddy, or so it seemed.

"This is Teddy Blue," Charley said. "We know each other from down Texas way."

Hickok cut his gaze to Teddy, nodded, but didn't say anything.

"I saw you once in Chicago," Teddy said. "You and Bill Cody and Texas Jack at Nixon's Theater."

A muscle twitched in the long face of the shootist.

"You could have gone the rest of the year without mentioning that," Hickok said. "I was a damn fool for letting Cody talk me into thinking I could stage-act."

"It wasn't so bad," Teddy said.

"You must have been drunk or asleep."

"You scared hell out of everybody when you shot out that spotlight."

Hickok's sandy moustaches lifted slightly as his mouth fought a smile.

"I could have killed an innocent. It's another thing about that venture didn't work out so well. Cody was mighty upset with me."

"Can I stand you a drink?"

Hickok studied him for a moment, said, "Long as you're no newspaperman or some lawyer my wife sent to ask me for a divorce."

The three moved to a table away from the din as much as possible. Others who'd been occupying it were more than willing to give up their seats to Wild Bill—thinking it some sort of honor.

Charley said, "Listen, I got to go take care of some business. I'll be back in twenty or thirty minutes. Why don't you two get acquainted some." And before either Hickok or Teddy could say a thing, Charley worked his way off into the crowd toward the little dark-haired dove who was plying her trade along the bar again.

"Charley's a lonesome sort," Hickok said. "Can't stand being without the company of a woman long."

"He seems a decent enough pard," Teddy said.

"A man couldn't ask for none better."

"It's none of my business, Mr. Hickok. But I saw two men here earlier you might want to know about."

Hickok turned his cocktail glass between the fingers of his left hand.

"Hank Rains and Ned Loyal," Teddy said.

Hickok raised his glass slowly and took a drink, then set it down again with great care. "Why do you feel the need to tell me this?"

"I saw them in Ellsworth when I was there, and rumor had it they were looking for 'Wild Bill.' Only you were long since departed from that place. I just thought you should know."

Hickok swiped the dew from his moustaches with fingers fine as carved ivory. "They'd not be the first ones looking to make their reputation off Wild Bill," he said. "Thanks for the warning, Mr. Blue, but I saw them. They were at the end of the bar when I came over. They know where to find me if they want. Thing is, I know where to find them too."

Hickok took another drink of the cocktail.

"What do you do as a profession, Mr. Blue?"

"I have no particular profession. I did some cow-boying till that ran out. I guess I'm like everybody else here. I'm just waiting to go up into the gold hills soon as the weather breaks."

"And do what? You're sure no miner."

"Seek opportunities. I guess same as you."

"Then you're enterprising. Gambling man, maybe?"

"No, I'm just a fair hand with cards. I'm a knock-about. I pick up work here and there."

He could see the doubt in Hickok's eyes.

"I'll take you at your word. Any friend of Charley's is a friend of mine."

Teddy saw the dove leading Charley up the stairs, or maybe it was the other way around.

"Well, it's been a pleasure to meet you, sir," Teddy said. "I guess I've had enough liquor and cards for the night. Perhaps we'll meet again."

"You know this town very well?"

"I've just recently arrived."

"Oh," Hickok said. "Then you wouldn't know which is the best dope den a feller might find?"

"No, I'm afraid not."

"Some see it as a weakness," Hickok said.

"What's that, Mr. Hickok?"

"Opium. But it unlocks the mind, frees the soul, puts you in touch with the spirit world."

"I guess I never believed much in that sort of thing—the spirit world."

"Death's not the end of things, Mr. Blue. It's the beginning."

"I'm afraid I'll have to take your word for it."

"Go dream your dreams and I'll dream mine, sir. And watch out for those who would see you put in a grave unprepared . . ."

The light inside the Gold Room was bad, made worse by the smoke and shadows, but Teddy was certain that what he saw in Bill's gaze was something he couldn't explain if he had to—a sort of distant detached look, like he was seeing something nobody else could see. There wasn't anything in Hickok's dossier about his being a dope fiend or an occultist. Maybe Allan Pinkerton wasn't as good a detective as he thought he was. But if Hickok were a slave to the dope, then the task of guarding him would be all the more difficult, for what would make it easier for someone to kill him, than to be walking about with a head full of dope dreams?

Teddy was about a block from the boardinghouse when someone moved in the shadows of an alley that ran between the mercantile and the dentist office next door. He had the Colt Lightning out and cocked in one swift move—ready this time for trouble—when the kid stepped into the muted light.

"You can kill me if you want to, but there ain't no reward on me, not just yet, anyways," the kid said. "You'd just be wasting a bullet."

"What are you doing on the streets this late?"

"I shot me a man tonight."

"Jesus . . ."

"He deserved it."

"Nobody deserves it."

"He did."

"Your mother know?"

"Nobody knows except me and him. He might be dead. I could use some help getting in the wind."

"Best to turn yourself in, kid."

"That ain't going to happen. That damn Jeff Carr will either shoot me or hang me. It was his cousin I shot."

"You want to tell me why you shot him?"

"What's it to you, anyway?"

"You want my help or not?"

"It was over Lilly."

"Who's Lilly?"

"She works down at the Gold Room. He was jealous of me seeing her. Caught me in an alley and threatened to kill me if I didn't stay away from her. Stuck his gun in my mouth. I showed him, though. I showed him good."

"Which one is she?"

"Short, like me. Dark hair. Young, pretty, sweet. What do you care?"

Teddy recalled the dove, the one taking the miners and Charley Utter up to her crib.

"What were you doing, seeing a prostitute?"

"She's only a year older'n me. What's wrong with me seeing her?"

"Nothing, unless she's a dove and got the sheriff's cousin willing to kill for her."

"I shot him with his own goddamn gun through the neck. They want to hang me for that, let them . . ."

"You rob him after you shot him?"

"Go ask him if he was robbed. You going to help me or what?"

"I'm not in the helping business, kid."

"You see me hanging from a telegraph pole the next day or two, you remember you could have done something . . ."

Like a shadow, the kid receded into darkness.

Jesus, Teddy thought, is there a sign on my back says Good Samaritan on it?

He went straightaway to the boardinghouse. The lights were out. He didn't know if he should wake her. He thought about it, then knocked on her door. It opened after a few seconds, far enough that he could see her face, the puzzled look on it.

"I have to talk to you."

She looked doubtful. "Can't it wait until morning?"

"It's about your boy."

She stepped back, and he stepped inside the room.

"He shot a man."

He saw her flinch as though someone had slapped her.

"I don't know how bad or if he's dead, but I can find out."

"Where is William?" she said.

"I ran into him a few minutes ago on the street. He wanted me to help him get out of town."

She began to shake. He took hold of her, held her frail body until she calmed.

"My God . . . my God."

"It gets worse," he said. "The man he shot is a relative of Sheriff Carr."

She tried to stifle a sob but was unsuccessful. He held her tighter still, then led her to a settee and eased her onto it.

"If he comes back tonight, put him in my room and tell him to keep his mouth shut until I can get back here."

She looked at Teddy, her cheeks stained wet. "Why are you doing this?"

"I don't know."

But he did know. It was because of her.

Chapter 12

———•◦•———

Charley rejoined Bill, said, "That young lady knows how to turn a man's thoughts from violence."

Bill seemed not to be listening. Charley thought maybe he was drunk, for when Bill got drunk he grew quiet, detached.

"You oughter give her a go, Billy. I mean I know you love Agnes and all, but how long can a man last on this raw frontier without some female flesh?"

Bill stood suddenly, adjusted his pancake hat and strung the curls out of his coat collar so they fell over his shoulders, then adjusted his twin Navy Colts inside the red sash around his waist and walked out.

Charley thought it best to dog him to make sure his back was being watched. And just where the hell was that feller Blue at anyways? Wasn't he supposed to be guarding Bill?

Charley stayed several paces behind Bill, walking casual just in case Bill got wind of somebody following him and turned and shot, as had been his reputation—to fire first and ask who it was later, sorry to say for dear old Mike Williams. Bill may not be able to see worth a shit, but that didn't mean he couldn't get lucky. Even a blind dog finds a bone now and again.

Charley followed him up the street, which was less rowdy now because of the late hour, with most of the miners and dregs of Cheyenne society either dead drunk or bedded down with crib girls in their tents or wagons. That was exactly where Charley felt he ought to be at this late hour.

Charley followed Bill about two blocks when he saw Jeff Carr with several deputies come down the walk in Bill's direction and stop before him. Charley walked up close enough to overhear their conversation.

"Bill Hickok," Jeff Carr said. "If I see you on these streets tomorrow, I'm running you out of town."

Bill stood steady as a porch post. "State your reason," he said.

Charley could see Jeff Carr's was a tense crowd, the deputies flanking him all well-armed and ornery-looking cusses.

"Vagrancy," Carr stated.

"You must have been bit by a rabid dog and it's made you mad in the brains," Bill said.

"We'll see who's mad in the head if you're still cavorting come the sunrise."

"If I leave Cheyenne, you'll be going with me," Bill said, and brushed aside the knot of lawmen. Charley was sure there'd be gunplay—that Jeff would do something rash and fatal, like pull his gun on Bill. Charley knew Bill well enough to know that he was thinking the same thing and was probably prepared to turn and kill them all. But Bill was the sort that would never show his concern until it was critical. He would only show them his back and let them do with their lives what they would.

Jeff Carr must have known it too, or at least sensed it, and instead of making a bad move, he grumbled to his boys, "Let's go find that goddamn kid."

Charley stepped lightly the rest of the way as he trailed after Bill, sticking mostly to the shadows. He followed Bill to the chink's—a nondescript house on the edge of town where the Oriental folks gathered. Charley knew it was a dope den. In the windows hung red lanterns that just plain looked spooky.

Shit, Charley thought. I'll have to sit out here in this bone-rattling cold until he comes out and heads back to camp.

The chink attended to Bill with great care, for even the Chinese population of Cheyenne was aware of Bill's notoriety. They admired him as well because of his long hair, which he sometimes allowed one of the girls to braid into a queue, something the chink personally admired, who wore one too, as a show of submission to the Manchus who ruled his native China. Only Bill didn't know anything about Manchus and did not much care what the girls did with his hair once he was in the grips of what the chink called the "Sweet Desire."

Lying on the pallet, Bill felt as though he were floating through space, that whatever had kept him tethered to the earth had been cut, and it was a very pleasant feeling. It was more pleasant than drunkenness. It was more pleasant than being with a woman—even Squirrel Tooth Alice, who was about the most pleasurable woman he'd ever known. It was more pleasant than riding a horse across the prairies at a gallop with the wind streaming through his hair. It was more pleasant, he concluded, than heaven itself.

The only bad part was afterward. For after he left the chink's, he felt at loose ends, not wholly together for several hours. It was like walking through mud, and his head hurt, though his eyes felt better. He would always make his way back to his and Charley's camp, climb into the tent and rest and try to get reconnected to the earth. It was a paltry feeling that made him feel human and vulnerable. But while in the arms of the Sweet Desire, he felt invincible.

Charley shivered, huddled in his coat and watched the stars and wished he had a cocktail to at least warm his insides. An hour, maybe two or three, passed before he saw Bill emerge from the dope den. He stood for several minutes as though uncertain which way to go, then Charley saw him head toward their camp and felt a great deal of relief. The streets were all but empty now. Which was good for the both of them.

They were perhaps a city block from camp—Charley could see the white tents and canvas of the wagons—when there was suddenly two gunshots close together. *Pop! Bang!* Bill staggered and Charley thought him shot for sure. The shots had come from behind.

Charley had trouble pulling all that gun Ned Buntline had given him from its holster and swore a silent vow that he'd go and buy himself a regular Peace-maker Colt first thing in the morning, if he lived that long, and toss the Ned Buntline Special in a water barrel.

Then for several seconds nothing happened and it was as silent as though the sound of guns being shot never happened. Charley wondered if it had or if he was so tired and sleepy he'd dreamt it.

He looked again at Bill, who was now moving off toward the camp, seemingly unharmed and unshot.

Then a shadow from the rear came forward, and Charley aimed the long barrel toward it and said, "You best stop right there if you don't want your lights shot out!"

"It's me," the voice said. Teddy Blue stepped into the light fallen from a saloon window.

"What the hell!"

"Hank Rain," Teddy said. "He was following you."

"You shot him?"

"I might have, I'm not sure."

Charley was at a loss as to what to do exactly, go and look and see if he could find Hank Rain's body or follow Bill to camp.

"Back there," Teddy said with a nod of his head.

Charley saw him examining the sleeve of his coat. "He get you?"

"No, came close, though. You best go on with your pard back to camp. I'll look around and see if I can find a blood trail or if he's lain down somewhere up in that alley."

Charley look around. Bill was nearing the camp, his hat full of moonlight.

"You sure?"

"Go ahead."

Charley went without asking Teddy what he'd been doing out that time of night.

If he had asked, Teddy would have told him that it had just been good luck on his part because he wasn't dogging Hickok but instead looking for William Bonney. He'd even thought at first that the figure he'd seen lingering in the shadows was the kid, until the man stepped forward enough into the light that Teddy could see the blanket coat and realized there was only one reason he was lurking.

He'd called to him softly. But men like Hank Rain didn't hold conversations in dark places when they had their mind on other work, and so he'd fired once and gotten fire returned. Teddy hoped he'd hit something inside that blanket coat besides cotton.

He'd seen Charley turn, pulling that big silly-looking revolver, and thought he had better identify himself before Charley did something like get lucky.

Teddy drifted back to the place where he'd spotted Hank Rain, and looked for signs of blood or a body but saw nothing. Farther in the alley it was too dark to see anything. Shit, he thought, I'm not very damn good at this business. The only sense of safety he felt was that Hank Rain probably didn't know who it was shot at him, and that gave Teddy some advantage in case they ran into each other again. The downside was, there was nothing he could take to Sheriff Carr in the way of charges—it would just be one man's word against another. If Hank Rain was still of earthly bonds, Teddy knew he would have to deal with him again, of that much he was certain. A hungry wolf never stays hungry longer than he can help it.

He went back to the boardinghouse, found the light still on in the parlor, and found Kathleen Bonney still up, her pretty Irish face drawn with worry.

"I couldn't find him," Teddy said. "Did he come back here?"

"No. But Jeff Carr and some deputies came looking for him."

"For the charge of murder?"

"He didn't say. He just said William had shot a man."

"That's good news, then."

"Why do you say so?"

"Because the only ones who know he did is William and the man he shot, and it sure wasn't William who told Carr he shot his cousin, so it had to be the cousin."

Her eyes widened with hope. "Then perhaps . . ."

"Doesn't mean, however, that the cousin hasn't since died."

He saw her hopeful face crumple.

"Not to worry yet," he said. "Best get some rest. I'll find out what I can come morning."

She rose, and suddenly he wanted to go to her and hold her again, but it wasn't the time or place, so he went to his room and took off his coat and boots and the shoulder holster. He removed the Lightning and ejected the spent shell, replacing it with a fresh load.

He then reset the hammer down on an empty chamber like old John Sears had taught him, reclined on the bed and closed his eyes.

He lay there a long time thinking about the kid, and about her.

Chapter 13

———•◦•———

Teddy awoke to the knocking at the door.

"Come in," he said.

The door opened and she was there looking pale and more tired than before.

"Did he come back?"

"No," she said.

"You want to come in?"

She glanced nervously about. "It might not look right if I did."

"I'll get dressed and meet you in the kitchen."

She had them each a cup of coffee waiting when he got there.

"I'm sorry you're involved in this," she said.

"Don't be."

"I went to see Sheriff Carr. He said the man William shot was his cousin Henry and that he would survive but that he would never talk again—that the bullet ruined his voice box."

"There's something you need to know, Kathleen.

William told me the trouble was over a woman who works down at the Gold Room . . ."

"A prostitute?"

"Yes."

Her eyes fell to the contents of her cup. "I guess I didn't realize that William's a young man now, not a boy any longer."

"She was this other man's girlfriend apparently. I don't know what happened exactly, but the way William made it sound, it was self-defense."

She shook her head sadly. "What chance does he stand against the law in this town, considering the circumstances?"

"Probably slim to none."

Teddy could see that it was snowing again, could see it silently collide with the window's glass panes.

"I should have gone to New Mexico," she said.

He thought of old John Sears, who was probably down in that country now, or dead. "What's in New Mexico?"

"Nothing really. But my doctor advised me to go. You see, I'm a consumptive."

He'd heard her coughing at night, but figured it was nothing more than a cold.

"I was saving money to go," she said.

"What about your business here?"

"I just rent the house. I can do the same in New Mexico."

"Maybe you should start to make some plans for getting down to that country . . . take William with you."

"I'd like that very much, Mr. Blue. If only I could

find him and leave with him before Jeff Carr and his men find him."

"Let me do some checking around. Why don't you start making plans to clear out of here in a day or two."

Their eyes met again and something unspoken passed between them—somehow they both knew that had the circumstances been different, there would have been untold possibilities.

"Do you have enough for such a trip?" he asked.

"Yes."

He nodded ruefully and set his cup aside, then shucked himself into his coat and hat and went out into the falling snow.

He had not gone far when he ran into Charley Utter.

"It looks like one of them glass balls you can buy in San Francisco," he said, looking up at the snow.

"What, the weather?"

"She's pretty when she snows, but mighty damn problematic for a man who wants to get into the wind. I'm thinking me and Bill need to clear out of here and head to Deadwood soon. Last night was a bad omen in my book."

"If there is someone intent on killing your pard," Teddy said, "what makes you think they wouldn't follow you to Deadwood?"

"I figure once we get to Deadwood, everyone will be too distracted by the gold and riches to want to waste their time on assassination. I figure once there, Bill won't bother nobody and nobody will bother him."

"Where is he now?"

"Asleep in the tent. Once he's gone to see the chink, he'll sleep for up to ten hours straight."

"I'm looking for somebody," Teddy said. "I could use an extra pair of eyes."

"Sure."

Teddy told him the situation with the kid and Sheriff Carr.

"Well, I never cared much for that sucker," Charley said. "He always acted a little pompous for my tastes, and Bill sure as hell don't care for him. He told Bill last night if he saw him on the streets today he'd arrest him for vagrancy."

"I need to find this kid and get him the hell out of Cheyenne."

"Hells bells, I'll keep my eye peeled for him."

"By the way, it was a fight over that gal you went upstairs with in the Gold Room the other evening."

Charley's eyes filled with bliss at the thought of the girl.

"Lilly's the best dove in Cheyenne," he said. "I reckon if you're going to shoot a man in the windpipe over a gal, she'd be the one you'd do it for."

"I'm on my way over there now to talk to her."

"She has a way of distracting a man from his problems," Charley said.

"You see that kid, come let me know, okay?"

Charley nodded, still feeling fresh from his morning bath and hungry as a yellow dog.

Teddy found the Gold Room quiet that time of morning. One of the bartenders was asleep on one of the billiard tables and another in a chair. He shook snow off his hat and went over to a man swamping out the place—a fellow with long skinny arms and a long skinny neck who looked a little like a wild turkey when he stood in the light, blinking his eyes.

"I'm looking for Lilly, one of the girls that works here," Teddy said.

"They don't do no work before noon generally," the man said. "They're all asleep like everybody else . . ."

Teddy took a silver dollar and placed it in the man's vest pocket.

"Which is her crib?"

The man looked up toward the railing that encircled the second floor.

"Third curtain on the left off the stairs."

Teddy took the stairs two at a time, and when he got to it, pulled the curtain back slow. She was asleep on the narrow bed, a bare shoulder peeking from beneath the several blankets, her hair a black nest. The crib smelled of sweat and cheap toilet water and despair.

He eased inside, knelt by the bed and gently shook her awake.

She didn't act startled when she opened her eyes. Her breath was sour.

"Well, go ahead and shuck off your drawers," she said sleepily, rubbing her eyes. "I just have to go make water first."

"I'm not here for that," he said.

She blinked, stifled a yawn.

"I'm here to find out if you know where William is."

Suddenly she was more awake. "It wasn't his fault," she said.

"I don't care anything about that, I just need to find him before Jeff Carr or one of his deputies does."

"You going to hurt him?"

"No, I'm a friend of his mother's."

She looked doubtful.

"Tell me," he said.

"I'll show you . . ."

He watched as she threw off the blankets, un-ashamed of her nakedness, and dressed quickly into pants and a heavy shirt, coat and cap. She was about the size of the kid, and like he had mentioned, just a year older. Teddy did not divert his gaze but felt he should have.

She led him down the stairs, out the back door and down an alley flowing with slops and human waste in places with snow falling and collecting, making it seem more pristine than it really was. They came out the far end of the alley and crossed the street to a large tent at the edge of an encampment of tents. A stovepipe poking through the canvas roof spewed black smoke and soot. Lilly walked to the flap and called in. The flap was thrown back by a large woman wearing an eye patch.

The woman cast her good eye on him.

"What do you want, Lilly, and who's he?"

"He's a friend of William's."

The woman looked up and down the street. "Get in here quick."

They entered. Everything a body needed to subsist on the prairies was in that tent, including a wood stove, pallet, table, chairs, washtub, old animal pelts spread upon the flooring, clothes, piles of newspapers yellowed from age, and a large steamer trunk.

"What you want here, mister?"

"I'm looking for the kid. He needs to clear out of town before Jeff Carr nabs him."

The woman looked at Lilly. Lilly shrugged, uncertain.

"How do I know you ain't one of Carr's men come to trick me?"

"I'm a friend of the kid's mother—Kathleen."

The woman closed her eye. There was naught but the sound of the wind smacking the sides of the tent. The woman began to chant unintelligibly. Teddy looked at the girl.

"She's a spiritualist . . ."

The woman continued to chant, then stopped and stood silent, her good eye yet closed.

"Madam Moustache?" Lilly said.

Finally she opened the eye, looked at them, especially Teddy.

"Okay," she said, then called, "William, come out."

The steamer trunk opened and out stepped the kid.

He came and stood next to Lilly and put his arm around her. They hardly seemed more than a pair of children freshly in love and too innocent for all the trouble that surrounded them.

"I guess you believe me now," he said.

"I believe your mother is ready to sneak you out of the territory."

"Did the bastard die?"

"No, but he's pretty well ruined on conversation."

The kid smiled.

"It's not funny," Teddy said. "Shooting someone never is."

"He should have thought of that before he picked a fight with me."

"Can you keep him hid until I come back for him?" Teddy said. "Might be a day or two yet before his mother is prepared to leave."

"Yes," Madam Moustache said. "His name is written in the stars, it will fall from men's lips years from now. He is a flame that burns quickly."

"You stay out of sight," Teddy said to William. "Jeff Carr or one of his men pick you up, there's nothing anyone can do for you."

"I'm not afraid of Jeff Carr."

"You should be."

Teddy made his way back across town to the boardinghouse. He found her in her room with a bloodstained handkerchief she'd been coughing into.

"I found him," he said.

"Good," she said. "I'll be ready to leave Cheyenne by tomorrow."

He turned to go.

"I am sorry we won't get to go horse riding together," she said.

"I am too."

He walked down to the telegraph office and wired George Bangs:

INCIDENT LAST NIGHT INVOLVING H. ATTEMPT ON HIM WAS UNSUCCESSFUL. THREAT REAL,

HOWEVER. I EXPECT MORE, WILL KEEP YOU IN-
FORMED. T. BLUE.

The snow had stopped, but the sky was full of fat-
bellied dark clouds shuffled by a hard wind out of the
north. Teddy walked over to Jeff Carr's office and
found the sheriff seated behind his desk.

"There's something you should know," Teddy said.

Carr leveled his gaze on Teddy.

"Someone's out to take Bill Hickok's life."

"Why should this concern you?" Carr asked.

"It doesn't really. But since you don't care for trouble in your town, I thought you should know."

"I'll ask you again, what are you doing in
Cheyenne?"

"Just passing through."

"Somehow, I doubt it."

"You want dead men on the streets of your town,
Sheriff, that's up to you."

Teddy walked out and almost into the arms of
Charley Utter.

"I was just going to go in and tell Carr somebody's
trying to kill Billy."

"I've already told him."

"What'd he say?"

"He wanted to know what my reason was for being in town."

"He's a class A son of a bitch," Charley said. "Let
me take you over to the Gold Room and buy you a
cocktail, old son."

"It's a little early for me."

"A little known fact," Charley said, "is that the average life span for a man on these prairies is forty years. I'm thirty-eight, means I got two years yet to live, maybe less, maybe a few more. Either way, I ain't going to waste it on formalities, and you shouldn't either."

"Okay, but just one."

Charley smiled so broadly Teddy could see his back teeth.

Chapter 14

———————————

Paris Bass arrived in Abilene on such a blustery day that men's hats tumbled down its dusty streets like pie plates. His own was tied neatly on by the blue silk scarf he'd discreetly taken from the woman who loved Phil Coe; he'd already forgotten her name, but not the incident that allowed him access to her wardrobe. And when he thought about the woman who loved Phil Coe, which he did more often than he thought he might, he always recalled her thin pale limbs and the lovely smell of her freshly washed hair.

He saw a saloon—The Alamo—and reined in there and dismounted; his ass felt beat half to death from the long ride. There were several customers clutched at the bar, drinking and talking, spitting and smoking cigars.

He stepped up and ordered a whiskey—"Old Bandit," he said, and the barkeep poured him two fingers of the rye into a clean glass. He threw it back and it felt like he'd swallowed a hot brand, but that's the way he liked it, and he ordered another.

The barkeep looked at him, the dark hat and dark clothes, and said, "You the new preacher?"

Paris Bass smiled slow when he smiled.

"Just passing through, friend. Do you serve victuals?"

"Free lunch," the barkeep said, tossing a nod down toward the far end of the bar, where there were plates of luncheon meats, sliced bread, pickled beets, and a jar of hard-boiled eggs.

Paris Bass threw back the second rye and rubbed the bristle of his cheeks.

"Grateful," he said, sauntered down to the end of the bar and made himself a sandwich, then took it to a table and ate as he read his Bible.

I have seen all things in my days of vanity. There is a just man who perishes in his righteousness. There is a wicked man who prolongs his life in his wickedness.

He smiled, thinking about himself and men like Bill Hickok. Which of the two of them was wicked and which was righteous? Well, surely God would sort through them all when their hour came—Paris Bass only sent them to their heavenly home, he did not pass judgment.

Six-Toed Pete sauntered in. His hair stood like scattered straw atop his head. The bartender asked, "Where's your hat, Pete?"

"Halfway to Oklyhomer by now, the way that damn wind is blowing."

Pete ordered a glass of Mexican Mustang and nursed it like it was a sick relative, all the while looking around. His gaze settled on the new man.

"Who's that?" he asked the barkeep.

"The new preacher, I think."

"What's he doing in a shithole like this if he's a preacher?"

"Hey, how'd you like me to thump you over the head with my hickory club?"

"Oh, you know I don't mean nothing by it. Just that preachers don't usually do their drinking in public."

"Why don't you go ask him."

"I think by gar I will."

Six-Toed Pete carried his glass with its contents over to where the stranger sat and introduced himself.

"Jake says you're the new preacher."

Paris Bass looked up from his Bible. "An honest mistake, I suppose."

"You talk fancy."

"I assure you I am not."

"I never could understand why this town needs another church or school. It's gone plum to hell since the old days when the cowboys came up from Texas and created a stir. Back then we had ten piano players, twenty saloons, eight whorehouses, and four dope dens. Now we ain't got hardly shit but this place and the Bull's Head, and those ladies of the Righteous League is trying to close *them* down. It ain't nothing against you personal, but what the hell do we need another preacher for?"

"As I understand it, there were also dead men lying about on the streets every morning. 'A dead man for breakfast.' Isn't that what they used to say?"

"Oh hell, we had some troubles, but old Wild Bill put 'em to rest—toes up if they wasn't careful."

"Could I buy you another of those?" Paris Bass said, nodding at the glass in Six-Toed Pete's fist.

"You surely as hell could."

Paris Bass allowed as how Pete should sit there at the table with him, and Pete sat gladly and nursed the second drink much in the same manner he had the first, his lips nibbling at the firewater like a mouse's nibbling at cheese in a trap.

"Tell me," Paris Bass said, "do you know where Mr. Hickok went to after he left here?"

"No. There's been one or two reports he was killed, but Bill wrote the newspapers denying it. Don't guess a dead man could write newspapers, do you?"

"No, I don't suppose he could."

"You the only preacher I ever saw drink in public."

"I am in the world, but I am not *of* the world."

"Huh?"

"It's a quote, sir, from the good book," Paris Bass said, patting the Bible.

"I never got into it much myself. What little I read never did make no sense."

"Why do they call you Six-Toed? Do you actually have six toes, Pete?"

"On my left foot, wanna see?"

"No. I'll take your word for it."

"Was married once to a woman who didn't have any—got 'em froze off in the winter of 'seventy-two. Between us, we had eleven." Pete's laughter sounded like busting glass.

"Could you tell me one other thing?"

"Sure."

"You mentioned something earlier about the dens

of inequity that once existed here. Are there still any?"

"You mean whorehouses?"

"Yes, that's exactly what I mean."

"Just Squirrel Tooth Alice's place. She used to be old Wild Bill's gal."

"How charming."

Paris Bass got Pete to give him directions to Alice's. She answered the door wearing a black silk kimono, and he could see right away that she would be pleasing to him. They negotiated a price, and Paris Bass climbed out of his clothes and Alice out of her kimono and any jake walking down the street could have heard the iron bed rattling against the walls.

Afterward she said, "I never met a preacher who could do what you just did."

"And you probably never will."

They lay there in the bed a while, listening to the wind sing along the eaves.

"I understand that you were Wild Bill's paramour," Paris Bass said.

"Why, yes. Until they fired him as marshal."

"Why did they fire him?"

She remembered that night so clearly. It was the last time she ever tasted Bill's lips. It made her blue to think of it now.

"He shot some men," she said.

"That was part of his job, wasn't it?"

"One of the fellers he shot was his own deputy . . ."

"And the other?"

"Phil *Goddamn* Coe. I seen it all."

"I'd love to hear the story."

"I ain't in the story-telling business, or the free business either. And just because you're a preacher don't mean you get no discounts."

"Of course, here's five dollars more."

Later, as he tugged on his boots, tucked in his shirt, shucked into his jacket, he said, "Does he ever write you?"

"I get a letter now and then."

"May I see the last one he sent?"

"No. It's very personal what me and Bill got. Ain't for just anybody's eyes."

"I see," Paris Bass said, reaching into one of his inner pockets and producing a small silver pistol with mother-of-pearl grips that he pressed to Alice's wrinkled brow. "Well, I insist."

"Since you put it that way . . ."

The letter's envelope was postmarked *Cheyenne, WT*, and dated the month before. He placed the letter in his pocket, much to Alice's chagrin; she'd been hoping to someday sell the letter to, say, a newspaperman or the like; such types were always paying for *memorabilia* of men like Wild Bill.

"Say," she protested. "I'd like that back."

The Preacher cut his gaze toward her and said, "Of course you realize that a true gentleman would never shoot a lady. But then, I'm not such a gentleman, and you're hardly a lady."

He cut his gaze in her direction. His eyes were without hint of mercy.

"Well, love, it has proven interesting, and now I must go and find your Mr. Wild Bill and shoot him dead. But just in case you have it in your heart to save him—"

Alice would tell the others later that she didn't remember the shooting.

"I can't even recall the sound or what it felt like or nothing."

Of course, she was questioned as to why a preacher would pay for the services of a whore, then shoot her. But Alice sure wasn't telling the true reason, for fear he might get word his bullet had missed the vital part of her skull—gotten lost, as it did, in the tangle of her thick tresses piled atop her head—and did very little actual damage. It scared her so bad her hair turned white overnight, and she suspended business for several days. And when she finally did take her first cowboy to her room, she shook so terribly it scared him into thinking she was having a mad fit. A few days after this, Alice thought she heard the voice of God talking to her, telling her to leave Texas and go warn Bill.

"Is that what you want?" she said. "For me to go warn Bill?"

But the voice of God as she heard it began sounding a lot like the wind, and she couldn't be certain it wasn't the wind all along and not her nearly shot brains playing mean tricks on her. Either way, she knew that she and Kansas were quits.

Six-Toed Pete had watched Paris Bass ride out of town on a big stud horse before he knew that the

Preacher had shot Alice, and he said to a cohort, "There goes a mighty mysterious feller."

"He looks like a preacher," the cohort said.

"I thought he was too."

A week later, Six-Toed Pete and his companion watched Alice board the flier, and they continued to watch until the train and all its cars became lost on the wide prairies.

"I reckon that experience with the Preacher ruined her," Pete said.

"I reckon it did too."

"There goes the best whore this town has ever seen."

"Goddamn that preacher."

"Goddamn him all to hell."

Chapter 15

Charley shook Bill by the boots until his eyes popped open.

"You back among the living?"

Bill sat up and looked around, blinked twice and said, "Did I kill someone?"

"That's a crazy enough question, but no, you did not."

"I was dreaming I was surrounded by a posse of drunken cowboys. They had their pistols pulled and aimed at me. I was about to go down fighting . . ."

"You remember anything about last night?"

Bill's eyes were rimmed red and leaking tears, and he swiped at them and said, "Not too much."

"Somebody tried to shoot out your lights."

Bill shook his head. "I don't recall nobody shooting at me."

"That feller I know, the one I introduced—Teddy Blue. He might have took the feller out for you."

"Why would he do that?"

"He's a good pard is all I can say."

"I'm beholden to him then."

Charley looked up at the sky—it was part blue and part gray and didn't seem like it could make up its mind which it was going to stay.

"I'm thinking of heading out for a little while," Charley said.

"Where to?"

"I ain't a hundred percent sure, but I'm thinking of making a run down to Denver to see my wife."

"How long will you be gone?"

"I'll be back in time to go up to Deadwood with you."

Bill looked glum. He'd gotten used to Charley being there, Charley staking him to card games, Charley buying him cocktails, Charley making sure his clothes got taken to the laundry and picked up again. Charley was like having a wife, only not half as much trouble.

"You want me to go with you?"

"No, best you stay here and keep an eye on our camp. But I was thinking that while I was gone, maybe it would be all right with you to have that Teddy Blue as your pard. How would you feel about that?"

Bill crawled out of the tent, stood with some degree of difficulty and said, "I've got to piss," and walked off toward the trees where men did their business, since the only public outhouses were several blocks away into town. The big pines seemed to have walked right up to the edge of the town and stopped. They made good places for a man to stand behind to do his business.

Charley waited until Bill returned, then the two of

them walked into town for breakfast and a chance for Charley to take his morning bath.

Bill was a fastidious person himself, but he didn't bathe every morning the way Charley did, and so he sat upon an old chair in the back of the barbershop while Charley did his bathing and pared away at his fingernails with a pocketknife.

"How long you say you think you'll be gone?" Bill asked.

"Two, maybe three weeks."

"Weather might break before then. Everybody might beat us up to the hills and stake the best claims."

"You ain't seriously contemplating digging into the earth, are you?" Charley said, his head a crown of soapy lather.

"No, but we oughter stake a claim or two and hire somebody to work it."

"True enough. Maybe if the weather breaks before I get back you should go on up ahead of me and stake a claim or two for us just in case."

"Maybe I oughter."

"You hear anything from Agnes lately?"

Charley sort of held his breath in case Agnes had written Bill and confessed their secret. But Bill simply shook his head.

"I expect to hear from her any day now. I write her twice a week."

"You think any more on what I said back at camp?"

"I don't need no pard other than you, Charley."

"I was just thinking it might be good to have someone watch your back while I'm gone."

Bill stopped paring his fingernails and looked at Charley in that sad way he had of looking when he was disappointed in something.

"I know what you're thinking. That my eyes is gone on me and I can't take care of myself. But I'll tell you this, old son, if it gets to that point, I'd just as soon somebody shoot out my lights."

"Ah, Bill, I wasn't thinking that at all. We all can stand to have us a good pard. Why you said yourself there are fellers who'd like to put you as a notch on their guns. Like whoever that was last night tried to potshoot you . . ."

"I believe in fate, don't you? If it is meant to happen, it will, and if not, me and Agnes will live a long and happy life together. You can't stop what is already written on the wind, Charley."

The barber's chink came in and poured in another pail of hot water over Charley's soapy head, and he felt about three days better.

"You want to take a bath?" Charley said, getting out of the tub.

"No, I took one on Friday," Bill said.

Charley and Bill were eating their breakfast in the American Café when Teddy Blue walked in. Charley waved him over.

"You ate yet, old son?"

Teddy could see Charley wanted him to join them. Bill seemed completely neutral, busy as he was eating the hash off his plate.

"I wouldn't want to intrude," Teddy said, and started to find himself another table. But Bill looked up from under his sandy brows and said, "Come on and have a seat."

Teddy ordered flapjacks and coffee, his mind still on the kid and Kathleen Bonney, but a little on the shooting last night as well.

"Charley tells me you killed a feller last night," Bill said.

"I don't think I killed him, I'm not even sure I hit him."

"Charley said he was stalking me for assassination . . ."

"I can't say for sure. He was lurking in the shadows, had his gun pulled. I called to him and he snapped one off at me and I snapped one off back."

"You know who the feller was?"

Teddy and Charley exchanged glances.

"I couldn't say for sure, it was dark."

Bill must have bit a piece of bone in his hash, for he grimaced then picked something small and white from his teeth and looked at it before wiping it off his finger.

"I once ate dog in a Pawnee camp that tasted a lot like this hash," he said, as though the whole subject of assassination hadn't even come up.

Teddy ate his flapjacks and Charley his scrambled eggs and the three of them glanced out of the plate-glass window at the traffic trying to navigate the muddy street. Finally Bill finished, dabbed at his mouth with a linen napkin and said, "Charley's leaving for a time to go visit his wife in Denver."

Teddy exchanged looks with Charley, who offered a rather sheepish portrait of himself.

"Said he thought it'd be a good idear if me and you were pards if the weather broke while he was gone. What would you say to something like that?"

Teddy measured his response.

"I'd say that would be all right with me if it would you. I'm sure I'd not make you as good a pard as old Charley here, but I can be trusted."

"Are you in the habit of bathing every morning?"

"I like to stay clean about my person, but I can't vow to taking a bath every morning out here on these prairies. It isn't always practicable."

Bill smiled. "That's my philosophy exactly. But old Charley here would rather drown in his bath than to skip it."

Charley feigned indignation, and Bill said he was going back to camp for a siesta, that he was still feeling a bit "floozy" and that he wanted to write Agnes a letter. He stood, settled his hat down on his head, and shifted his revolvers around so they rode just so inside his red sash, then wandered out into the half-sunlit, half-gray morning.

"Bill ain't the early kind," Charley said.

"When are you leaving for Denver?"

"This afternoon on the flier. Do you think you'll be all right watching Billy by yourself?"

"I'll wander over to his camp later after he's had time to take his siesta. It'll give me time to get a few errands done."

"Say, you ever find that kid you were looking for?"

"Yeah."

"Looks like Jeff Carr found him too," Charley said, staring out the plate-glass window.

Teddy saw Jeff Carr and two of his deputies marching the kid down the sidewalk, his hands and ankles cuffed.

Teddy made his way to Jeff Carr's office just as they were putting the kid in a cell to the rear of the place. Jeff Carr was racking his double barrel.

"I'm here to pay his fine," Teddy said as Carr turned to look at him.

"You his daddy?"

"No. I'm a friend of his mother's."

Carr got a look on his face that Teddy didn't much care for.

"He ain't been arraigned yet so no bail's been set. And if I have my say, there won't be any bail either."

"What's the charge?"

"Attempted murder."

"I'd like to speak to him."

"That ain't even a consideration."

"I'm his lawyer. She hired me to represent him."

Carr looked skeptical. "Thought you said you were a friend of his mother's?"

"And an attorney . . . He has a right to legal representation. You want, we can go find a judge."

"The judge won't arrive for three days."

Teddy held his gaze.

Jeff Carr still looked doubtful but could see the man across from him might be more trouble than he was worth. Carr wasn't a man who liked complications cluttering his sense of duty.

"You've got five minutes with the prisoner."

*   *   *

The kid sat on the cot looking unafraid and unconcerned.

"Thought I told you to stay put," Teddy said.

The kid looked at him, said, "You think this shit-hole can hold me?"

"I think Jeff Carr is hoping you'll do something stupid so he can blow your brains out and save the time of a trial."

"Jeff Carr will be the one ends up with a hole shot in him, like that fool cousin of his did . . ."

"I'll need you to lay it out for me in complete detail what happened that night if I'm to represent you at trial."

The kid's eyes narrowed.

"Unless, of course, you'd rather have the judge pick you a lawyer. Maybe someone who is a friend of the sheriff's."

The kid stood from the cot, walked over to the bars and put his hands around them, felt how cold and hard they were as he looked through them into the face of Teddy Blue.

"You doing this for me so you can get to her?" he said.

"Don't be a bigger fool than you already are."

"She tell you about my pa?"

"We haven't exactly been sitting around in the parlor having tea and conversation."

"He left out one day and didn't come back. Dead maybe. Most likely, though, he ran off. She still pines for him, and I do believe if he showed his ugly face I'd shoot it off. But make no mistake, I ain't looking for another daddy and she ain't looking for another husband."

"We're not here to discuss what happened to your pa or about what your mother wants or anything other than how I'm going to try and keep you from going to the nearest state prison. You know anything about what it's like in prison?"

Something flicked through the kid's eyes, traveled down to his mouth, ticked in his jaw.

"Tell me what happened that night between you and Carr's cousin?"

"Sure I'll tell you. But it ain't going to matter. They done caught the rabbit. But this old rabbit ain't done running yet."

"I'm listening," Teddy said.

After leaving the jail with the kid's story in his head, Teddy headed toward the boardinghouse, where he found Kathleen elbows deep into a vat of hot wash water, beads of sweat dotting her face.

"William's in jail," he said.

The news seemed to stagger her. He pulled a chair out and set her in it.

"I am going to represent him at trial."

She seemed not to understand. He explained it.

"If you don't mind," she said afterward, "there's a bottle of cognac in the cupboard . . ."

He poured her a small glass. She drank it, coughed. He poured more.

"William told me about his father . . ."

"Inconsequential," she said. "It's been years. I obtained a divorce. William still holds out hope he'll return someday. He won't, and William won't admit he wants his father back. The damn bullheaded Irish . . ." she said.

"It can't have been easy for you."

"No, but who ever made any of us a promise that life would be easy?"

"I still think you need to be making plans to leave as soon as possible," he said.

Those warm sea-green eyes searched his own quizzically.

"There always has to be a backup plan in case the first one doesn't work out."

"You're not thinking . . ."

"Anything's possible, Kathleen."

He left her and went to the camp of Wild Bill, whose feet he saw protruding through the end of his and Charley's tent. Charley was trimming his moustaches with a pair of ladies' scissors in one hand while looking into a small mirror held in the other.

"Have to look presentable for the missus," he said.

"What time you leaving out?"

"Noon flier."

"You want to leave me a way I can send you a wire in case I need to?"

Charley wrote it out on a piece of paper from Bill's notebook. "I surely hope you don't need to," he said, handing him the address.

"I might."

"I hope not."

"Me too."

* * *

Wind sang through the trees and the sky grew more gray and it sure enough looked as though the weather might not ever break good enough for men to go to the country north, where the gold and riches lay.

It felt somehow like the end of the line, this place.

Bill slept like a child. Or a dead man, maybe.

Chapter 16

————◆————

Temptation comes in its many forms, and Bill wasn't sure if Alice was really there or he was dreaming she was.

The sun had crossed the sky from one end to the other, and shadows were starting to encroach upon the land—the shadows of the pines lay twenty feet long along the ground, the same with wagons and horses and every man and every woman standing.

Before he saw Alice's face, Bill was in the arms of a nightmare. Phil Coe had his revolver pressed to Bill's ear and he could feel the cold steel and hear the click of the hammer being thumbed back and Coe saying, "You thought you kilt me in Abilene but you never did and now I've come to shoot out your lights!" Then Phil killed him, and he saw himself lying in a casket with all his old pards marching past and several women he'd known and fought over, including Sara Schull that time he shot it out with McCanles. Even that bone-faced Calamity Jane was in line, drunk as usual, spouting off to anyone who would listen how sad she was her "lover" had been kilt by Phil

Goddamn Coe and what she was going to do about it—"seek revenge and blow his melon to shreds." Somebody had put his trusty rifle in the coffin with him—as if it were going to do him any good in the place where he was going.

Then he looked up, unable to move so much as a whisker—for dead don't feel nothing and can't move nothing—and there stood Squirrel Tooth Alice with tears running down her pretty rouged cheeks.

"Oh Bill, oh Bill," she sobbed, and he half felt sorry for her, for she was a good old gal as there ever was and he pretty much loved her at one time, but then he saw Olive and fell in love with her. But Olive wasn't a true heart and took turns going back and forth between him and Phil Coe, and that's what got it all started. Phil Coe's drunken display and loud-mouthed threat was just the capper; they both knew it was going to end that night—each thinking it would be the other shut up for eternity.

He come up out of the dream gasping and clawing for his pistols, and had one cocked and aimed and the other about there when he realized it wasn't a dream and Alice was real. Only thing was, her hair was pure white, not dark and pretty like it used to be.

"Lord God, don't shoot me, Bill!"

That was the trouble with sleeping in the day, he always had those bad, bad dreams.

He put away his guns, crawled out of the tent and said, "You was in a dream I was having all about my funeral . . ."

"You always had them awful dreams, Bill. Sometimes I was afraid to sleep with you. Afraid you'd wake up out of one of them and blast me."

"Oh, I never would."

"Ain't you glad to see me?"

He chewed on whether he should tell her about Agnes. Decided it could wait just a little.

"What are you doing here?" he said.

"Come to find you, Bill. I got to warn you about something! I come all this way to prove my love for you."

"Warn me of what?"

"A man is coming to kill you, Bill. He come and ask me where you was. I didn't want to tell him nothing, but he made me tell him. Then he shot me in the head, and except for the providence of God and the fact he had shot me with a little bullet and my hair and all, I'd be dead this very minute."

Bill sat on a stump and pulled on his boots one at a time. Alice was always an excitable sort, especially if she got into the whiskey too heavy, which Bill figured she was to be telling such a fantastic story. The sky was turning the color of a plum, and clouds were stretched across it like fingers. Bill always admired what the sky could do when there were clouds and a setting sun together.

When Alice saw Bill's lack of concern, she said, "You believe me, don't you, Bill?"

"You been drinking, Alice?"

"Some, but not so much I'd—"

Bill cut her off: "It don't concern me fellers is out to kill me. Fellers has been out to kill me from the day I set foot in this country. And I reckon if there is one who will kill me, it will be a stroke of fate or pure madman's luck. Now get on along there, Alice."

"Bill, is there room enough in that tent for two?"

Bill looked back as if it was the first time he noticed his and Charley's tent.

"It wouldn't be right," he said.

"Why wouldn't it?"

"I've gone respectable, Alice."

"What's that supposed to mean?"

Bill figured he'd made a vow to Agnes to stay loyal and true, and besides, hard as it was getting to piss anymore, he realized he had caught a case of the drip and wasn't exactly sure when or from who. It took all the urge out of him for women. Just the thought of it made him cringe a little. Life's pleasure doors were starting to close to him and he didn't know how much more of it he could stand. Sometimes when he thought about death, he thought it would be a blessing.

"You'll have to excuse me," he said. "I have to go make water."

Bill walked up behind the trees and stood there a time, leaning as he could against the trunk of one especially large pine, and tried not to think too hard on anything because the more he concentrated on the task at hand the harder it became to perform it.

You've sure enough started to come apart at the threads, old son, he told himself, the darkness creeping closer and closer to his boots. *Your eyes and dick are all but gone to hell on you. They ain't much left . . .*

*   *   *

Pretty soon he came back to the tent, beads of sweat riveted to his forehead and a cool wind starting to chase after the shadows.

"I know something bad's going on with you, Bill," Alice said. "What is it?"

"I got married, Alice. But it ain't a bad thing, I reckon."

He could see it took her breath away, and he offered her a bucket to sit on and said, "No use getting all melancholy on me. It's done and can't be undone."

"Who'd you marry, Bill?"

"Agnes Lake—the circus lady."

Alice ran it through her mind, that name, tried to put a face with it. The only one she could see was one that was plain and older by several years than Bill.

"That doughty widow came to Abilene that time with lions and horses and trick shot artists?"

"Now I'll take your description of her as just a case of simple jealousy, Alice. I know you aren't in your right thinking so I'll overlook it this once."

Alice began to shed tears, but Bill knew them to be of the crocodile variety for he'd seen them shed before.

"You've not been in your right head since you shot Phil Coe that night," she sobbed.

"Phil Coe didn't have nothing to do with it."

"Yes it did, Bill. Yes it did."

Alice grew inconsolable, as she always did when drunk. Bill figured to let her air out, get sober again and get in her right mind. Instead of running her off like he knew he oughter, he told her she could put her valise and herself in the tent for that night but come

the next day she'd have to find new quarters. He tried
to pass it off that Charley would not care much to
find a woman in his tent when he returned. Of course,
Charley would probably be delighted to find a female
in his tent, and especially one as bosomy as Alice. Bill
wandered into town feeling lower than the run-down
boot heels of a Texas cowboy. A good poker game
was what would cure his mood. He headed for the
Gold Room.

Teddy had stayed off a little ways and seen the
whole thing. He didn't want to be underfoot of Bill
but rather to gain his confidence slowly while main-
taining an aura of casualness. He saw the woman
talking to Bill, saw Bill walk off toward the trees then
return, and saw them talking some more before Bill
meandered off toward town looking less noble than
he usually looked.

He angled in from his position of observation and
fell in step with Hickok.

"I was just on my way over to your camp to see if
you wanted to join me for supper."

"That's a good idea," Bill said. "I don't suppose
you could stake me to some poker money after?"

"Yes, I could stake you say twenty dollars."

"Twenty oughter do it. I'll have it doubled in half
an hour."

Charley had not mentioned Bill's skill with the picture cards, but Teddy figured it must not be very good
for he was always getting Charley or someone other
to stake him to a game.

They went to the oyster bar at the Union Pacific
Railroad Hotel and dined on fresh oysters, Bill say-

ing, "A feller has to eat a lot of these to fill his belly, but they're tasty when dipped in melted butter."

Later, after Bill had lost the money Teddy staked him to and they stood having a cocktail at the bar, Bill said, "I'm thinking I need to clear out of town for a while myself."

"Why's that?" Teddy asked.

"It'd just be best . . ."

"Oh."

Bill sipped his cocktail while looking around the room. Teddy saw Ned Loyal and Hank Rain standing at the far end of the bar together. Hank had a red mark across his cheek that wasn't there the last time Teddy had seen him. It looked like it could have been made by a knife, or a bullet.

Teddy saw the two men eyeing him and Bill.

"Yes, maybe it's best you left for a while if you feel like leaving."

"Squirrel Tooth Alice showed up at my camp this evening unexpected. Maybe if I get into the wind for a few days, she'll leave without my having to ask her."

"Somebody from your past?"

"Old flame, but one that's still got some heat to it."

"And you being a married man . . ."

Bill looked at him. "A man's only as good as his word, in my book. I took a vow to my wife and I intend on keeping it."

"That's admirable."

Bill drained his glass, choosing to pass on the story Alice had told him about somebody coming to kill him. Hell, if he had a plug nickel for every yahoo intent on killing him, he'd be living in a mansion. But he wasn't living in no mansion and he sure wasn't dead yet!

"I guess I'll go and sleep out on the prairies tonight."

Teddy took out the key to his room and held it forth for Bill. "I have a room over at the widow Bonney's boardinghouse. You can sleep there tonight if you want."

"That's positively generous of you, old son. But where will you sleep?"

"Not to worry, Bill."

Hickok held forth his hand and Teddy shook it. Teddy felt he'd won Bill's confidence and respect in that simple gesture.

"Charley was right about you making a good pard."

The manager of the hotel came up and shook Bill's hand and asked if he could buy him a drink, and Bill accepted and said, "Buy one for my pard here too, Harry." He did, and then Bill asked Harry if he'd stake him to a poker game, and the manager said sure and gave Bill fifty dollars. Bill thanked him, then went off and bought his way into a game, making sure he got the seat where his back could be against the wall.

"That Bill's got the worst luck of any man I ever seen at the card tables," the manager said. "He calls it luck, I just think he's a piss poor hand at the game."

"Why'd you stake him then?" Teddy asked.

"Why? Hell, he's Wild Bill, that's why."

Teddy stayed put at a place along the bar where he could keep an eye on Bill. Ned Loyal and Hank Rain continued to collaborate about something, and finally Hank made his move, but Teddy intercepted him.

"I wouldn't if I were you."

Hank looked at him, a scowl troubling his features. "You wouldn't what?"

"Do whatever it is you're planning on doing. He'll kill you, and if he doesn't, I will."

Hank touched the fresh scar on his cheek. "Then it was you last night," he said.

"You think what you want."

"Maybe I'll do you first, then him."

"Your play."

Hank look around toward the bar, but Ned wasn't there any longer. Then suddenly it was as though a shadow moved in, and Bill said, "Trouble with you third-raters is you're never good enough to be first-raters. Like my pard said, 'Make your play.' "

But there wasn't any play to be made, for Bill had the barrel of one of his Navies pushed against the ribs of Hank Rain with the hammer thumbed back, and it wouldn't have taken anything at all to send a bullet into him. They all three knew and understood that much.

"There's been some sort of mistake here," Hank said.

"You goddamn right there is," Bill said. "Now pull that iron or clear out of town."

That's about when Hank started to sweat like it was July and he was bailing hay. "I'd be a fool . . . with you already drawn and cocked."

"You are a fool and about to be a dead fool," Hickok said.

"Shit," Hank said. "You shoot me like this, they'll hang you. I ain't drawing."

"Then get in the wind."

Hank Rain turned and walked away with as much pride as he had left.

Bill said to Teddy, "I can't see too good at more than ten feet. Let me know if he turns or goes for his six-banger."

Teddy waited until Hank cleared the room, then said, "You would have killed him and not given him a fighting chance, wouldn't you?"

"You damn right I would have. It's something you better heed too, old son."

Bill twisted his Navy about, stuck it butt forward in his sash and went back to his poker game. Teddy could still see that look in Bill's eyes that said he'd been a split second away from blowing Hank Rain's innards out.

About three in the morning Bill rose from his chair, shoveled his hair up under his hat, and headed for the door. Teddy joined him, making an excuse as to why.

"I need to get some things from my room before you bed down."

"That was a brave and kind thing you did back there tonight, old son."

"He's the one took a potshot at you the other night. Just so you know."

"I figured as much. That scratch on his cheek wasn't made by any woman."

"What if he tries again?"

"He won't. Whatever he had in him, ain't in him no

more. He had a look at the other side of the river and didn't care for what he saw."

They entered the boardinghouse and Teddy grabbed his valise, saying, "I know you're not normally an early riser, but I'll be down at the café for breakfast if you change your habit. I'd like to talk with you about your plans before you head out."

"Where's the privy?"

"Out back."

Bill nodded, stepped out through the rear door and closed it behind him.

Teddy headed back up the hall, but she opened her door when he went past.

"I waited for you to return," she said.

"I had to be somewhere."

She looked at the valise in his hand. "You're leaving?"

"Just for tonight. I gave my room to Wild Bill; I hope that's okay with you."

"Where will you stay?"

He shrugged. "The hotel's lobby maybe."

She stood back away from the door. "No."

"Are you sure?"

She reached for him and took him by the wrist, and he went in and closed the door behind them.

Chapter 17

————•◦•————

A cardinal, its blaze of red feathers, stood perched on the windowsill, and she said, "Look."

It was a thing of beauty in a most unbeautiful place, just as he saw her as a thing of beauty. She expressed the amazement of a child. She lay there with her back to him watching the crimson bird, and he was glad that they had not made love the night before, for he would have felt ruinous now, as though he'd stolen something.

He remembered waking sometime in the night and finding her there in his arms, her breathing like the purr of a cat, and she seemed so frail and vulnerable to him. Now she lay looking at the bird in simple amazement, her skin sallow in that early light, her body warm against his, her hair soft, and he thought about her dying sooner than seemed fair.

"What did the doctors say about your consumption?" he said.

For a moment she lay silent. The bird flew away, the windowsill became empty again, this place less beautiful again.

She shrugged slightly but did not turn her face to him.

"There are good doctors back East," he said.

"I could not afford to travel East," she said.

"I could get the money."

"No. The air in New Mexico should help."

"The farther west you go, the less the chance of—"

She turned suddenly and placed her fingers to his lips, and he kissed them gently. Then she brought her mouth to his, and he kissed it gently too.

"It is too late for any of that," she whispered. "I'll live my life as I must, I'll take care of my son as I must, and God Himself can do with me what He will."

He held her for a long time in that morning light as it came farther into the room and fell across the bed and climbed the opposite wall.

"I must get up and fix the morning meal," she said.

"I don't want to let you go so soon, Kathleen."

She gazed at him, their faces inches apart, and he thought that if he stared long enough into her eyes, he could immerse himself in the sea that crashed upon the shores of Ireland, the country of her beginnings.

She kissed him again and rolled away, and together they dressed. He tried very hard not to look at her as she dressed, but his desire for her wouldn't let him divert his eyes from her completely. She was thin with small round breasts, whose tips were the color of pale rose petals. But beyond her beauty showed her illness—the ladder of her ribs, the ridge of her backbone as she bent. She caught him looking and did not try and hide herself from his eyes, and he felt a bit of shame flush his cheeks.

"I'll go out first and you follow in a few moments," she said. "I'd hate for the boarders to talk."

"What does it matter?" he said.

"A woman's reputation means everything to her . . ."

"I just meant that you'll be leaving here shortly."

"I'd not want to have them think of me as a whore," she said.

He started to protest but saw the look in her eyes and finished buttoning his shirt instead and waited for her to go out, then followed moments later.

He could hear Bill snoring through the door, and remembered what Charley had said about Bill not being a morning man and so went instead to the jail to see William.

There was a dark-eyed man of short square stature talking to Jeff Carr when Teddy entered the office. Both men turned and looked at him.

"I'm here to see my client," Teddy said.

"You know the way back," Carr said.

Teddy started to the rear of the jail when Carr said, "Wait a minute." He came around the corner of his desk. "You armed?"

Teddy drew back his coat to show the sheriff the shoulder rig with the Colt Lightning in it.

"Put it on my desk."

This he did.

"Five minutes, Blue, same as before."

The kid was sitting on his cot eating from a tray some mush, a biscuit, and a cup of black coffee. He had crumbs on his lips that he wiped away with the cuff of his shirtsleeve when Teddy stepped up to the bars.

"How they treating you?"

"They like to talk rough, threaten, but I ain't afraid of none of 'em."

"I'm going to find out when they're going to convene a court and arraign you. The judge might set bail. If so, we can probably bail you out until the trial."

"How's my mother?"

"She's worried about you."

"That all you got to tell me about her?"

"Don't push it, kid."

"I could use a smoke."

"It's not a habit of mine, but I'll see you get some makings."

"They make me piss with my hands cuffed."

"It could be worse. You want to go over your story about that night one more time?"

Teddy learned from Jeff Carr the name of the circuit judge before he left the jail with the same story in his head the kid had told him the first time. The judge wouldn't be in town for another two days. Teddy went to find Lilly. She was still asleep, and he woke her and asked her to tell him what she knew about that night.

She shook a little inside the blanket wrapped around her as she said, "I wasn't there. I just know what Billy told me. He said Henry caught him and threatened to kill him if he came around me again. He said he got the gun free from Henry, mostly because Henry was blind drunk, and shot him because he was scared. I believed him . . ."

"Would you testify to this in court?" he asked.

"No."

"Why not?"

"Jeff Carr would run me out of town."

"That might not be the worst thing that could happen to you."

"What would you know about the worst thing that could happen to me?"

"I don't."

"I've got a life here . . . and a few friends. I don't got a life or any friends in other places. Look at me. I am only sixteen but I look forty. I'm about worn-out. What would I do in other places I can't already do here?"

"I understand, Lilly. Thanks anyway."

Lilly wouldn't be of any help, and Teddy knew that no matter how they presented William's story, there probably wasn't a jury in town that would buy William's version put up against one of Jeff Carr's kin. The kid would end up in the Wyoming State Penitentiary breaking rocks.

Teddy walked to the post office and asked the clerk if any mail had been sent to him General Delivery. No, nothing had been sent. He then went to the telegraph office and inquired as to the same, and the clerk gave him a telegram.

WIRE EXCHANGE ARRANGED WITH LOCAL BANK—WYOMING SAVINGS & TRUST. ALL FUTURE MONEY REQUESTS THROUGH THEM. FORWARD ON EXPENSE SHEET VIA EARLIEST MAIL. I TRUST H. IS IN THE NEST SAFE AND SOUND. G. BANGS.

He went to the bank and withdrew the money, decided it would never be enough to accomplish everything he had in mind, and returned to the telegraph office. This time the telegram he sent was to his mother, the libertine:

CAN YOU MAKE ARRANGEMENTS TO SEND $1000.00 IN TRANSFER TO WYOMING SAVINGS & TRUST, CHEYENNE, WT? WOULDN'T ASK IF I DIDN'T NEED IT. DO YOU STILL PLAN TO GO TO EUROPE WITH THE POET? WILL BE HERE FOR A WEEK OR TWO MORE. AFFECTIONATELY, THEODORE.

Coming out of the telegrapher's he had it in mind to walk back to the boardinghouse, but his plans were set aside when he saw Hank Rain crossing the street, heading straight toward him.

Christ, he thought.

It was the unsteady way the gunman moved that troubled him most. He held a half-empty bottle of liquor in one hand and a black rope of hair in the other. He was drunk. He began to shout curses.

"You honey-faced little son of a bitch!"

The lessons old John Sears had taught him spilled through his mind:

Take your time. Pick a spot you want to hit—torso's easier, head's a sure thing. Turn yourself sideways to make a smaller target of yourself, keep to the shadows if you can, let 'em get close enough you can't miss, but not so close they can't either. Tell yourself you only got one shot, because that's probably all you really got.

Teddy held up a hand.

"You stop where you are."

Hank Rain laughed at the gesture.

"What the fuck, you think we're schoolkids in the play yard!"

A crowd was quickly forming there, on the edges of the invisible circle that encompassed the kill zone.

"I don't want trouble from you, but I won't run."

Hank Rain snorted his derision.

"Shit, boy. I'm going to kill you easy as a rabbit."

Teddy could see Jeff Carr coming down the walk from across the way—a napkin flapping at the top of his shirt, his double barrel swinging in one fist.

Teddy eased himself sideways, never taking his eyes off Hank Rain, nor stepping into the sunlit street where the gunman stood now, maybe because instinct told him he'd gotten close enough to become cautious in spite of his bravado.

He'd just reach up under his coat and pull free the Lightning, aim and cock it in one motion. *Take your time.*

Maybe if he could stall for another few seconds Jeff Carr would break it up and nobody would have to get shot this day. The sheriff was still coming down the street, coming slow, deliberate, a man who knew not to rush into unnecessary danger until he figured out the situation, because he'd done it early on in his career and learned from it.

Jeff Carr's progress proved too slow.

Hank Rain let loose of the hair, jerked a Colt Peacemaker from his hip-high holster and took aim, the barrel wavering because the whiskey running through his blood was doing its job.

Teddy's fingers had encircled the Lightning's grips and brought it free without so much as conscious will. His concentration was such that he could see the gun that Hank Rain gripped had a seven-inch blue barrel; he could see the nubs of the cartridge points in its cylinder; he could see the slow turn of that cylinder as Hank thumbed back the hammer. He could see the hair rope falling.

He wasn't sure he even heard the shot from Hank Rain's pistol.

He had Hank lined up down the front sight—the blade just there in the middle of his fat head. *Don't jerk the trigger, old son, it'll throw off your aim, and missing 'em by an inch is as good as missing 'em by a mile.*

The bullet from Hank Rain's Peacemaker exploded the window glass of the telegrapher's office and the glass fell like a pail full of diamonds.

Jeff Carr was pushing through the crowd now, his throat still trying to swallow a chunk of beef tough as boot leather, so he couldn't even call a warning.

Teddy could see the look in Hank Rain's face when he missed, could see he didn't believe it, could see the anger coming on him again, but he didn't wait for Hank to thumb the hammer back a second time.

A calm passed through him, and with true aim, the bullet found its mark and shattered Hank's skull with such force that it blew his hat off. He dropped to the ground like he'd been held by strings that some invisible hand had just snipped.

"Dead as hell," old John Sears would have said.

There was a full moment when nobody moved.

Then Jeff Carr managed to swallow down the chunk of meat just as he stepped into the kill zone. His hard stare went from the now defunct Hank Rain to the aimed pistol of Teddy Blue.

"Well?" said Jeff Carr.

Teddy lowered his piece. "You saw it," he said.

"Yeah, I saw it."

Carr looked around, saw heads nod in ascent that it was a shooting of self-defense.

Carr bent for a closer look at the grievous head wound, then straightened and called to some men to carry the corpse over to the undertaker's. He approached Teddy like he had to walk over eggs to get to his side of the street.

"That was a hell of a shot," he said when he got close enough to speak in a normal tone of voice. "Or lucky."

"Maybe some of both," Teddy said.

"So I was right about you, you're not a miner or nothing but another damn shootist, only why ain't I ever heard of you?"

Teddy tried hard not to let it show—the nerves that were screaming inside him.

"I'm not a shootist," he said to Carr. "I'm just a man doing my time, same as everyone else."

"Shit, I don't believe that for a fucking minute. What was the trouble between you two?"

"He's the one tried to take Wild Bill out. I stopped him twice, I guess the third time wasn't any charm, at least for him."

"Why would you risk your life for Wild Bill or anybody else?"

"Because nobody deserves to get potshot."

"Well then I guess I had you all wrong. I guess you ain't no shootist at all—you're the Good Samaritan come straight out of the Bible. Get the fuck out of my town!"

"When I'm ready, I will leave your prairie dog town, Mr. Carr." Teddy remembered Bill's similar comments in several newspapers. He challenged one and all who would try and kill him, no matter where they might lay in wait.

"We'll see about that," Carr said, then turned and strode off, still mad about his dinner being interrupted and the fact the Chinese population would be all in a fury about Hank Rain cutting off some chink's pigtail—probably that of the head chink when he'd gone to the dope den looking for Bill. Well, if the goddamn chink wanted his pigtail back, there it was, floating in a pool of Hank Rain's blood.

A few men came up to Teddy, slapped him on the back and insisted on buying him drinks, the ones who had derogatory remarks about the character and personage of the late shootist.

Teddy shoved his way past them. He wanted nothing to do with the celebration of killing a man.

Chapter 18

———◆———

Bill awoke with his eyes aching him fiercely. It took several minutes of swiping at them and patting them with the silk handkerchief Agnes had given him before he was able to see clearly.

"Take this as a reminder of my love for you," she had said. The handkerchief had their initials embroidered on it—*JBH* and *ALH*—inside a little heart.

He dabbed at his eyes until the handkerchief was damp through and through then tucked it into the pocket there over his heart.

He remembered Charley saying as how the mercantile had gotten in tinted glasses a feller could wear to lessen the effects of the sun and other bright light, and he thought he'd dress and walk over there and get himself a pair. He'd seen some dandies back in New York wearing them that time him and Billy Cody and Texas Jack were playing at stage acting. They thought them silly, but now he was ready to try about anything if it made his eyes hurt less.

It wasn't even the pain so much that troubled him as it was how his eyes blurred, causing him to feel most vulnerable. Sometimes he couldn't see beyond ten feet. All an assassin would have to do would be just stand beyond his line of vision and it would be all over for him.

He dressed in his usual finery—white shirt, brocade waistcoat, checkered trousers, soft calfskin boots. Around his waist he wrapped the red sash Squirrel Tooth Alice had given him when they lived together in Abilene for a time. She said it came out of a Denver bordello—the first one she ever worked in when she was just seventeen. He wrapped it twice around his waist then tucked in his Navy revolvers. His frock coat could stand a good cleaning, he noticed when he went to put it on. And the cuffs were beginning to fray. He combed out his hair as best he could with his fingers then smoothed his moustaches. He looked like a banker with guns.

Wild Bill saw that the small red-haired woman took notice of him when he passed by the kitchen. He touched the brim of his pancake hat, said, "Mornin'," then walked out into the brisk but sunny air of Cheyenne and started up toward the mercantile with tinted glasses in mind.

He had not gone a block when he saw Jeff Carr standing out front of his office, leaning on a post and looking for all the world like a mad old bull. He felt disinclined to acknowledge Carr and so remained silent as he continued up the street.

"Hickok!"

Bill felt that old feeling he got when somebody wanted something of him he wasn't prepared to give.

Thing was, Jeff Carr stood at the very outer edge of his vision, so he looked fuzzy and indistinct.

"What is it, Sheriff?"

"There is a corpse cooling on a block of ice right this minute on account of you."

"I've no idey what you're talking about, nor do I much give a damn."

"Hank Rain is now defunct. Some feller killed him a bit ago because of you."

"Hank Rain, huh? Well, that's no great loss to anyone unless you was counting on him voting for you in the next election. Who was it killed him?"

"Your new pard, Blue. Least the word I get is he's your new pard since Charley Utter cleared out. Take my advice and clear out too, and take Blue with you, or you both might be the next ones cooling on a block of ice."

Bill knew if he were going to shoot the man, he'd have to get closer. Carr must have sensed it too because he took two backward steps as Bill took one forward.

"I don't clear out of no place I don't want to clear out of, and I don't run from a man, badge or no badge. You want to arrest me or shoot me or otherwise get to fighting, then get to it if you got the nerve."

Jeff Carr held up a hand. "I've got no legal right to arrest you . . . unless of course I prove you've no visible means of supporting yourself. Then I'll arrest you for vagrancy."

"I'm about sick to death of threats. Do what you feel you must goddamn you, or get gone from my sight."

Jeff Carr's confidence that he could manhandle Wild Bill faltered, and in that moment both men knew it.

"When I do come to arrest you, Hickok. I won't be alone."

"Bring your sister, for all I care. But between now and that time, stay clear of me."

Bill knew he offered a tempting target when he turned his back on Carr, and he knew the sheriff could have easily raised his double-barrel and blown him into hell. But Bill was good at reading the intentions of men and knew what Carr was probably thinking: what if he missed, or didn't get a clean kill? It was the self-doubt that did many men in. They could be faster and better shots than their adversaries, but the self-doubt would get them killed every time.

Jeff Carr had in his years thought a lot about what it was like to die, and he didn't care much for the feeling it gave him. He'd seen plenty of men die like Hank Rain had earlier. It was the suddenness of it that caused something cold and metallic to ripple through his blood. He wasn't sure he was ready to die, or that he would ever be ready, unlike men of Wild Bill's caliber, who didn't seem to give death a moment's thought. So instead of taking the risk, he simply watched Hickok stride down the street with such bravado that it seemed even the mud wouldn't stick to his boots.

Teddy rented a horse and rode it hard out onto the prairies until he came to a stream where the water tumbled cold out of some distant mountains and he could look back and barely see the town where he had killed his first man. He reined in and let the horse drink. The sun seemed shattered in the water where it rippled over rocks, and he thought that if he scooped up handfuls of it and drank, he'd be drinking part of the sun and it might warm him inside. But when he tried, his hands shook so badly he barely got a thimbleful to his mouth. His nerves felt as shattered as the sunlight. If whatever it was coming on him now had come on him back there in the streets, he would have been the one dead and not Hank Rain.

He thought about his brother Horace and that night he was killed, how he was alone except for the ones who killed him there in some run-down brothel where the light was dim and the air was scented with sin. He wondered what thoughts raced through Horace's mind in those last fatal seconds, or if he had time to think at all.

He thought about Kathleen Bonney and how she would die still a young woman and there would be no saving her. Death seemed lately to be in the mood to pick the youngest flowers of the field, and now it had picked Hank Rain too. Teddy guessed Hank to be hardly older than himself—twenty-five, maybe—but a young man given an old soul, one that was now departed to that place where souls young and old alike resided for eternity.

Resting as he did upon his heels, he saw a small herd of antelope some distance out cropping the sage, lifting their heads—alert, ready to spring away from danger. They grazed and switched their tails. Then something spooked them and they fled as a group, zigzagging across the plains until they were less than dots on the horizon.

He felt as though he should be spooked and run too. But a man isn't an antelope. He can't run from his obligations, and he can't run from himself. And so he mounted again and rode the horse at a gentle trot back to Cheyenne, more prepared now for everything than he had been two hours previous.

Bill was there in front of the Gold Room's double glass doors, a single tall man leaning against the wall watching everything that passed down the street.

Teddy reined in, rested his forearms atop the saddle horn.

"You have a good night's sleep?"

Bill was wearing tinted glasses, and Teddy couldn't tell if Bill was looking at him or everything but.

"Passable," Bill said.

"You waiting on somebody?"

"No one in particular."

"Well, I better get this horse back to the livery."

"Come around see me after you do."

"Where will I find you?"

"Here or there," Bill said.

Teddy nodded and reined his horse around toward the livery, wondering if Bill had gotten the word yet about the shooting.

Bill saw that Alice had spread several freshly washed pieces of her undergarments on the sides of the tent to dry in the sun. She stood brushing her long hair when he walked up. Bill took a bucket and overturned it, using it for a seat as he watched her. She smiled at him, and he remembered how much he had once cared for her. Finally she stopped brushing her hair and stood there looking at him.

"You'll have to go, Alice."

"Why, Bill?"

"It's just not right your being here. I am a married man."

"I don't mind you're married. She ain't here, but I am. She don't have to know nothing. You need a woman, Bill. You've always needed the company of a woman."

"That was in them old days, Alice. It's a tempting offer that nine times out of ten I'da took. But I'm a new man now and I've made a vow to Agnes and that's it for me. Having you around would just prove more temptation than I could withstand."

She leaned forward and took his hands.

"I always admired your hands, Bill. You've always had such pretty hands."

He pulled them free because he knew it was like holding hands with the Devil, in a way. He was not by nature a religious man, but he knew enough to know that the Bible talked about the many forms in which Satan would take to tempt a man. So maybe it was Alice and maybe it wasn't really her. He didn't want to make no bargains with the Devil.

She saw then in his face how sad he looked, how old he'd become since Abilene and since that night he shot Phil Coe and Mike Williams. She wanted to kiss his sore eyes and beg him to take mercy on her and let her stay in the tent with him, even if it wasn't to be a permanent arrangement.

"I so miss the old days, Bill, what we had, you and me. I'd give anything for just one more time in the saddle with you."

"I wished it was different," Bill said. "It ain't. The next flier leaves this afternoon, I'd appreciate your being on it."

"I'm busted, Bill. I'll have to stay around and work for a time to buy a ticket."

"I'm busted too, or I'd give you the money for a train ticket."

Seemed like the last hope she had fled from her at hearing those words. Tears brimmed her eyes.

"Go see Harry Young at the Gold Room," Bill said. "He's always happy to take on a new working girl."

"You'd see me working cribs before you'd lend a hand to help me out?"

"That's what you do, Alice. We all must make our way through this old world with the talents God gave us." Bill patted his pistols and looked at Alice's wide hips. "I'm good with these, you're good with those . . ."

Alice knew then that what she and Bill had had ended that night in Abilene and that all that was left of the two of them was what she'd been keeping alive in her mind these several years. Their love was as dead as Phil Coe and Mike Williams and all the other men Bill had killed. It was like he'd just killed their love with his words like bullets.

"Fine," she said with the last ounce of false dignity she had left to her. "If I have to work cribs until I can get back to Abilene or someplace decent, then I'll work cribs, and don't you come around begging me to return to you, Bill Hickok, because such is just not in the cards anymore. The only reason I came to see you in the first place was because I heard you was sick and going blind and thought I'd take pity on you. But what good is all my pity in the eyes of a man who'd see me work cribs instead of lending a hand?"

Alice could be confusing when she got heated up, but Bill felt too worn-out by everything to care. Let her have her false dignity.

"Tell Harry I sent you," Bill said. "My word's gold with him."

Bill sat and wrote a letter to Agnes until his eyes wouldn't let him finish.

Dearest Darling,

The weather here will soon break, I think. My rheumatism tells me so—it is not near so bad as it has been. Charley has left out for a fast trip to Denver to see his wife. If you were nearer, I would leave out too to visit you as well, but as it is I expect the road to Deadwood to be open soon and will advance on without him. I know you must be worried about me, but don't fret my pet. It will be an uncommon day when anyone but you can corral yr. William . . .

Some of Bill's tears leaked onto the paper, and it was his last sheet and he didn't even have pocket change to buy more, so he stopped writing, hoping he could finish the letter later when his eyes eased up.

Lacking anything better to do and not feeling like a nap, he walked into town thinking he'd get Harry Young to stake him to another poker game. Then too, he had to talk to that young rascal Teddy Blue and get the details on how it came to pass that he shot out Hank Rain's lights.

The business with Alice and the trouble with his eyes left him feeling glum. Maybe what he ought to do is go see the chink first; he couldn't swear to it, but it seemed when he smoked the opium pipe his eyes got better for a time.

Well, it could wait, he reckoned, until after he spoke to Teddy Blue about the shooting and how much of it had to do over him. Bill was starting to feel like he was a place where at evening the light starts to leave and the darkness moves in. What with Charley gone, Alice angry at him, his eyes so bad he couldn't finish a letter to Agnes, his troubles pissing and his pockets empty, life was starting to feel like a cruel joke. It didn't seem like he'd ever fallen on such hard times. And just the thought of Jeff Carr trying to arrest him as a vagrant—well, it sure wasn't the same as it was when they used to call him *Prince of the Pistoleers*.

He half wished Cody would come to town just so they could drink together and talk about all those good times they had, and talk about New York and the waterfalls at Niagara and all those other swell places they'd been to, even though the acting itself had been an embarrassment.

And as though the gods had been listening and

granted him a final wish, when he reached the Gold Room, there amid a crowd holding court was none other than Buffalo Bill himself. Tall and handsome and decked out in new buckskin britches and entertaining the rubes like they were his own children.

Seeing Cody was akin to seeing the past brought back one more time, and it took the edge off an otherwise miserable day.

Chapter 19

Nearly two months had expired since Paris Bass had left El Paso and the woman who loved Phil Coe. He wondered often while he felt so obligated to finish the job she'd hired him for. But underneath all the weariness and temptation to do otherwise, he knew the true reason he felt such obligation. It was a reason that had nothing to do with honor, but one that had everything to do with vanity. He would add the name of the famous pistolero to his book of the dead, and then he would go and find the woman and tell her and she would feel the need for him greater than she felt it for other men, greater than she'd felt it for Phil Coe. He felt longings he'd not felt before.

He would have thought after that day in El Paso that he would have all but forgotten the woman who loved Phil Coe. But instead she'd clung to his mind, most especially so on those long prairie nights encamped on lonely stretches of land by moonlit streams. He'd heard her name spoken in the stars and in the wind.

She called to him in his sleep, and twice he awoke

and thought he saw her there beyond the dying coals of his fire.

He tried hard to decipher what it was about her that made her follow him. What sort of woman would save her money for five, six years just to pay to see a man dead? She had the same Devil's soul in her that he had in him. Fate had brought them together, and fate would reunite them.

He knew after he'd shot the harlot in Abilene that he would not stop until he killed the famous Wild Bill. And once he did this thing, he would return to El Paso and take up with this Olive, with this woman who loved so strongly nothing could keep her from loving, not even death itself.

So there he was in those waning hours when the last of the sun lit the snowcapped peaks of the mountains at whose base sprawled the city of Denver. He had ridden as far as he would ride. He would sell his horse, take the train to Cheyenne and do what he had in mind, and then he would leave that country, go home to El Paso and take up with the woman, and that would be the end of his killing.

The air without the sun in it turned cold quickly. And he knew that a man could get caught in that open high country by a sudden snowstorm and freeze to death, and it held no appeal to him. He rode down the last slope of loose shale, glad that things would soon come to an end.

He took a modest room in a hotel near downtown where the clatter of horse trolleys rang against the cobblestone streets and brick warehouses. He divested himself of his riding clothes, putting on fresh, then went and found a restaurant to take his supper and ate roasted elk and boiled potatoes, washing it down with a nice claret.

He saw a woman across the way watching him. She sat under a large hat and was with a man wearing a necktie. They were both large people. Spoiled no doubt by wealth, he thought. *A banker and his missus out for the evening. Fatted calves who will not matter in the end days. Their existence is temporary and they will pass through this life without consequence. They will live in their expensive home and entertain their friends and bear children and then die and be buried, like everyone else. They will be no better off than Phil Coe or the harlot I shot in Abilene, or any of a thousand others like them.*

He stared at the woman until she turned her eyes away, then finished his claret and walked out into the black cold evening.

His thoughts again turned to Olive and to El Paso with its warm southerly winds that brought the smell of the Rio Grande into his room at night. It was a place and a way of life that had made him forget his past for the most part. He had not killed anyone in an entire year before the woman came to him and hired him to go and kill Hickok. He tried not to think of her now as he walked in and out of the shadows created by street lamps and night turned black as pitch.

Paris Bass sensed rather than saw the two figures emerging from the shadows.

The smaller of the two stepped out to block his

progress while the other scurried around behind him. He saw the sap raised high, smelled the stink of desperation in them even as he heard them shuffling into position.

Too late for them when they saw the flash of something silver in his hand—the barrel of the pocket pistol he'd used to shoot the whore. He fired once into the chest of the man in front of him. The force of the slug lifted the fellow off his feet and dropped him to the curb. Wheeling about, he punched the barrel of the pistol into the slablike hardness of other man's body and pulled the trigger again, causing the man to fold in half, dropping to his knees, grabbing for something to hold him up, then toppling onto his side.

Paris Bass stopped near the man, leaned in close, his face just inches away. He could smell the acrid breath, see that look of astonishment in his eyes.

"You're in a bad way, my friend," he whispered to the man. "What is your name?"

"Otto . . . Schmidt . . ." The words came out guttural, choked with rising blood.

Paris Bass took the book from his pocket and wrote the man's name in it.

"And who's the other one?"

The man's eyes darted to his fallen companion, saw only a pair of heavy black shoes angled like a V pointing toward the heavens. He tried to speak but found it difficult. He swallowed the blood back down when he felt the cold steel of the revolver's barrel against his temple.

"His name?" Paris repeated.

"Karl . . . that's my brother . . . Karl."

Paris nodded and wrote that name in the book—
Karl Schmidt—Killed this day, September 14th, Denver. He would fill in the details later.

The man watched as Paris rose and walked over to
the body of his brother. He saw the bright flash of
light at almost the same time he heard the shot. Then
he saw the man turn and walk back to where he was
lying, saw the man's boots inches from his nose and
turned his head in time to see the white flash again.

Paris Bass returned to his hotel room and removed his
coat, taking first the pistol from his pocket then setting it atop the dresser so he might clean it and replace
the spent shells. Next to these he set a cheap brass
watch and a lead sap and several silver dollars—some
stained with blood. These he'd taken from the dead
men. In the corner stood the hand-tooled scabbard
with the *Schutzen* sporting rifle and its long brass
scope—the primary tool of his trade. He didn't much
care for pistol work, he decided.

He took out his *Book of the Dead* and wrote a
short paragraph below the most recent names.

Two fools, petty criminals, hardly deserving of a
bullet, tasted mine this pleasant evening and experienced perhaps the greatest consignment
conceivable. Oh, I doubt the lads were quite
prepared. But, truly this pair know what I do
not. I could see it in their eyes, that look that
comes just before the moment of death—that
sweet bliss. The spirit knows what the flesh cannot, and I envy them this. Surely I am like the

concubine to those poor devils and other like them—the one they seek when they have fallen into ruin. The one who gives them the fatal kiss.

Well, neither of them were comparable to Wild Bill, he thought, putting aside his pen, seeking the sleep he prayed would come before the tortuous headache flamed and burned inside his skull. To help the matter, he swallowed two cocaine pills and it did the trick.

Chapter 20

————◆————

Teddy found Hickok easily enough—he was sitting at a table in the Gold Room with Buffalo Bill. He wasn't sure if he should interfere with their conversation. Standing behind Cody was Texas Jack. Jack looked like an Eastern dude, dressed the way he was in a suit of black broadcloth, paper collar, and standing under a sugar loaf hat. Others approached the table, shook hands with the trio and offered to buy them drinks, even though there were several filled shot glasses on the table already and one or two unopened bottles of champagne.

Teddy decided he'd wait for a bit for some of the others to settle down, and give Bill and Cody and Texas Jack a chance to talk. He went to the bar and ordered a whiskey. It was then that he noticed the dark-eyed man he'd seen talking to Jeff Carr earlier in Carr's office. The man picked up his glass and offered a casual salute to Teddy, who wasn't sure why.

He looked around for Hank Rain's partner—Ned Loyal. Surely Ned knew about the shooting by now and might well be seeking to take his revenge. But then again, Ned could just as easily have figured that maybe Cheyenne wasn't as easy pickings as it seemed. Teddy had no proof that Ned was there to kill Hickok, or no proof that he wasn't. Either way, he needed to keep a sharp eye for Loyal.

He stood nursing his drink and watching the trio of frontiersmen. He had to admit, they seemed to have a certain aura about them that other men did not have. He knew he would never be their equal, nor was he sure that he ever wanted to be.

"That was a hell of a shooting," the dark-eyed man said, suddenly standing next to him.

Teddy turned, his hand reaching in under his coat. The man held forth an open palm.

"You'll get no trouble from me, friend. Name's Masterson. Most call me Bat."

"It wasn't my idea, what took place earlier," Teddy said.

"I know that. I was there. That damn fool has been looking to get himself killed for three years and he finally done it. Here's to Hank Rain and his latest success." Masterson raised his glass then threw back his whiskey.

"I saw you earlier today talking to Jeff Carr," Teddy reminded him.

"I was looking for work. Heard Jeff might be hiring on new deputies. Unfortunately for me, he wasn't. I half thought about going to the goldfields, but I doubt I'd be much good at mining. I think I'll swing down to Abilene. Good friend of mine is the city marshal down there. Earp, you ever heard of him?"

"No. But I've been to Abilene, and it can't be much of a town to be tamed these days."

"Bad enough still."

"If you'd been wearing a badge this morning and could have stopped it . . ." Teddy said.

"I don't think nothing would have turned out different than it did, do you?"

"I guess not."

"Were you down in Kansas when Bill was the law?"

"No, later."

"A man that can keep a cool head the way you did ought to consider taking up the law as a profession."

"I've no interest in the law," Teddy said.

"I can appreciate that. I've little interest in it myself, except a feller can usually find himself a job in it if he's cut from the right cloth. Anyway, just thought you might be interested to know that Hank used to run with a gun name of Ned Loyal. You might want to keep an eye out for him. He's a back-shooter mostly. And because of that, he might outlive us all. Keep to the shadows my friend."

Masterson set his glass upside down on the oak, touched the brim of his bowler, and started to leave.

"A question," Teddy said.

"What's that?"

"You ever hear of John Sears?"

Bat smiled. "Yeah. Him you'll want to stay clear of."

Teddy watched as Bat Masterson pushed his way through the crowd and disappeared. Teddy turned his attention back to the table where Bill sat with Cody and Texas Jack.

"Me and Jack are putting together a new combination," Cody was saying, both he and Jack sloppy drunk with smiles on their red faces. Cody was especially in good spirits.

"Count me out," Bill said.

"I got married to Josephine," Jack said. "You know she's all about show business, and so am I now. No more wrangling those sharp horns or eating dust on the plains for me."

"You've become dandified," Bill said, "but I don't blame you. Josephine's a fine woman. Why I got married myself."

Cody expressed surprise. "I never thought you'd have a lasso tossed around you Bill. Who was it?"

"Agnes Lake. She owns a circus."

Cody whistled, said, "What ever happened to men like us that we got tamed so?"

They all drank a rueful drink, but deep in their hearts they were not disappointed in the men they'd become as much as they were disappointed in the men they'd once been and were no longer.

Teddy approached the table, said to Bill, "I'd like to talk to you when you're through here."

Hickok glanced up from under the broad sweep of his hat brim.

"Fellers, this here's my most recently acquired pard, Teddy Blue. He's already saved my skin once."

Teddy felt embarrassment down to his toes.

Cody tugged him by the sleeve, said, "Glad to meet

yer. Sit and have a drink with us and tell us how you saved old Bill's hide."

"I appreciate the invitation, gents, but I really must be somewhere. Perhaps another time."

Teddy could see Bill watching him closely. He didn't want to offend, but he had no true desire to sit around and swap stories with men of such brotherhood—not tonight he didn't.

"I reckon the three of us will be here till the sun comes up tomorrow," Bill said. "Come look me up when you're ready."

Teddy nodded, glad that Bill would have Cody and Texas Jack as companions for this night and that it was unlikely anyone would try him with those two in attendance.

It was still relatively early, and he made his way to the jail fully prepared to face the wrath of Jeff Carr. But he had a legal right as the kid's lawyer to speak with him, and Carr would have to put aside their differences whether he liked it or not.

As it turned out, Jeff Carr wasn't there. In his place was one of his deputies, an older man who yawned a lot as he sat with his heels propped atop Carr's desk reading the *Police Gazette*.

Teddy explained the reason for his presence, and the deputy said, "Go on back," acting indifferent, not even bothering to ask him for his pistol. The thought occurred to him how easy it would be to just break the kid out of jail. But it was a thought not born in logic.

The kid lay facedown on his cot.

"You doing okay?"

He did not move.

"William . . ."

"What?"

"Sit up, boy. Look at me."

The kid eased himself up. Teddy could see his eyes were rimmed red.

"The judge will be in Friday . . . two more days. Can you last that long?"

"She came to see me today."

"Your mother?"

"I hated her seeing me this way."

"She doesn't think less of you."

"I didn't do nothing wrong."

"You shot a man, kid."

"You shot one too. I heard them talking about it earlier. What's the difference between you and me?"

"Probably not much."

"I need to get out of this place."

"Sit tight until I can talk to the judge."

"Talk . . ." the kid said. "Ain't you about sick to death of talk? I sure as hell am."

Teddy said, "Here," and handed him the sack of tobacco and papers and matches he'd bought earlier. "Maybe this will help some."

The kid came off the cot and took them. "It's decent of you," he said.

"You need anything else?"

"Just some freedom."

Teddy left the jail and headed back to the boarding-house. Kathleen wasn't there in the kitchen and she wasn't in the dining room, nor the parlor. He knocked on her door. She opened it slightly, looked at him through the narrow space.

"I just left seeing William."

"Oh," she said, and tears coursed her cheeks.

"You okay?"

"No," she said, and closed the door.

He felt a lot more hurt by her action than he thought he would.

Texas Jack fell out about four in the morning, but Cody was still going strong trying to promote with Bill the idea of a new combination show to take east.

"I'm thinking of taking the whole shebang to Europe—England maybe, to see the Queen. What do you think of that? Wouldn't you like to see what's on the other side of that big water before you go off to your heavenly home, old pard?"

Bill shook his head. "I'm fearful of deep water."

"Why, they got sailing ships big as this whole saloon. You'd not even know you were on the water."

"Yes, I would. I'd just look over the rail and there she'd be, and lots of her—a lot more than I'd care for. I came close once to drowning on the Red River, and that about ruined me on deep water."

"Well, how about going with us just as far as back East again—would you go that far? I'm thinking of including live buffalo—a whole herd of 'em."

"Buffalo is mighty tough to train to do tricks," Bill said. "They got little brains."

Cody laughed from all the booze and because he just naturally found Bill funny. Bill was a straight shooter and a straight talker and said what was in his heart and in his mind without any attempt to be humorous; it just came out that way.

"Boy howdy," Cody said, slapping his thigh. "What do you think of my new clothes? Had them done by Sioux squaw."

"You always were a fancy cuss."

"Ned says I'm so fancy looking he's tempted to marry me."

Bill smiled. "I'd keep a close eye on him—he'd marry a mule when he's drunk, which is about most of the time."

"Will you at least sleep on the idea of joining me and Jack?"

They both looked over at Jack, who had his head laid on a table with his eyes closed, probably dreaming of Josephine Morlacchi, his recent bride.

"You boys are the showmen, not me," Bill said. "Can I tell you something in confidence?"

"Sure," Cody said, leaning close.

The Gold Room was abandoned except for the trio and one bartender who mopped the floor.

"My eyes is near gone," Bill said.

Cody peered into Bill's eyes as though trying to judge the degree of blindness Bill was suffering from.

"There's some good doctors back East. Come back with me and Jack and see one of them New York City medicos. You don't have to work the boards if you're against it. But Jesus, old son, you can't stay in these frontier towns. Not if your eyes is gone. It ain't safe."

"I've made up my mind," Bill said. "I'm going up

to the Black Hills soon's the weather breaks. I'm going to put together a stake for me and Agnes."

"I just can't feature you working a pick and shovel, Bill."

"Picture cards. Me and Charley are going to set up an establishment. He'll run the liquor and girls and I'll run the gambling. It's what I do best anymore—picture cards is."

Cody knew of Bill's skill and luck with the picture cards, and it wasn't very good. But still, you didn't tell a man like Wild Bill he wasn't worth a damn as a gambling man. In fact, you didn't tell Wild Bill much about himself.

"I sure hate to leave without you," Cody said.

Bill started to say something when Jack fell off his chair and awoke with a start. Both men looked at him and he at them.

"I dreamt I was being chased by Indians and I rode my pony off a cliff," he said, feeling around his person for broken parts. "I'm sure glad it was just a dream."

Bill stood, shook hands with them and said they'd get together again when they were all fat rich men.

"Someday they'll be telling about us in history books," Cody said.

"I doubt anyone will remember us more than two Tuesdays after we're dead," Bill said.

Jack said, "I thought I was already dead."

They parted company and Bill walked back to his and Charley's tent. He was pleased to see that Squirrel

Tooth Alice's underthings were gone off it, and so was she. Though he didn't care much for the fact she'd still be in town, probably working for Harry Young as a crib girl. He'd have to find himself another "office" until the weather broke and he could go up to Deadwood Gulch.

He sure missed Charley.

He climbed into the tent just as sun broke over the eastern horizon. It gave him pause to look at it, thinking Agnes was probably already up and had her breakfast and was worrying about him. He figured to go down to the post office later and see if he had a letter from her.

He pulled off his boots, then soon as he did, felt the urge to make water. He pulled them back on again, climbed out of the tent, and walked off to the trees.

As he stood there doing the best he could to make water, he thought what a cruel thing it would be for one man to sneak up on another and shoot him while he was pissing. Instinctively he looked around. But nobody was sneaking up on him. All he saw were the tents and the wagons and some folks waking up and stirring around. He never could understand that regular sort of life some folks kept—of going to bed when it got dark and waking up when it got light. Nothing really interesting ever happened during the day.

He finally finished up and walked back down to his tent and pulled his boots off again, wrapping himself in the buffalo robe, keeping his pistols close at hand. He fell into the gunman's sleep—the kind where a man isn't full asleep nor full awake but about halfway between and ready for anything.

Sometimes Mike Williams showed up in his dreams, and sometimes it was Phil Coe who did. And sometimes it was McCanles, and sometimes it was others he'd shot over the years. And sometimes it was just an angel that he couldn't tell whether it was male or female, but one with golden hair and bright blue eyes and a cherub's mouth.

He always liked it better when the angel showed up than when the others did.

Chapter 21

———•◦•———

Two days of domesticity and Charley was feeling as restless as a cat outside a cage full of birds. The company of a wife just wasn't the same in the quiet district of Denver as it was in the wild place of Cheyenne, or just about anyplace else in the company of Wild Bill.

Mrs. Charley Utter was a kindly soul, plain-faced, and practical as a hammer. She loved Charley greatly in spite of his wanderlust ways. And Charley's daughters looked exactly like him, except for Emma, who favored her mother both in features and temperament. Lottie and Hortence were restless creatures and fat-cheeked little things with happy dispositions like Charley. He loved them all equally and truly, just as he loved his wife. But love was hardly enough to scratch the itch in his feet.

Rain spilled down the windows while Charley read an article in the newspaper about two men found shot dead on Colfax Avenue: *Assailant unknown. Victims were Otto and Karl Schmidt, late of Des Moines, Iowa. Apparently robbery was the motive. Both men*

*found with empty pockets sans wallets and personal
items. Both known to local police as bunko artists
and pickpockets. Bodies to be interred at Potter's
field.*

Charley looked up from his paper and across to his
wife, who sat quietly knitting. The girls were away at
school, and Charley could hear the clock in the parlor
ticking and the cat breathing as it lay curled by his
wife's feet. It was about like death, he thought, all
that quiet.

"I'm fixing to leave in the morning," he said.

His wife looked up. It was plain to see her disappointment.

"Where to this time, dear?"

"Why, back to Cheyenne, of course. Bill needs me
to go up to the goldfields with him. Of course I hate to
leave you and the girls, but this could be my big
chance to strike it rich. We could all move to a big
house with plenty of room. Why, I could even have a
greenhouse built for you where you could raise roses.
Wouldn't you like your own greenhouse?"

"I fear for you both," she said.

"Ah," he said, knowing she was about to pester
him with her dreams.

"I've been having bad dreams lately."

"What kind of bad dreams?" He did his best to be
polite at such times, but he knew the dreams she
would tell him about would be the same dreams she
always had.

"Ones where you and Bill get yourselves mur-
dered."

He rolled his eyes. "Never going to happen," he

said. "Bill's the best pistol shot in the whole West. Cautious too."

"You said yourself his eyes have gone bad."

"When'd I say that?"

"The other night . . ."

Charley tried to think when he would have said anything about Bill's eyes.

"When we were upstairs," she said.

"Oh." He remembered now. He always did tend to talk too much right before and after fornicating. "Well, I believe it to be a temporary thing, Bill's eyes."

"You wouldn't be the first to pay the price for keeping the wrong sort of company," she said.

"I don't suppose I even know what that means."

"I think you do."

Charley went back to reading his paper. There was no way he was ever going to win an argument with her. She was far too clever with words and the thoughts that came out of her head. She'd gone to college. Why she ever agreed to marry him remained a mystery to Charley. It wasn't as though he wasn't smart, he just wasn't educated.

When he first caught her attention and began to court her, he told her he was the sort of man who didn't believe in a lot of thinking, that a man ought to just go ahead and do whatever he had his heart set on doing. This impressed her for some reason. She was practically the opposite of him in every measurable way, including the fact she was a good seven inches taller than he.

He'd said the morning of their wedding, "How do you think this is going to work out?"

And she'd said, "How what will work out, Charley?"

And he'd said, "Me being a lot shorter than you."

At first she still didn't know what he was talking about, but then that night when they finally got undressed and in bed together the first time, she understood his concern and laughed.

"See," she said, after a bit of amorous positioning, "it all just naturally works out."

And Charley sort of settled in and said, "I guess it does." And after that the difference in their height never bothered him any. In fact he thought it a badge of honor to be seen with her, knowing that others would take notice of how much taller she was than him; they'd wonder what it was a short man had to make a tall woman want to be married to him.

Even Bill made mention of it once.

"She's tall," he said.

"Sure is," Charley said with a smile.

"I don't suppose . . ."

"No. It all works out, you'd be surprised how it does."

"I never been with a lady taller'n me," Bill said. "I'll have to take your word for it."

"But you been with women a lot shorter, right?"

"Well, yes."

"Same difference, only the reverse."

Bill thought some on it and then said, "I see your point."

"You don't have a problem with me going back so soon, I hope?" Charley said to his wife.

"If you're asking me am I happy that you are, the

answer is no. But I've known you were the way you are since the first and I'll not try and change you now."

"I think that's the part about you I love best," Charley said.

She smiled and said, "It's nicely quiet without the children home."

"You want to go upstairs and show me again about how things work out between a tall woman and a short man?"

She set aside her knitting and stood from her chair.

"You've forgotten already? It has just been a day or so since I showed you the last time."

"I think it's that sulfur water I been drinking up in that country," he said. "Makes me forget easy."

She offered him an exaggerated sigh.

"Maybe you ought to take pen and paper with you this time and write it down," she said.

Charley folded his newspaper, stood and came to her, offered her his hand and said, "No, I'll remember this time—I'm clear-headed now."

In a way, it was powerful hard for Charley to wave good-bye to his family as they stood waving to him there on the train station platform the next morning. Mrs. Charley Utter was a good wife, and his daughters were good children, and he vowed to change his ways this time and not visit any more crib girls. Bill had gone celibate, why couldn't he? Yes sir, he'd be celibate too, no matter how much the urge came over him for female flesh. Him and Bill would go up to Deadwood and open an establishment and make a fortune each, then he'd return home and that would be it for him. They were both getting a little long in the tooth to be running all over God's creation, drinking and gambling and whoring and generally carrying on.

The tears of his dear, dear family seemed to fall straight onto his heart like a cold rain, and he had to swallow hard to keep his own tears from flowing. The train lurched, and he felt like jumping off right then and there and running to their arms. But he knew it wouldn't be long before he'd be hankering to run off again. When he was home he longed to be gone, and when he was gone he longed to be home. It seemed like a curse, all that longing for the other thing.

He couldn't hardly stand thinking about his longing, and so instead of dwelling on it, found his way to the dining car, ordered a drink and drank it, then ordered another and drank it too. Then he ordered a third and so on, until he washed all the longing out of his blood and began to feel more like his old self again.

It wasn't long before he was thinking about Lilly, the pretty little crib girl who worked at the Gold Room. Then he started thinking of all the reasons why it was wrong for a man to go too long a time without female flesh and how it got some men in trouble who tried to be celibate. He'd heard a lot of theories about what going too long without a woman did to a man. He knew most fights between men were over women, because men gone too long without the company of female flesh were prone to violence. It just wasn't a normal condition for a man to be celibate like it was a woman. It clouded a man's mind and led to unnatural thoughts that generally led him to untold troubles.

Charley had known of a few men who had "wives" in different towns so they were never without one when they traveled. It made good sense, in a way. He ordered another drink and thought about it further. Bill sort of used to be that way, but not any longer.

By the time the train was halfway to Cheyenne, Charley had figured out it might be a good thing for him to ask Lilly to marry him—as long as she was willing to be his wife only in Cheyenne or Deadwood and didn't ask too many questions of him about his need to often travel without her. He thought maybe he'd ask Bill his opinion of such an arrangement, Bill being wise in the ways of women as he was.

He was feeling plum better about things by the time the sun settled low in the distance and threw the shadow of the train out across the prairie. He saw some antelope running, but it was the buffaloes he missed most. Hell, he'd be happy to see a few Indians riding free and wild—their hair and the tails of their ponies fluttering in the wind. It wouldn't be long before even the antelope would disappear and there was a town sprung up every twenty miles.

Maybe him and Bill should go up to Alaska when they finished in Deadwood. He didn't know exactly where Alaska was, but he figured he and Bill could find it.

Charley went back to his seat unsteadily now and nearly stumbled and fell on a man reading a Bible there in the coach car. The man wore a black hat and coat.

"Pardon me, Preacher."

The man looked up, but Charley didn't see no milk of human kindness in those eyes. He figured it was because he'd lost his balance and nearly sat down on the man's lap.

The man didn't say anything, and Charley made it on to his seat and flopped down thinking that train riding had gotten to be an awfully damn more difficult a business then it used to be.

He hunched down under his hat feeling much like a prairie dog in its dark burrow, and quite enjoyed the scent of the hair oil his wife had used to comb his hair with that very morning while he bathed.

She was too good a woman to play fast and loose with, he determined in a single moment of lucidity. He'd just have to tell Lilly he wouldn't marry her no matter what she would agree to. Then a moment later his resolve crumbled and he was back to thinking about her in carnal ways—those little doe eyes and that young slender body of hers.

Oh, what to do?

He drifted in and out of fitful sleep and dreams that alternated between his wife and Lilly until he could no longer stand it and got up and made his way back up the aisle again to where the preacher sat staring out the window at the purple haze of a night fallen.

"Pardon me," Charley said. "But I was wondering if you could help me out on a matter of a spiritual nature?"

The man cut his gaze to Charley, his countenance this time less unfriendly.

"You need to talk to me of your sins?" the man said.

"Well, something like that. Seeing's how you're a man of the cloth."

"Go ahead and confess what is troubling your heart, friend."

Charley took the seat opposite and began telling the preacher about his dilemma, and the man listened with great patience even as he sized Charley up for a coffin. It was Charley's good fortune that he couldn't begin to know what the man was thinking.

When through explaining his situation, the man said, "For by means of a harlot, a man is reduced to a crust of bread; and an adulteress will prey upon his precious life."

Charley said, "That's a bit confusing . . ."

"Proverbs six, verse twenty-six."

Charley scratched his head. "I guess I get your point."

"Are you a believer?" the preacher said.

"I believe in things I can understand, but I do confess to not understanding a lot of the good book, or what you're talking about."

"Do you have your house in order?"

"It was fine when I left."

"I'm speaking of your spiritual home."

"Oh, I don't know too much about that, no sir."

"Be prepared, my friend, for death comes like a thief in the night . . ."

That done something to him he didn't care much

for. There in that dim light of the rocking railcar with night hard up against the windows and everybody else asleep in their seats, Charley felt the cold hand of fear he'd only felt once or twice in his life.

"I'm sorry to have troubled you, Preacher. I guess all that fruit wine I drank in the dining car has laid waste to my senses."

He couldn't swear to it, but it almost looked as if the preacher's eyes were glowing. He hadn't felt this way since that time he got into some bad snakehead whiskey in Manhattan, Kansas.

It was the conductor who woke him and said, "Cheyenne . . . Final stop, sir."

He uncurled himself out of his seat, sat up and wiped the slobber from his chin and the weep from his eyes and looked around. He didn't see any preacher, and thought maybe he'd dreamed him. He shucked himself loose and stepped from the car onto familiar turf again and felt like he was at last back in his element. First thing was to go see how Bill was. Then go and get himself a drink of something decent to take the hair of the dog off.

Charley still felt plagued by the bad feeling the Preacher put in him. Whatever it was, it seemed that feeling would remain for the rest of his days. Only whiskey and a turn with Lilly might hold it off for the time being.

'Least, he hoped it would.

Chapter 22

Teddy was having coffee alone with his thoughts there in the now-empty dining room and hoping that she might yet make an appearance so he could speak with her about last night.

And finally she did appear, and he said to her, "What's wrong, Kathleen?"

She was drawn and more pale than usual and her hands trembled a little, causing him to want to take them into his own and hold and comfort them.

"I received a letter yesterday," she said. "It was from a constable in Kansas City informing me that my husband was dead."

"I'm sorry," he said.

"He said he was going to the goldfields . . . I don't understand what he was doing in Kansas City."

"You sort of expected the worst, didn't you?"

She slumped into a chair at the table. "I suppose I did. I mean I expected never to see him again. But having it confirmed that he's dead . . ."

He stood, went to the stove and poured her a cup of coffee, and remembering how she liked it sweet, put in a teaspoon of sugar and set it before her. He touched her shoulder and said, "There's only so much you can do. It's not your fault."

They sat in silence for a time, then she raised her eyes and said, "The sun is out, did you notice?"

"Yes."

"I think, if the offer is still good, I'd like to go for that horseback ride today."

"Then I'll be back to pick you up in twenty minutes," he said, put on his hat and went out.

He rented her a small palomino mare and himself the same gelding he'd ridden before, then led them back to the boardinghouse. She was waiting for him, dressed in a wool shirt and corduroy trousers. She'd pinned her hair and tucked it under a slouch hat she said was one of William's. He gave her a hand up into the saddle, then said, "Is there a river nearby?" She told him there was one off to the east, and they rode out in that direction for almost an hour, going at an easy trot and sometimes a gentle gallop. She was a good horsewoman, and he liked the feel of the wind in his face when they galloped and liked to watch her running slightly ahead of him like a spirit set free.

They came to the river—she said she didn't know the name of it, and it didn't matter to him one way or the other. They dismounted and let the horses drink. There were scattered clouds flung across the blue sky, and they cast shadows that floated across the land like dark creatures in search of prey. And where the shadows fell on the water it changed it from glass blue to a metal gray.

They found a grassy spot and sat on it cross-legged, facing off toward the river and beyond to the unending sweep of land that was yet brown from the retreating winter but would soon be green again with rich grasses.

"I would love to have a house right here," she said.

He had to agree; it was peaceful and far removed from the realities of the world.

"Kathleen, I'm really sorry about the news and I'm sorry about William's troubles and all the rest . . ."

She turned her head slightly to look at him, and he saw as much peaceful beauty in her face as he did in the land. He drew himself close to her and kissed her and wanted to steal from her the sickness she carried, wanted to steal all of her troubles.

She relaxed in his arms and he held her like that— the two of them looking into what could have been a future together, but they both knew the impossibility. Still, it did not prevent them from dreaming about it.

"You must promise me," she said, "that you'll get William free so that I can take him with me to New Mexico."

"I promise," he said, but doubted his ability to keep such a promise unless he took the law into his own hands. What would it matter if he did? West of the Mississippi the law was mostly what a man made it, and if he had to become a fugitive to keep his promise to her, then maybe that's just how it would have to be. He thought briefly of Horace. What good had serving the law done him?

He held her closer still, and she turned her face up to him, offering her mouth. He kissed it more passionately this time, her touch causing his blood to race hot under his skin.

"Is this what you want?" he said.

"How do I know?"

Her eyes were filled with tears. He couldn't tell if they were tears of sadness or joy, and he didn't want to ask.

He lay her back upon the old grass where new grass was just starting to sprout through and began to unbutton her shirt. She took her hat away and her hair spilled free. He kissed the hollow of her throat as she unbuttoned his shirt. The shadows of clouds played over the ground as she closed her eyes, and she could feel the clouds playing over them too, could feel the altering warmth and coolness. She could feel her own passion rising like a great bird winging toward the heavens.

Afterward, they rode back to Cheyenne feeling stunned and happy, and beneath their happiness lay the ever present sorrow that seemed to grow larger and more real the nearer to town they came.

"I could go with you to New Mexico," he said.

"It's such a nice thought to think that you would."

"You don't believe me."

"Yes, I believe you, but I think that it will never happen . . . that it can't ever happen."

"Why not?"

"I've always known since I was a little girl that I would never be as happy as I feel right now—that such happiness, though it has found me for a little while, is not mine to keep."

"Don't be so sure," he said.

"We shall see," she said.

He left her off at the boardinghouse with much regret in his heart, then returned the animals to the livery. From there he went to the bank and completed the transaction of funds his mother had sent: close to a thousand dollars. He would give it to Kathleen for a stake to get her set up in New Mexico—hopefully enough to buy her own boardinghouse. He knew she was right about everything, but he didn't want to accept it.

He went to the telegrapher's office and sent two telegrams, the first to his mother:

RECEIVED FUNDS THIS DATE, MANY THANKS. WILL PAY YOU BACK. HOPE YOU'VE CHANGED YOUR MIND ABOUT GOING TO EUROPE, BUT IF NOT, BEST WISHES. AS ALWAYS, YOUR SON, T.B.

The second he sent to George Bangs:

YOU SHOULD KNOW THERE WAS A SHOOTING INVOLVING MYSELF AND SOMEONE TRYING TO ROUST H OFF THE NEST. ATTEMPT UNSUCCESSFUL. MAN DEAD, NO LEGAL COMPLICATIONS. WILL SEND GREATER DETAIL IN LETTER. WEATHER SET TO BREAK ANY DAY, MAY BE ON THE MOVE TO THE GULCH SOON IF H GOES. ASSUME YOU WANT ME TO STAY ON THE HUNT. DO ADVISE AT YOUR EARLIEST CONVENIENCE. T. B.

Coming out of the telegrapher's office, Teddy spotted Charley ascending the train station platform steps. He was relieved that Charley was back. It might just mean that if he had to, he could resign his job with Pinkerton's and go with Kathleen to New Mexico. He walked over and shook Charley's hand, who shook his in turn like he was trying to pump water out of a dry hole.

"Well I'm glad to see you ain't killed," Charley said. "Because if you were, it might mean Bill was killed too. Where is he?"

"Left him last night in the Gold Room with Cody and Texas Jack. The rate they were going, they might still be over there chewing the rag."

"Shit and be damned!"

"What's the problem?"

"Cody will try and talk Bill into going East again, if he ain't already done it. Cody's got a flannel mouth, could talk a Eskymo into buying snowballs. I hope I ain't too late."

Teddy and Charley marched over to the Gold Room, but Bill wasn't there; the place at that early hour was as empty as a church on Monday. Charley was inwardly hoping maybe Bill had broken his vows of celibacy and was lying up with one of the doves somewhere. For if Bill had broken his oath, it meant that he could probably break his too and not feel overly bad about being a weaker man than Bill when it came to such things as carnal desires.

"Let's try the camp," Teddy said.

Sure enough, Bill's feet were sticking out through

the tent's flaps. Charley didn't see any feet other than Bill's and it disappointed him greatly that he didn't. Charley peeked in, and Bill was lying there like a corpse, but one that snored.

"There's something I need to tell you," Teddy said, then he told Charley about the gunfight with Hank Rain.

"I'd like to have been there when you dusted him," Charley said.

"It wasn't a pretty thing to watch."

"Never is, but I'd still liked to have been there. What about his pard, Ned Loyal?"

"I've not seen him."

"You can probably bet you will, sooner or later."

"That's what I'm thinking too."

Bill snored like a locomotive.

"You sticking around for a while?" Teddy said.

"I'm here for the long haul, unless of course something catches my fancy, then you never know. I've been thinking about Alasky lately."

"But for the present, you'll be going with Bill to Deadwood?"

"Yes. I've done been home to visit my wife and daughters, so I've done that for now. All I need is a nice hot bath and some victuals."

"You want me to hang around while you go take your bath?"

"I surely would appreciate it, old son."

"You don't think anyone would try and shoot Bill in his sleep, do you?"

"Hell, I think there are those who'd shoot him

while he was trying to piss. Some's bad in that respect, sneaking up on a man and just plum killing him outright with no warning, especially when it comes to a feller of Bill's reputation."

Charley dropped his valise next to the tent and said he'd be back in a couple of hours. Teddy made a chair out of a bucket, turned his back toward the sun so it would fall over his shoulder, then took out his book of Shakespeare and opened it at a random spot and read: *You and I are past our dancing days.* Then lowering the book, he glanced toward the narrow opening of the tent where Bill slept peacefully and knew that it was probably true—that men like him and Charley and all the others were past their dancing days.

But still he'd taken the job of guarding Hickok, and guard him he would until the last dance was over.

Charley bathed and sang, making up words from his joyous heart. He'd determined that anything could happen at any time, and as that strange preacher reminded him on the train, death she does come like a stranger in the night, and maybe she was coming for him and maybe for Bill and all the rest of them. And if it were so, then he might just as well live out what time he had left in the most bodacious possible way.

He had the chink scrub his scalp until his hair squeaked. Then he repaired from the bath, put on fresh duds and went straightaway to the Gold Room prepared to propose marriage to Lilly and offer to set her up with a nice little house he could visit and spend nights at. The cold ground of Cheyenne was putting a soreness in his bones that ached him most all of the time. Even Bill had begun to complain about rheumatism, and Bill was a good five, six years younger.

Then when he and Bill went up to Deadwood, he would send for Lilly to follow, and have a nice little house set up there for her as well. He sang loud and off-key, and the chink stood back and smiled the whole time Charley got dressed, Charley knowing the chink couldn't understand a word but that chinks were pleasant souls and smiled a lot. Chinks were generally agreeable and good fellers all around.

When Charley found Lilly, she was having her lunch along with several of the other crib girls. They were chattering like squirrels at the end of the bar in the Gold Room. Mostly they were telling stories about their odd encounters with customers. Charley interrupted such palaver and told Lilly he needed her to accompany him upstairs.

"It's my lunch, Charley. Can't it wait till after?"

"No, it can't," Charley insisted.

Lilly knew Charley to be a rambunctious little fellow when he got his mind set to something, but usually this didn't happen till late in the evening after he'd had several cocktails. It was just barely past noon.

Once in the crib, Lilly began removing what little clothing she wore, but Charley stopped her.

"It ain't about that, Lil . . ."

"What is it, Charley?"

"I come to ask you to be my wife."

Lilly tried to suppress a laugh. Charley got down on one knee.

"I'm serious," he said.

"I know you are, but you're already married, Charley."

"How'd you know?"

"Why, you told me plenty of times, mostly when you were drunk and maudlin and it was after we did it."

Charley forgot how much he talked before and after fornicating and how maudlin he could get when he was through fornicating but still in his cups and thinking of home and his wife and children.

"Well, it don't mean we can't still get married," he said. "It just wouldn't be entirely legal—you'd be more or less my common-law wife. And I'd treat you good, Lil. I'd treat you like a regular wife . . ."

"No, Charley, I won't marry you. You told me how sweet and nice your missus was and how pretty your daughters. I could never do nothing like marrying you and hurting them. And besides, I already love another."

"Ah, Lil . . . What's his name? I'll fight him over you."

"Oh, Charley, you're so sweet."

He couldn't be mad at her no matter how hard he tried. Lilly was right, he did have a sweet wife and children. He should be thanking her for reminding him.

"I'm just not in my right mind, is all," he said. "These wild prairies make a man feel lonely. They's other things too been troubling me something terrible lately . . ."

"What Charley?"

The crib was small and cramped, with just a bed

and a small trunk taking up most of the room. Charley sat on the side of the bed.

"I met a preacher man who put the willies in me," he said. "That's some of it."

"What's the rest?"

"I guess I don't know."

"I bet I do."

Lilly sat on the bed next to him and took her finger and run it around in Charley's hair, twisting a strand into a curl, and he felt himself falling for her wiles all over again, then remembered what that glow-eyed preacher said about seductresses and jumped up.

"I can't do it, Lilly. It ain't that I don't want to do it, it's just that I can't."

"Since it's still early in the day I'll give you a discount if you want."

It was a tempting offer. But he saw the face of his wife and daughters waving to him through the train window of his mind.

"I guess I was led here by God to learn the truth," he said. "And the truth is I need to become celibate. It ain't nothing against you, girl. And if I was going to be my old self, I'd be it with you, but that old me is long gone to somewhere other and I doubt the old Charley will ever show his face again. Good-bye, Lil."

And with that Charley went out and down the stairs, out the front double doors, and almost straight into the arms of Squirrel Tooth Alice.

She said, "Whoa there, buckaroo, I sure never laid eyes on you before. You're a cute little cuss."

And Charley fell instantly in love all over again.

Chapter 23

————◆————

Teddy was in the courtroom when the deputies brought William in. The circuit judge was a man named Pierce. The jurist had long white hair and tufts of more white hair sticking out of his ears. He had a pinched eye that looked like it had seen about everything bad there ever was to see in the way of the human condition and didn't care to see any more of it than was absolutely necessary. He had ridden in from Laramie, this Judge Pierce, and his coat was shabby with dust and his paper collar yellow with sweat stain. Beyond that he looked thirsty and disillusioned and tired.

Teddy saw Kathleen there in the front row, and she offered him a sad smile.

Jeff Carr served as bailiff and announced the court come to order, and everyone stood until Judge Pierce waved them back down into their seats. Then Carr announced the first case on the docket—a man named Haybarrow, on the charge of being drunk and disorderly in public.

"How do you plead?" Judge Pierce said to the sot.

"Guilty, I guess."

"Ten days or ten dollars."

This Haybarrow was, like many of his kind, a prankster, and said, "Judge, I'll take the ten dollars," and Pierce scowled and slapped his gavel hard down on the desk and said, "Make her thirty," and told the bailiff to take him away. Jeff Carr hooked a thumb at one of his deputies, who stepped forward and hauled the happy lush away.

"Next case?"

"William Bonney, felonious assault and attempted murder."

"How do you plead?"

Teddy stepped forward, said, "I am the legal representative of this boy, your honor?"

The judge rested his pinched eye on Teddy.

"He pleads not guilty."

The judge read over the charges before him, looked up again.

"Says you shot a man through the throat. That's an onerous place to shoot a man."

William started to speak, but Teddy stopped him with a hand clasped firmly on his forearm.

"My client will claim self-defense, your honor."

"Can you prove that, sir?"

"The victim was shot with his own revolver—the defendant does not possess nor own a firearm. If he had not been set upon by the victim, well, there simply wouldn't be a victim and this case would not stand before the court."

"Is it true that the victim was shot with his own

gun?" Judge Pierce asked Carr, who offered a reluctant affirmation. "Why'd you shoot him, boy?"

Teddy started to intervene but the judge waved him off.

"I want to hear it from his mouth."

"He was beating me up over a gal. He had her beat plenty of times too. He stuck his gun in my face and threatened to blow out my brains. I figured he would, so I stopped him the only way I could."

"Says here the dispute was over a prostitute. This gal you were fighting over, was she a dove?"

"She's only doing it to feed herself. She's a good gal doing what he told her to do."

"The victim was her pimp?" The judge settled his weary gaze on Jeff Carr. "The victim a relative of yours, I assume?"

"Cousin."

"You wouldn't be biased in this case, would you, Sheriff?"

"We ain't never been that close, him and me."

"Any witnesses to the event?"

"Nobody except the victim himself and the defendant. One ain't talking and the other can't."

"Yes, as I'd suspect a man shot through the gizzard would have a difficult time carrying on a conversation. Where is the woman in question?"

"I've already questioned her, your honor. She refuses to testify one way or the other."

The jurist closed his eyes. Dust moats floated in a shaft of morning sunlight that fell through a window. Then with great effort, he resumed his position of arbitrator and said, "How big a man is the victim?"

Jeff Carr hesitated, but not for long under the impatient pinched stare.

"Nearly six feet tall, sir."

"How much does he weigh?"

"He's as big as a dang horse," William blurted.

"Hush your mouth, son."

"About two hundred," Carr said.

Pierce looked at the kid, saw a boy not five and a half feet tall, maybe all of 120 pounds soaking wet, and not even the hint of peach fuzz on his cheeks yet.

"Not guilty," the judge said. "Next case."

The courtroom characters stirred like flies on a manure pile that had been bothered by something invisible, then settled down again to hear the case of a woman who stabbed her husband with a paring knife.

Outside the courtroom Teddy watched the warm exchange between mother and son, then went over and said, "This is for you, Kathleen," and handed her the envelope that contained the thousand dollars. "To give you a start down in that country where you're going."

She tried to push it back into his hand. "You've helped enough," she said.

"It's something I want to do, Kathleen. Take it."

William stood silent between them.

"You have a place in New Mexico picked out?"

She said, "Silver City."

"I got an old friend who went down in that country. Who knows, maybe I'll see you down there sometime."

"William, will you go to the boardinghouse and start packing your things?" Kathleen said to her son.

"We leaving now?"

"Yes."

"I need to say good-bye to somebody first."

"Then go ahead."

He started to turn, then stopped, turned back around and stuck out his hand for Teddy to shake. "I guess I was wrong about you."

"Get to know a person before you judge them," Teddy said, shaking the small hand. "It might just save you a lot of heartache down the line."

"It ain't easy trusting nobody."

"That's not always a bad trait."

The kid smiled. His front teeth were like those of a squirrel's.

"I'll remember," he said, and Teddy watched him head off to the Gold Room, no doubt to say good-bye to Lilly.

"Why did you do this?" Kathleen said, holding the envelope.

"Can it be enough to simply say I care about you and what's there will make me worry less about you when you're gone out of my sight?"

"You know I'd ask you to come with us if I thought it was the right thing, don't you?"

"Yes, I know."

"You could write me."

"I will."

"I will worry about you too," she said.

"I'll be fine, Kathleen."

She touched his face, and he wanted her fingertips to stay there forever.

"You could help me pack," she said.

"It would be my sad pleasure."

As they turned to start to the boardinghouse, Teddy saw Jeff Carr on the courthouse steps. His demeanor was that of an unhappy man. It won't be long before he makes his move to run Hickok and me out of town, he thought. Looking at the sky and feeling the warm Chinook winds, Teddy reasoned that maybe the move would be more voluntary than forced. He hoped so; he had no desire to be in another shooting contest.

Bill sat out front of the post office reading the letter he'd gotten that day from Agnes:

Sweetest James,

I've missed you so terribly. I pray that you change your mind about staying in that country and return to me soon. Or at the very least, that you send for me. I worry about you and cannot sleep well for worrying. I know there are jackals in that country who would prey upon you at the first opportunity. It gives me nightmares when I do sleep. I'm selling the circus in order that we may have a stake. I should have all the money soon. For what good is a circus if I've no one to run it, and what good is a husband if I cannot be with him? Has your eyesight gotten better or worse? If worse, please, please consider return-

ing to me soon. I would dread receiving bad news about you—it would destroy me. You do not know how great a woman's love is for her husband or you would not have gone off without me. I find no pleasure in your absence and none in my current existence. Please write me every day if you can and vow your love for me so that I will know that I'm not being foolish and that ours is not a one-way love.

With the greatest affection,
Yr. Darling wife, Agnes

Bill read the letter three times, having to pause often to wipe tears—not of sorrow but of affliction—from his eyes. He told himself several times how much he loved her, but something seemed lacking. Why, he asked himself, if he loved her so much, had he left her after just two weeks of marriage to go West again? It wasn't a question he had any good answer for.

This got him thinking about all the other women he'd known and loved and wasn't with, and he wondered about that too. Women were creatures he admired and felt great desire for, but ones he knew very little about. They had minds as mysterious as those of antelope. It was hard enough for him just being *Wild Bill*. It seemed to demand overly much of him to figure out women too.

He was thinking about such things when he saw Charley coming out of the glass doors of the Gold Room.

Charley strutted like a peacock, the fringes of his

jacket arms swaying with every strut. He had the brim of his hat pinned back to the crown and he looked a bit clownish, especially with that long-barreled Buntline Special pistol slapping against his hip.

Charley came over to where Bill was sitting, noticed the piece of lavender paper on which Agnes had written the letter clutched in Bill's pretty hand.

"From your wife?"

"Yes," Bill said. "It's a sad one too."

Charley felt that little niggling guilt creep into him as he wondered if Agnes had spilled the beans to Bill about Teddy Blue being a Pinkerton man, and worse, about him being in cahoots on the secret.

"What'd she say?"

"Said she misses me. Wants me to come to Cincinnati."

"You thinking you might go?"

"No. I might as well be dead as to be living in Cincinnati. I'd never be no good back in that country."

Bill almost constantly seemed to wear a sad face, Charley thought, and he felt mighty sad for him.

"Hey, guess what?" Charley said.

"What?"

"Harry Young's got himself a new crib girl. I just paid her a visit, and by gar I think I'm about half in love."

"Thought you were half in love with that sprite, Lilly?"

"Oh, it's all over between us. She's in love with another."

"You're the most romantic feller I ever met," Bill said. "Who's the new gal?"

"Her name is Alice—"

"Jesus," Bill said.

"What?"

"Nothing."

Charley saw Bill looking suddenly more sad-faced.

The kid was smart enough to know you just didn't barge in on a crib girl unannounced, not even one you were in love with and who was in love with you. Lilly might well be busy entertaining another feller; he didn't want to see such a thing, and so he stood outside the curtain listening. When he didn't hear anything, he called to her.

"Lilly?"

She eased the curtain back. "You get set free, or did you break out?" she said.

"Got set free, self-defense."

She pulled him inside the crib. "Best we don't get seen together," she said.

He saw an open valise on the bed, some clothes stuffed into it.

"You going somewhere?"

"Hell yes. I got to get gone, Billy." She called him Billy instead of William, something he liked about her.

"Why?" he said.

"Jeff Carr come up and told me to get out of town or he'd run me out, which is the same thing, the way I see it. I think he told Harry Young to fire me too. I think they already got a new girl to take my place. Only she ain't no girl, young and pretty as me, but a older gal calls herself Squirrel Alice."

She could see the mad go up into his eyes and said,

"Don't. It ain't worth no more trouble from old Carr. I got an aunt back in Indiana I am going to go stay with for a while. I'll be all right."

"I got to get gone too," he said. "Ma's taking me to New Mexico. Doctors say she needs to breathe the air down there."

"Well, you better get started then."

"Lilly . . ."

"What?"

"You know you've been my first true love, and it sure enough makes me sad we never done anything. I was sorta hoping . . ."

"You ain't never had yourself a girl, is that it?"

"No, I never have. But now that I shot a man, I guess I'm old enough to, don't you?"

"Well, Billy, I'm officially out of the whore business. I done told Harry I'd quit and leave out of her on the noon flier."

"It wasn't no whore I was hoping to do it with my first time, Lil."

She stopped her fidgeting and taking things from the trunk and putting them into the valise.

"I think that's about the sweetest thing anyone has ever said to me," she said.

"I was hoping it was."

"Well, shuck them clothes off if you think you can get done what you need getting done in ten minutes. The flier leaves out of here in fifteen."

"I was wanting it to be more romantic than this, wasn't you?" Billy said when they finished and were getting dressed again.

"I was wanting to be wearing a wedding dress my first time, hon. We all got dreams just waiting to be broken."

She kissed him quick and rushed out. He tried following her but had a hard time keeping up wearing just one boot and carrying the other he hadn't had time to put on. The last he saw of his sweet Lilly was the hem of her skirts disappearing into the train car. He felt happily sad.

Teddy tied the strap on the trunk and the two of them stood in the long shaft of midday light that had found its way into Kathleen's room. The empty bed seemed lonely without them in it, and he thought of what it would have been like waking up next to her every morning.

She caught a coughing spell and he held her until she stopped trembling. She looked at him with a wan smile.

"I wish we had more time."

"I do too," he said.

He kissed her, and she lay her head against his chest.

"Maybe someday you'll come to New Mexico and tell me who you really are," she said.

"You know who I am."

"I know your name and I know you've a kindness in you most men don't. But beyond that I know practically nothing about you."

"Isn't that enough?"

"It is for now, or if we never see each other again. It won't be if we do."

"Then we'll just have to have a long, long conversation when I get down that way."

"Yes, we will."

They heard the front door open.

"Kiss me before my son comes in," she said.

And he did.

Chapter 24

————•◆•————

The bullet whistled through the twilight and struck Charley's horse in the skull.

Charley and Bill were walking around the camp discussing the impending trip to Deadwood when they heard the shot. Both turned in time to see Charley's horse shudder then topple over.

Bill eased away from the firelight and so did Charley. They pulled their revolvers, but as Charley was quick to comment, "You can't see shit with all this dark coming on and I ain't sure what I should shoot at and what I shouldn't."

Bill said, "I think it come from up in them trees where I usually go make water."

Charley looked, but he couldn't tell if the shot came from the trees or not. Several others in the encampment came running and paused to look at Charley's dead horse.

"What happened?" came the collective question.

Charley said, "I wouldn't stand in that firelight unless you all want to end up like my cayuse." They quickly retreated back to their own tents and wagons.

Bill tried to peer into the gloaming but he could barely see as far as Charley's defunct horse, which the darkness was quickly swallowing.

They waited a long time, it seemed. They waited until the fire burned itself down to just glowing embers that breathed and sighed and breathed then winked out at last.

"I don't think we should stay around this place much longer, do you?" Charley said.

"It could be whoever it was weren't out to get me," Bill said. "They might have been out to get you, or your horse maybe."

Charley still had that bad feeling in him from talking to the stranger on the train.

"I don't know why anybody would want to shoot me or my horse, Bill."

Charley looked over to where the horse, Abe Lincoln, had been standing and now was fallen and stiff-legged and unmoving.

"You and me both know it wasn't nobody out to shoot Abe."

"I know it," Bill said.

"I'll bet it's that goddamn Ned Loyal," Charley said.

"It could be. It was his pard that Teddy Blue shot the other night."

"I'd put my money on it being him, wouldn't you?"

"The question is, wouldn't Ned be taking potshots at Teddy Blue instead of us?"

"I don't know," Charley said. "Figuring out the mind of assassins is about the same as it is figuring the mind of women."

"I can't argue with you there. Either way, we better go find Blue and warn him."

Then a figure moved near their camp, and Bill came around with a Navy in his hand while Charley was waving his long-barreled Colt and Teddy said, "It's just me, boys."

"Step on in," Bill said without lowering his revolver.

Teddy came close enough that they could both see it wasn't an assassin and lowered their pistols.

"I was on my way over here and heard a shot. What happened?"

"Somebody shot Charley's horse," Bill said.

"Yes, and it is a sorry son of a bitch who would shoot an innocent horse," Charley said, feeling true grief.

"The general consensus is it was Ned Loyal," Bill said. "Took a potshot at us, missed and hit old Abe Lincoln instead."

"You want to go see if we can find him?" Teddy asked.

"Nothing can be done this night," Bill said. "Only an Indian can track a man in the dark, and neither one of us is Indians, unless you are."

"I think we all ought to go into town together and get us a drink to steady our nerves and hoist one in honor of poor old Abe," Charley said, hoping to veil his concern for Bill's safety by suggesting they stick together. But Bill would have none of it.

"I don't need no bodyguards," Bill said. "Let the son of a bitch who wants to kill me fill his hand and come on."

"Ain't nobody going to kill you face-to-face, Bill," Charley said. "Ain't nobody's got that sort of nerve."

"He's right," Teddy added. "They'll try and assassinate you."

"Like that old horse, yonder."

"Yes, just like that old horse, yonder."

"I feel about like Abe Lincoln," Bill said. "Plugged and down for the count. Charley, next horse you get you oughter name him after somebody with more luck. I think it was unlucky you named your horse what you did."

"I say hurrah to that," said Charley. "My tongue is dry, ain't you boys about ready for a cocktail?"

"What about your horse?" Teddy said. "You just going to leave him there?"

"I'll get some fellers to drag him out a ways from the camp in the morning—it's a sad thing, but even the buzzards need a free meal now and again."

"Let's walk into that damn prairie dog town and see does anybody have the nerve to buck Wild Bill," Bill said, and tugged at his lapels and fixed his pistols just so inside his sash, making his way through the multitude of campfires and tents and wagons and onlookers with Teddy flanking him on one side and Charley on the other.

The Preacher knew that from that far away and with the light poor as it was, it would practically be impossible to hit his target. He felt bad about killing the horse, but not terribly so; it would at least send Wild Bill a message, if nothing else—a small price to pay for striking a bit of fear into a man whose name he'd al-

ready written in his *Book of the Dead*. There would
be more opportunities to fill in the details; of that he
was sure. And into the dark he faded, prepared to
strike another time. But at that moment he was in sore
need of more genteel pursuits.

Madam Moustache said, "Death is upon you."

Ned Loyal said, "When and where?"

"This I cannot say."

"You're a fortune-teller, ain't you?"

"I communicate with the spirits."

"You able to get in touch with my old pard Hank
Rain?"

"It is possible."

"Ask him does he require revenge?"

She opened one eye, saw the rather ravenous-
looking man sitting across from her, his gaze intent on
her in the way a wolf would look at a sheep. He
hadn't shaved in many days and probably hadn't
bathed since Christmas—if then. But oddly enough,
he wore the fanciest boots she'd ever seen on a man—
hand-tooled with big white stars on them.

"Go on, ask him."

She muttered a few incantations, then said, "He
says you need not bother to revenge his death, that
what he did, he did on his own account and that's just
the risk he ran and it was a lucky shot that got him
and nothing more."

"Good. Ask him what he did with the plans for
that bank in Laramie."

Again she peered at him, hoping against hope that
her little false conversation with the late friend would

put an end to any further violence by men of his—and no doubt his defunct partner's—ilk. But what she saw was a man with fevered, wretched eyes, and it troubled her more than just a little. She went into her routine again.

"He says he knows of no plans."

"Goddamn, you sure it's him you're palavering with, that this just ain't some damn fast game you're running on me?"

"He says that you should repent."

"Repent!"

"He says that the place he is in is terrible, full of fire and misery, that his soul burns night and day and that you will suffer the same fate if you do not repent."

Ned Loyal ran a fist full of fingers through his greasy hair. He looked about the room, but other than the lamplight flickering against the walls and ceiling of the tent, he saw nothing else there but himself and the fortune-teller. No sign of any sort of Hank.

"He says you need to abandon your current ways and seek forgiveness for your sins."

"Shut up, you damn witch!"

Madam Moustache opened her eyes fully. "You must leave now."

"I ain't got for what I come for."

"I've told you everything I can. You must leave now."

"I need to know where those bank plans is."

"You must leave now!"

"Stop saying that!"

And when she said it again, he pulled his revolver and shot her.

At first she saw a tunnel of white light. Then the light turned to many wonderful colors and it felt as though she had wings and was gently soaring above the ground. *This is the most wonderful feeling . . .* she thought. She could see Ned standing there below her, the gun in his hand still smoking. She could see herself lying faceup on the floor of the tent, a flower of bright red spreading across the bosom of her kimono. She saw Ned bend and open fully the kimono and touch her breasts and bring his fingers away dripping blood. Oh, he was the most terrible man she'd ever encountered, and she'd encountered quite a few in her day.

She lay there gasping, and Ned thought about shooting her again, but he was scared now because he'd never shot a woman before. Then he got to wondering what it would be like to fornicate with a dead woman and bent down and opened her kimono and felt her tits, but blood ran warm against his fingers and he didn't like it much and lost all carnal desire for her as quickly as it had come on him.

A glowing figure appeared to her, and without speaking, she knew that some great spirit was calling her and she gladly went. The nearer she drew to the formless shape of light, the more she felt filled with light. She reached toward that glowing figure.

* * *

Ned was startled nearly witless when the woman stretched out her hand as though reaching for him. He stumbled backward and tripped over the stool he'd been sitting on and fell hard, banging the crazy bone in his elbow, which caused him to drop his pistol. He had to pick it up with his left hand, which felt awkward.

Come daughter, the glowing figure seemed to say.

Ned scrambled out of the tent, but not unseen by several of Madam Moustache's neighbors, who'd come out of their tents at the sound of the pistol shot. They saw a man in fancy boots running up the street. Boots with big white stars tooled into them.

Jeff Carr was summoned.

"That Gypsy's been shot. The one who tells fortunes—Madam Moustache."

They described the man and the boots he was wearing, and Jeff Carr knew who it was right off. Only a goddamn dandy or cold-blooded killer would wear such prissy boots.

Somebody said they saw the man running toward Frenchy's Saloon. Jeff rounded up three of his deputies and marched down to Frenchy's.

Sure enough, prissy boots was standing at the bar tossing back drinks. Jeff sent his deputies left and right, then thumbed back the hammers of his shotgun and walked to within good killing range of Ned Loyal.

"Ned Loyal, I've come to arrest you for shooting that Gypsy. Stand away from that bar."

Ned looked up, his face a sheen of sweat. "I don't shoot women. I'm a man killer pure and simple."

"Drop your pistol in that spit pot."

"Why that damn bitch was nothing but a fraud, claimed she could talk to the dead. She couldn't talk to the dead no better'n you and me."

"You don't drop your iron in that spit pot, you'll get firsthand knowledge of what talking with the dead is really like. Stand away now or make your play."

"Well, shit, the way I see it is you'll hang me if I throw my iron away and let you arrest me, and I hear that is a terrible way to die. So I guess I won't."

Jeff Carr raised his shotgun to eye level and sighted down the barrels.

"This here will tear you up pretty good," he said. "No way of knowing for sure it'll kill you. Might just tear you all up and you'll end up dying slow and hard. Seems to me a broken neck at the end of a short rope would be the sure thing."

"Well, I say fuck that. Get to shooting, Jeff Carr!"

A cardplayer was killed by one of Ned Loyal's stray bullets, and a crib girl was shot through the leg by another. Ned Loyal was himself flung head down across an upturned table with most of his insides spilling onto the floor in greasy gray ropes, and one arm near shot off as well from the double ought buckshot Carr loaded his scattergun with.

Carr couldn't hear a thing from the loud blasts, and

his two deputies were still holding their unfired pistols, wondering who, if there was anyone, they needed to shoot. The scattergun breathed smoke, and all anyone could see of Ned Loyal through the haze was fancy boots with stars on them sticking up above the table.

"Jesus Christ," Carr said, working his jaw up and down, trying to get some of his hearing back. He could hear ringing, that was about it.

As she was being carried to the physician's office three blocks away, Madam Moustache felt immersed in the light, warm and happy to be so. But the light began to fade and her wings seemed to fail her and she felt herself being pulled harshly toward the cold earth again.

Why?

"Why, why, why?" she cried in her semiconscious state.

The doctor, who was himself under a great deal of laudanum influence, said to those who'd carried Madam to his office, "She'll live, but don't ask me to explain how."

She'd been shot through the brisket, which usually was a fatal place to be shot through, and had lost a great deal of blood. Still, she breathed and her heart beat in a steady patter and the doctor couldn't help but notice the bloody fingerprints upon her bosoms. He shook his head, thinking of how much violence he'd seen perpetrated over the years in the name of love and God.

*   *   *

Word arrived in the Gold Room via a miner who'd just witnessed the shooting.

"Jeff Carr just killed Ned Loyal over in Frenchy's. Shot him half in two!"

Bill and Teddy and Charley occupied a corner table where Bill could keep his back to the wall.

"Well, what goes around comes around, I reckon," Bill said, lifting his glass.

"Here's to them who would shoot horses," Charley said. "May his soul be damned in hell."

"I guess that about plum cleans up the assassins," Bill said. "What with that 'n' you shot the other day."

Teddy knew he should feel relieved, but realized that the world was probably full of men who would yet see Hickok dead. And he knew Bill was simply putting on a brave face, because Bill knew better than anybody that there would never be a world without assassins in it—at least not his world.

Chapter 25

———————

They drank until the dice quit rolling, until the roulette wheel was spun a final time, until the last hand got tossed in. Bill had himself a good night with the picture cards and won nearly $250.

Twice Charley drifted off up the stairs to Squirrel Tooth Alice's crib with her. Each time Alice put on a big show of it for Bill's benefit, but Bill hardly seemed to notice, which put a fury in her she took out on Charley, which only made Charley that more enamored with her.

"You fornicate like a madwoman," he said breathlessly after each time.

"I got my reasons," she said.

"It's all right with me whatever they are. Say, you wouldn't consider being my common-law wife would you?"

"What, and give all this up?" she said sarcastically.

"I'd rent us a house when me and Bill get up to Deadwood. You could grow petunias in a flower box and be a regular gal. Nobody'd have to know you were a crib girl."

"You don't know, do you?"

"Know what?" Charley said.

"About me and Bill."

"What about you and Bill?"

"We was practically married when we lived in Abilene."

Charley felt a great disappointment. He wondered if there was any woman in the West Bill hadn't had at one time or another. There went love, it felt like to him. Twice in a day his offer of marriage had been turned down by doves. Charley figured sure the preacher had put some sort of curse on him with all that talk about death and seductresses.

"It never was me you was interested in, then?" Charley said.

"I was hoping to make Bill jealous."

"I never seen him that way."

"Did he ever mention me before?"

"No. If he had, I think I'd remember that. But Bill never talks much about his paramours that I know of. He's respectful in that way. I am too."

"I came all the way from Abilene to find him and he spurned me," Alice said.

"Look at us," Charley said. "We're pretty pathetic, ain't we, Alice?"

"Speak for yourself."

Charley knew what it was to swallow his pride, and when he looked at Alice there in the bed beside him with little to cover her but a crème chenille bedspread that come up only as high as her waist, leaving everything else exposed for his eyes, Charley caved in on his resolve not to be a beggar.

"I guess I could get over the fact of you and Bill if you could," Charley said.

"I've been a dove for a long time, Charley. And I don't know much about life in general except that it's hard most of the time and never gets its foot off the back of your neck. And I know girls of my profession would do just about anything to be something other than what they are, including marrying the first feller that would ask them. But I am not fool enough to jump from the fire into the frying pan, and that's what I'd be doing if I was to go with you to Deadwood. You're already a married man, Charley. I can spot married men from here to Kansas. I'd just as soon nest with my sisters and be a free bird as to be one man's dove in a gilded cage. No offense."

"None taken, Alice."

"I do believe that is the longest speech I ever made."

"It was inspiring."

"You want to go again, or have you run out of cash?"

"I always keep a little reserve in my poke, girl, but I'm feeling about like a winded horse that's done run his race and don't see how I could possibly get my money's worth a third time around. I'd just peter out on you." Alice laughed at the pun.

"Would you be up to buying a girl a drink at least?"

"That I could do."

Teddy was trying hard not to think about Kathleen. She and the kid had left on the flier to Denver, but in a way it seemed as though she'd only been something his imagination had conjured up, so short had been their relationship. Everything about the West had a most temporary feel to it—life most especially.

It felt like he'd aged ten years in just the last week or so. He'd been blooded—had taken a life and nearly had his taken. And now he'd known love and had it taken from him as well. *Innocence lost*, he thought.

He watched Bill at the poker table from across the room. The famed shootist hardly seemed real either. Teddy wondered if he weren't just in a long dream he couldn't wake from, and maybe he was still in law school and Horace and his father were still alive and his mother wasn't enamored with some English poet she was preparing to go live with in Europe.

He felt an ever-growing sense of uncertainty, that too many things were unfinished, that there were too many questions without answers.

Maybe he was just tired, he told himself. His mood was as black as the last hour of night before dawn began to seep across the plains, crawling slowly toward that outpost called Cheyenne.

Bill stood finally, his pockets full, his face a mixture of the sorrow, which had become almost permanently affixed in those watery eyes, and one of modest satisfaction at having finally had a streak of unbreakable luck.

Charley was near asleep by the door but came alert when Bill slapped him across the back and announced, "I just earned us our expense money for the journey north."

The three of them walked back to the collection of tents and wagons, and Bill said, "Come with me and Charley up to Deadwood, old son. You're a good pard and we'd be privileged to have you in our camp, wouldn't we Charley?"

"Sure enough," Charley said, still a bit dazed from all the rejection he'd suffered, and from too little sleep.

"I might could go with you boys," Teddy said. He wasn't sure what George Bangs would want of him. "When are you fixing to leave?"

Bill paused, made a visor out of his hand and looked at the growing light, the way the sky shone over the land—white at its core and pink around the edges. Then he sniffed the air and said, "I reckon we can leave about any time, the weather is broke good enough to suit me. How about this afternoon after we've had a good catnap?"

"I could stand a change of scenery," Charley said. "But I'll have to buy myself another horse to replace old Abe Lincoln."

"See if you can find one that has a nose for gold," Bill said. Charley hadn't seen Bill's spirits so high in months.

They walked into camp, and Charley went and paid some men to put ropes around Abe Lincoln and drag him far out onto the prairie. "Far enough where I won't have to be reminded unnecessarily of my old pard," Charley told them, paying each five dollars for the onerous task.

Bill started off toward the trees to make water, and Charley made like he had to go too, but Teddy knew it was just so he could keep an eye on Bill's back. They were up there maybe fifteen minutes, and Bill walked sort of funny on the way back then crawled into the tent and fell fast asleep.

"He says when he has to piss it hurts for some time after," Charley explained about the funny way Bill was walking.

"You want to stand first watch or second?"

"I'll take first," Teddy said.

"I got a bad feeling for some reason."

"You think there'll be another attempt on his life?"

"Don't you?"

"It's possible."

"I feel like somebody's always watching us."

Teddy looked off toward the trees. "It could be somebody is. A man with a good rifle . . . wouldn't none of us be safe if he had bad intentions."

"I know it," Charley said, then yawned. "But I guess we could worry ourselves to death as well."

Charley crawled into the back of his and Bill's wagon. Teddy took the old bucket and turned it upside down, setting it against the wagon wheel so he could rest his back against it. He couldn't say whether Charley was right about the possibility of another attempt on Bill's life, but he knew that certain men had certain gifts when it came to knowing about things yet to happen, and Charley might well be one of those men.

The sunlight came easily along the ground until it touched the toes of his boots, then climbed up his legs and settled in his lap like an old house cat and warmed his hands. Bill was right, the weather looked like it had finally broke. He wondered what Deadwood would be like—that country he'd heard stories about nearly every hour from the mouths of men who wanted to go there, and some who'd gone and come back again.

He thought in a way how nice it would be if he could stake his own claim in that country and perhaps make a strike. He played loose with the ideas of what he'd do with all that money, but his ideas kept taking him down roads that led to Silver City, New Mexico, and the frail but lovely Kathleen Bonney. It was a thought as pleasant as the new weather.

Jeff Carr looked out his window at all that morning sunshine and said to his deputies, "Boys, it's going to be a good day. The weather's broke, and that mean's all these yahoos and miners and gunslingers and pimps and whores will be busting out of camp and heading to Deadwood and points north, and that's good news for us."

"Hooray," they said.

He might just as well announced Christmas was due to come early, for the smiles it put on their faces.

The sight of all that sunshine just put a good feeling in a man's bones, and Jeff thought maybe he'd take the day off and go on a picnic with his Molly, and he said as much to his men.

"You boys hold down the fort for a few hours and try not and kill anybody and try not and let anybody kill you." And they all agreed that it sounded like a good idea.

Jeff left his office and went straight home, where

his wife by common-law marriage was baking a cobbler with peaches she'd canned the summer before. She and Jeff were childless, and it was just as well with him that they were because he'd not want to raise sons and daughters in such a lawless place as Cheyenne, though admittedly, it was getting tamer with each passing season. Still, he'd not want to have to explain to little boys and girls that had his eyes and Molly's sensibilities why he had to shoot a man so badly at Frenchy's Saloon the other night.

"That smells frightful good," Jeff said.

"Peach cobbler," his wife replied. "Your favorite."

"I love you like money."

"You always did know how to talk romantic to a gal," she said teasingly. She was a bit French, some of her people were—on her father's side—and Jeff knew she leaned toward fancy words and genteel mannerisms, which was something he didn't possess much of, being a man originally from the backwoods of Kentucky.

"I was thinking it's such a pretty day we should go for a picnic," he said.

It surprised her, his thoughtfulness.

"I bet we could swing by Carson's Café and get us a basket of fried chicken and some cold beer to go with it."

Sometimes he surprised her a lot more than she ever thought he was capable of. Mostly he was a taciturn man with a grim view on life, a view born out of his chosen profession as law keeper.

"How's the weather, warm enough, or should I take a shawl?"

"Take a shawl," he said, "you know how fast the weather changes in this country."

"*Oui,*" she said. He loved hearing her say things like that.

He went out of the house and hitched up the chesty bay he called Bob to the hack and whistled while he was at it. His wife came out of the house carrying a bowl of the cobbler and a shawl draped loose over one arm, and he helped her up in the hack then snapped the reins over Bob's haunches, setting the bay into a nice clip-clop walk.

He wheeled in at the café for a basket of fried chicken and some fresh warm biscuits and a pail of cold beer. He had given some thought to what they'd do after they had their picnic, and was pleased with himself for having slipped an extra blanket in under the seat. It had been a long time since he and Molly had gone on that kind of a picnic, and he figured it was about time they did again.

They rode along at a gentle but steady pace toward Crow River, where he knew of a little copse of cottonwood trees that would offer friendly shelter and just enough privacy that if they got around to it, they could put to use that extra blanket.

"I do wish you'd consider taking up another profession," Molly said.

"Where'd that come from?"

"I don't know. I just worry sometimes that something terrible will happen to you. Pretty days cause me to worry, I guess."

"It ain't yet and it ain't going to," he said reassuringly. "I'm a careful man, you know that."

"I know you are, Jeff."

He patted her hand as they rode along, and he was glad he'd met and took up residence with her instead of remaining a bachelor. That was no kind of life for a man.

They came to where Crow River twisted down from the plateaus and squirmed through the stand of cottonwoods, and he pulled in there and climbed out of the wagon. Then holding the reins steady in one hand, he gave Molly a hand down with his other.

"It is such a lovely day, I feel young again," she said.

Jeff ground-reined the horse to a place where it could crop the new grass sprouting up so fresh and green there along the river, while Molly spread one of the blankets along the ground and set the food and herself on it.

They ate in quiet pleasure but Jeff felt his heart stirring more rapidly with every bite for thinking about being there alone with his wife. At one point he took her hand and kissed it, and she looked at him and saw that particular look he got in his eye at certain times.

"Why Jeff Carr, did you bring me out here on the pretense of a picnic just so you could dally with me?"

"I did," he said.

"Eat your chicken," she said.

He smiled, said, "Woman, you'll be my consternation all the rest of my days."

Her laughter was like that of a songbird.

He hardly ever knew such happiness, and swallowed hard to hold it in himself and keep it there.

* * *

Perhaps it was the hand of God, or the lack thereof that caused her to move just when she did, to unknowingly put herself in harm's way. Whatever it was, something slammed into her, knocking her suddenly forward, and she lay there twitching as though lightning struck before his stunned eyes.

Jeff Carr gently turned her over and saw the bloody maw of flesh and torn dress, saw her mouth moving as though to tell him how terrible the pain, but nothing coming from her except little gurgling gasps.

"Molly, Molly!"

Then her eyes rolled heavenward, and with her cheeks yet warm from that pleasant sun, she stopped moving at all even as blood spilled from her onto his hands and stained his clothes.

He drew her close to him as though to pin the death that was in her trying to flee, and in the fleeing leave her forever still. But too late, he realized when her cheeks began to cool against his own.

Eventually he reclined her back onto the blanket, now soaked with more blood than he ever saw come from a human being so small as she, and stood shakily turning this way and that in every direction to see where the death had come from.

Several hundred yards distant stood some boulders, the remnants of a forgotten flood in the history of time, and from these he determined the shot must have come.

While in his agony, the wind shifted around to the north, herding before it a mass of dark restless clouds. He knelt beside his wife, bringing the shawl up over her shoulders, and said, "This place, you cannot trust it, Molly. For, didn't I warn you that the weather changes every five minutes? I knew it was best you bring your shawl along."

He stood and went to the hack and took free the spare blanket and wrapped her in it, careful not to disturb her more than was necessary. And with the greatest effort, he lifted her, placed her inside the hack, and drew her over close to him, his free arm around her. Then he rode back to Cheyenne with haste and grief in him colder than the rain that began to fall from that unpredictable sky.

He could not even think of revenge, or feel any emotion except the one that was eating him up as he whipped furiously the flanks of the startled horse.

Paris Bass waited among the rocks—the rain pelting his hat. He pried with the knife tip to eject the jammed shell, his luck all bad now. He knew of such possibilities—how a man's luck could turn on him suddenly. But until he shot the woman quite unexpectedly, he had never made such a miscalculation.

She'd moved even as the shot rolled like small thunder across the span of what he judged a good four hundred yards—an inch or two, is all it was, but it made all the difference between life and death.

He had not traveled all this way to kill a woman!

He should not have strayed from the task at hand, he told himself. And yet temptation to exact an old revenge proved too much.

The rain was cold, as cold as he'd ever known it to be.

He pried with the knife blade to free the shell from

the rifle's breech. But it would not budge. And by the time he finally did free it, the target he'd sought was gone, fled with misfortune's victim.

And what truly had he hoped to prove by killing Jeff Carr—slayer of an old friend those many years ago? A friend who most likely deserved the death he got at the hands of the lawman in a border brawl. It was a stupid sense of justice, he realized now, and not at all the sort of thing a king of the old testament would do . . .

" 'Vanity of vanities,' " the Preacher said aloud, " 'all is vanity. In the place of judgment, wickedness was there; And in the place of righteousness, Inequity was there . . . ' "

He felt raw inside. Raw and cast out like the dark angels of God's heaven.

The pain started just behind his left eye and radiated inward until it felt as though a hot poker was piercing his brain. Nothing but laudanum would do, and he scratched through his clothes for the bottle, but when he found it, there was barely a swallow, hardly enough to sustain him for more than an hour, maybe less.

He drained what was there, flung the bottle against the rough rocks and saw it shatter into a hundred blue pieces, and tried tracing back the path that had led him to this moment. And the backward journey led his aching thoughts to the woman who had approached him on the streets of El Paso saying it was love that drove her to tempt him. *The love of a bandit.* Ha! he laughed most bitterly. She'd offered him money. *Greed!* But greed did not tempt him. She'd offered him her flesh. The Devil had known his weakness and had sent her to him. *Temptress, seductress, harlot, whore*. He knew now the snare that had been set.

Too late, too late.

For vanity would not let him simply ride away from this thing.

And he would kill Wild Bill and anyone who tried to prevent it, and free himself from the Devil's snare. And he would find the woman who loved Phil Coe and kill her as well.

The pain grew sharp as a cleaver's edge that cleaved his brain in two.

Chapter 26

Bill was picking out Charley a horse among a corral full of them. Charley trusted Bill's judgment when it came to flesh of any kind, horse or woman.

"That paint yonder looks like a pretty good cayuse," Bill said, pointing with his nose toward a little black and white mare.

The livery man said, "You want me to throw a rope around her?"

"Yes," Charley said. "Bring her over so I can have a look at her teeth."

Teddy liked the looks of the horse as well.

"You decided if you're going with us to Deadwood or not?" Bill said.

"I'm thinking I probably will."

"Better decide sooner rather than later. Charley and me get restless easy, and I've about had all of this prairie dog town I can stand."

"You still thinking of leaving today?"

Bill looked up at the sky, saw the dark clouds moving in from the north and rubbed his hip.

"Rheumatism tells me it's going to rain, and

Charley thinks we oughter put together a wagon train—lead them up there. Be good protection against Indians and bandits. Most likely go tomorrow or the next day, depending on the weather and how fast we can put a train together."

"Okay then, it will give me a chance to make up my mind."

Bill watched as the livery man tossed a rope over the neck of the paint and led her over so Charley could inspect her teeth.

"You looking for cavities?" Bill said with a grin, knowing Charley didn't know much more about a horse than it had four legs and a tail, but would not admit to his ignorance.

Charley said, "They're big and yeller and look all right to me, what do you think?"

Bill ran his hand over the back and haunches of the animal, then down along its legs, lifting one hoof at a time then setting them back down again.

"She'll do."

Teddy excused himself while Charley dickered with the livery man over a price for the mare.

"I'll swing 'round to your camp in a bit, I've got a few things I need to do if I'm going." He heard Charley tell Bill he thought he'd name his new horse George Custer, and Bill said, "That's more like it. That son of a buck will become president some day and live a ripe old life."

Teddy went to the telegrapher's and sent a telegram to George Bangs:

H IS READY TO MOVE NORTH, DO I GO? INFORM
IMMEDIATELY.

He waited while the telegrapher sent the wire—
waited nearly half an hour before a response came.

STAY WITH SUBJECT UNTIL INFORMED OTHER-
WISE. G. BANGS.

That settled, he would need some supplies and a
horse for himself. He thought a good rifle would
come in handy as well.

He walked over to the mercantile, looked at the selection of long guns and eventually settled on a Henry
rifle with brass fittings. He liked the feel and balance
and he liked its looks too. He bought two boxes of
cartridges, a slicker, beef jerky, a can of peaches, a canteen, and a set of saddlebags to put all but the rifle in.

He wandered back over to the corral and bought
the gelding he'd ridden the day he and Kathleen rode
to the river.

"I've got better horses," the man said.

"No, I want that one."

The horse cost him thirty dollars, the saddle forty.
He was about as fixed as a man could be for a long
ride into that country he knew nothing about except
that it held men's dreams of becoming rich the way
doves held their desire for eternal happiness.

He could think of a lot worse company to ride up
to that country with than Wild Bill and Colorado
Charley.

* * *

He found them both back at camp, Charley going among the wagons signing up folks who wanted to go to Deadwood under the protection of one Wild Bill Hickok, and of course himself.

He was finding plenty of takers, even at a charge of fifty dollars per wagon.

Bill was writing a letter to Agnes using an upturned bucket for a table. He held his face close to the paper and Teddy pretended not to notice. Bill looked up when Teddy approached.

"Just writing my wife news of our soon departure," Bill said.

"Don't let me interrupt you."

Drops of rain big as silver dollars fell, and Bill folded the letter carefully and put it inside his coat. Glancing up, he said, "We'd have gotten soaked to our union drawers if we'd left today. Started out good, but look at her now."

The sky hung low over the land like the dark belly of a great beast, so low a man's head would poke through it if he were riding a horse. He heard thunder rumbling off in the distance.

"Where you from originally?" Bill said.

"Chicago."

"Well now, ain't that something. I'm from Illinois myself originally—Homer, you ever heard of it?"

"I can't say honestly that I have."

Bill smiled. "You'd not be the first that hadn't. So small you can spit from one end of town to the other. My daddy's a farmer, my brothers too. I was back there last when Cody and me was on stage tour. I guess it'd be that time you saw us in Chicago." Bill looked wistful.

"You miss it much, that country?" Teddy asked.

"No, you?"

"Not like I did when I first went off to Texas. But a year gone from there might just as well have been a lifetime for me."

"I know that. I couldn't ever go back and live in that country. Don't see how anybody who's been out here anytime could."

"There's something about all this that ruins you on places back East," Teddy said.

"Ruins you in a good way."

"You miss your wife?"

Bill nodded. "I guess not as much as I should, but enough. What about you, you got one waiting for you?"

"No."

Bill looked around. "Charley's got one, and three daughters. Imagine living in a house full of females. I think it's half of why he's so restless."

The rain fell harder now, and Bill said, "I don't feature sitting out here getting wet, do you? Let's go into town and get a drink."

"What about Charley?"

"He'll follow along eventually."

So they went, two men in stride with one another, Teddy feeling somewhat Bill's equal as men who had been ruined by the West and men who knew what it was to be unfettered by the rules. Men who knew that when it came to the law or self-preservation, they had to play the game in their own way or not play it at all.

They went to Frenchy's this time, Bill saying he preferred it over the Gold Room but not saying why the change. Teddy was unaware of Bill's former consort, Squirrel Tooth Alice, and her employment now as a crib girl and Bill's not wanting to be witness to her newfound work. Bill still had some affection down deep for her but could never allow himself to admit to it, or to admit the little flames of jealousy that singed the edges of his heart.

There were still bloodstains on the floor from where Ned Loyal had fallen when Jeff Carr shot him near in half. Dark, like old barn paint. Frenchy had tried to scrub the stains away with a mop and hot soapy water, but to no avail. A man's blood spilled in violence was a forever stain. So he had set a table over the spot, hoping folks wouldn't notice so much. It wasn't the sort of notoriety he craved.

Bill sipped his cocktail, then said, "I used to get two bits each for shooting stray dogs in Abilene. It was added to my regular marshal's pay of twenty-six dollars a week."

"Did you regret having to perform such work?" Teddy asked.

"I do now, but not then."

Other men drifted in, shaking rain from them like wet dogs. Even the pewter light seemed listless and cold.

"I reckon I'll go over to the chink's," Bill said. "You're welcome to come along."

"I'll walk over with you," Teddy said, "but I'll forgo the opium pipe."

"It has a mysterious effect on you. Puts you in touch with the dead, among other things."

Teddy thought how unsettling it would be to see Horace again, even if it was in nothing more than a dope haze.

They finished their cocktails and were crossing the street when Jeff Carr nearly run them over with his hack. Teddy snatched Bill by the elbow, and the wheels of the hack flung mud against the legs of their trousers.

"What the hell!" Bill said, looking down at his muddy pants.

"You didn't see it, did you?" Teddy said.

"See what?"

"The woman that was with him."

Bill shook his head.

"She was covered in blood."

Potts, the undertaker, was accustomed to seeing the dead. He'd learned his trade as an apprentice on the battlefields of Bull Run, Cold Harbor, Gettysburg, and other such hallowed ground whose earth was soaked through with the blood of men who looked the same but were different in their hearts.

But rare was it a woman he'd had to tend whose wound was as grievous as that of the wife of Jeff Carr.

Jeff had brought her, accompanied by Doc Carver.

"Do the best for her you can," Doc Carver whispered before leaving again.

And Carr waited in the anteroom until Potts came and said, "You can view her now."

Potts always found women and children most difficult. They were frail and tender creatures, like spring flowers yet in their bloom. Last week it had been a young prostitute poisoned by her own hand. Pretty and fair, she seemed only to be sleeping, and Potts had kissed her before closing the lids.

"She did not wear her hair like that," Jeff Carr said, upon viewing the pale face.

"If you have a tintype or a photograph, it might help. And . . . whatever dress you'd like her in, bring that along when you return."

"I won't leave," Carr said.

"Then if you would, send someone for those things."

Jeff Carr couldn't ever imagine leaving her.

News of the killing spread through the town quick as fire. But Wild Bill did not hear of it until the next day when he went to piss out the last strains of the opium there among the trees. He wandered back into camp and Charley told him.

"As much as I don't care for the man," Wild Bill said, "I feel sorry he's lost his wife."

"I was thinking," Charley said.

"About what?"

"The way she was shot and all."

"How was she shot?"

"From a long ways off with a rifle."

Bill was still heavy-limbed from the effects of the dope. His mind was a bit sluggish still and he couldn't put together everything that was being said.

Teddy sat listening to Charley talk, said, "You

think it could have been the same one that shot your horse the other night?"

"I don't get it if it is," Bill said. "Why'd he want to shoot Jeff Carr's wife? Besides, I thought we all agreed it was Ned Loyal."

"I don't think it was him now," Teddy said. "I think whoever it was shot her for the same reason he shot Charley's horse. He wasn't aiming to."

"He killed the wrong one?"

"It's a possibility this shooter isn't any good with a long gun."

"Or maybe he is and just enjoys shooting women and horses," Charley said glumly.

Teddy watched Bill closely. Maybe he should have shown fear, but he didn't. Instead he just looked a little more morose than usual.

"I guess somebody wants to shoot Jeff Carr's wife and Charley's horse and you and me and all the rest, he by gar will," Bill said. "As long as he's willing to hide and do it with a long gun where nobody can face him down, who's to stop him?"

Charley shivered, and when Bill saw him do it, Charley said, "Cold morning, ain't it," and poured himself some coffee from a pot he'd been heating over the campfire.

Bill sat off by himself to finish writing the letter he'd started the evening before. Teddy squatted next to Charley.

"Any ideas?"

Charley sipped his coffee, said, "No, you?"

"I was just thinking, the next time he tries, he might not miss."

Charley looked off to the trees. "He could be up in there right now."

"He could be."

Charley flung the dregs of his cup into the fire, which hissed like a snake. "Old Bill's right about it all. He wants to kill us, I guess he will."

"It's my job not to let that happen," Teddy said.

"Then you better get to work, old son."

"I guess I better."

Chapter 27

Jeff Carr thought what a cruel joke it was that the day he was to bury his love had turned so beautiful.

Potts, dressed in formal funeral attire—black cut-away coat and trousers, a stovepipe beaver hat—came and said in a low whisper, "Anytime now, Sheriff . . . whenever you're ready, we can proceed."

Jeff had been sitting in the front pew of the small church hardly noticing anyone else. Among the mourners: his deputies, the mayor and city fathers, old friends, members of the Ladies Benefit Society, and the curious. All had come to bear witness to a man and his grief. The leaders of the community were less certain now than they had been a year previous, when they'd hired him, that he was *their* man. For, he did seem to arouse a certain antipathy from the rough trade—the shootists, pimps, and whores. And now there had been three murders in the span of as many days. And though the community leaders were sympathetic to his current situation, they privately wondered how much longer they could go with the man. Perhaps someone with a bit more diplomacy, someone who didn't stroll about cradling a shotgun, might be better suited for the task. Still, this day they would abide him his position and let him have his bereavement.

Some of the businesses Jeff Carr and his crew protected day and night draped their windows in black crepe out of respect. Even Frenchy closed his bar till noon—announcing the shutdown with a hand-painted sign out front. A few of the doves took up a collection the night before to help pay funeral expenses.

But none of this was of any consequence to Jeff. He thought only of his Molly, of the brief days of her life, the moment of her death, and the man who'd killed her.

Potts's sister, Adele, played a collection of mournful dirges on the organ—music that floated toward the rafters, rattled around, then fell heavy on the ear and heart, heavy and ethereal and dark as bad dreams. And when she came to the end of the selection and looked at her elder brother, he signaled with a look that she should continue, and so she began again, while the gathered began to grow restless.

Finally Jeff Carr stood, went to the coffin and gazed down at his wife. He felt compelled to say: "I should have made it official, given you a ring." Then he closed his eyes and thought how much better it would feel if he were any sort of believer so that he might call out his distress to some god or other. And perhaps he would get some sort of an answer as to why the sort of god Molly believed in would need her more than he would. But he could find no such sense of faith, and so in his sorrow and regret, he felt completely alone, like one of the living dead.

Potts waved forth the pallbearers. To the six, the weight of the coffin with Molly in it seemed hardly anything at all. They carried her forth to the waiting hearse hitched to a dandy pair of Percherons.

The Catholic cemetery was a half mile distance, the Baptist a quarter mile the opposite direction, and potter's field a mile farther still. Molly had been Catholic but not practicing. Jeff thought the God of Catholics wouldn't mind if he buried her where the other Catholics were, and so bought her a plot there and paid the local priest to perform the service.

Jeff mounted his horse sans shotgun or any arms whatsoever—and walked it alongside the hearse with its high-glass sides and ebony wood, brass lamps and black crepe trim. The horses had black feathered plumes sticking from their headstalls. He didn't care much for the garish display. He could see Molly's polished mahogany coffin inside with its brass handrails. It had cost him a hundred dollars, but he wouldn't have cared if it had cost a thousand. He would have robbed the damn banks to pay for it if he had to.

He tipped his hat one last time, then took the lead so the hearse and mourners could follow, and did not acknowledge the presence of those who stood along the street observing this utterly sad procession.

Teddy Blue was one of those on the street, and he truly felt bad for Jeff Carr, a man who looked broken in spirit as he rode with slumped shoulders, his eyes cast downward.

But more than simple interest in the funeral procession had him watching the crowd. Teddy was observing them collectively to see if anyone caught his eye. He wasn't sure even what to look for, but instinct told him he'd notice something unusual if it were there.

He saw nothing on first glance. He worked his way down the walk—first one side of the street, then crossed over to the other and up that way.

Then someone did catch his notice. A man standing dressed in black, like a preacher. There was nothing very unusual about him, and Teddy would never have noticed him on a normal day except for one thing: he was writing something in a small book.

Teddy stopped several feet away and continued to observe the man with the book. He saw him write something in it then close the book and slip it into a side pocket of his coat. It was no proof of anything; he could have been a journalist—God knows there were plenty of them in the territory. When the funeral procession passed, the crowd of onlookers drifted back to whatever they'd been doing before; clerks to their stores and cafés and banks, barkeeps to their saloons, doves to their cribs.

The man with the book turned north and walked alone to the American Café. Teddy lagged behind several paces and entered as well. The man had taken a table near the window. Teddy took a seat at the counter where he could observe the man in the mirror that hung on the back wall.

The man ordered breakfast and ate it with deliberation, pausing once mid-meal to take the book out again and write something more into it. Teddy knew he'd like to get a look at that book.

The man finished his meal then stood and left, and Teddy stayed on his trail, keeping a dozen paces behind him.

He followed the man to the Union Pacific Railroad Hotel. He watched as the man went up the stairs, then he walked to the desk.

"Say, wasn't that Buffalo Bill Cody?" Teddy said.

The clerk blinked. "Who?"

"That fellow that just went up the stairs?"

The clerk snorted. "No, Cody and them checked out the other day. That feller is Mr. Bass."

"Bass, huh. I could have sworn he was Cody."

"Don't look nothing like Buffalo Bill . . . well, except they're both dark-haired."

"My mistake. Bass, you say? Not Jake Bass from Kansas City, I suppose?"

The clerk shook his head. "No, that feller is Mr. Paris Bass. Odd name, ain't it, Paris?"

"Damn odd. Well, I've wasted enough of your time."

Teddy went to the telegrapher's and sent a short wire and told the clerk he'd wait for the reply:

WHAT INFORMATION DO YOU HAVE ON ONE PARIS BASS? INFORM IMMEDIATELY. T. BLUE.

Silence filled the little office. Silence and sunlight with dust moats dancing in it. The sort of silence that eats time slowly and leaves a man fidgety. It seemed like nothing at all moved except for the steady tock caused by the pendulum's swing of the regulator clock.

Five minutes passed, ten, twenty.

Then the telegrapher's key started ticking and the clerk wrote down the message and handed it to Teddy. Teddy read it, looked at the clerk, who shrugged.

"I just work here, mister."

"Keep it that way."

Out he went, straight to Charley and Wild Bill's camp.

Charley was braiding his hair and Bill was shaving.

"There's something you should know," Teddy said.

Charley stopped and Bill stopped and both men looked at him.

"There's a man in town named Paris Bass, either of you ever heard of him?"

"Paris," Bill said. "That's a funny name for a feller to have. What about him?"

"That's just it, I don't know, except he's in town and he was watching the funeral procession this morning."

Bill went back to shaving, his interest already lost in a man whose first name was Paris.

Charley cast a sidelong glance toward Teddy, indicating they should walk off a ways from the camp.

"You think this Paris Bass is the one who shot my horse the other night, don't you?"

"I can't be sure."

"You think he meant to kill Bill."

Teddy pulled the telegram from his pocket and handed it to Charley, who read it:

PARIS BASS. CURRENT OCCUPATION: UNKNOWN. FORMER U.S. SECRET SERVICE AGENT. FORMER 1ST REGIMENT SHARPSHOOTER/U.S. VOLUNTEERS. SUSPECT IN SEVERAL SLAYINGS FOR HIRE IN SEVERAL STATES. AMONG VICTIMS, TWO TEXAS RANGERS, U.S. DEPUTY MARSHAL, BANK PRESIDENT. LAST KNOWN RESIDENCE: EL PASO. CONSIDERED DANGEROUS TO APPROACH. IS HE IN CHEYENNE? DO WE NEED TO SEND ASSISTANCE? G. BANGS.

"You need to show this to Jeff Carr," Charley said.

"I thought about it, but there's no proof of anything here."

"Proof is a bullet already fired. By the time any of us gets the proof, it'll be too late. What you going to do?"

"Follow him."

"He'll probably know if you do."

"I know it."

"You want him to know . . ."

"Maybe if he does, he'll think twice before trying anything."

"Or kill you."

"Yeah, maybe that too. Thing is, if I'm following this Bass, you'll need to stick close to Bill."

"We're planning on heading out tomorrow for Deadwood."

"Might not be a bad move."

"It won't stop him, though, will it?"

"Not if he's come to kill him."

Charley's face suddenly grew ashen. "You think maybe he killed Jeff Carr's wife?"

"I think it's possible, I just don't know why he would."

Charley handed the telegram back to Teddy. "Say's he's a hired assassin, which if true, means somebody has paid him to come for Bill . . ."

"That would be my guess. Any ideas on who might do that?"

Charley shrugged. "Could be any of a dozen folks . . . Bill's made himself a lot of enemies over the years. You'd be barking in tall grass trying to figure that out."

"I've got to go."

"Go on, then. I'll stick with Bill. Hell, I'll even hold his pecker for him while he pisses if I have to so his hands stay free."

"You're a good pard," Teddy said with a grin.

"I always knew I was."

The pain was like lightning had shattered his skull. Paris Bass pulled the shades to stay the daylight and lay with a towel across his eyes. It had gotten worse over the years, and in the last several months had struck with greater frequency, and each time the effect was more debilitating than the last. A doctor in Dallas said he suspected a brain tumor. That was a year ago. He was thirty-four years old. It couldn't be a brain tumor. He stuffed his ears with cotton to dull any noises. He grew sick, threw up in the basin. He knew the routine. A derringer lay on the bureau. He wondered if he had the strength to rise, take it, put it to his temple and pull the trigger.

Except . . . except, he knew that once the spell passed and life seeped back into him again, he would feel well and whole and ready again for the pleasures of life. He doubted he had the strength to kill himself at that moment, and so abandoned the thought, as he always did.

Teddy camped out in the lobby of the Railroad Hotel, watched folks come and go: miners, engineers, couples, cowboys. The trains outside ground to halts and chugged away again. He had no plan except to follow this Paris Bass when he saw him and be ready for whatever might happen.

He thought of Kathleen in the intervening hours of his wait. She was somewhere on a train herself at that very moment, a young restless boy by her side, each heading toward uncertain futures. But then again, he was heading toward an uncertain future himself, and so was Bill and Charley and all the rest of them.

Something greater than them existed, held the reins to their destinies, and would eventually guide them along like wild horses before a drover.

There in his room, the dull light of dusk now descended, his pain a cooling fire inside his head, he hears voiced . . . a voice: *But you denied the Holy One and the Just, and asked for a murderer to be granted to you, and killed the Prince of life . . .*

* * *

He sat bolt upright, his skin flush and afire, his nerves twitching under his eyes, his hands trembling.

"*My time is short, I know it,*" he muttered to himself. "*I must go and kill the Prince.*"

Teddy saw the Preacher descending the stairs, a long rifle encased in a scabbard of rich brown leather. He's going out for the kill, he thought. The twilight hour has fallen and he is going to find Wild Bill and kill him.

He followed the Preacher from the hotel, down several city blocks, and up an alley that led to vacant lots. Across these, maybe five hundred yards distance, were the stand of the trees that lay between the town's limits and the encampment of the miners where Wild Bill and Charley had their tent pitched.

The twilight sky was a dusty rose color, like a harlot's faded dress. Teddy could see the dog star, could feel the heat of the earlier sun ascending out of the earth. The Preacher walked steady on across the vacant lots toward the treeline. He had to hold back in case the Preacher was to turn and see him. Surprise was key.

Bill was tugging on his boots and Charley was playing a game of solitaire with a deck of cards that had illustrations on them of scantily clad women. Charley had bought the cards in San Francisco from a sailor who said they came from Hong Kong, China.

"You winning or losing?" Bill said.

"Doesn't matter," Charley said. "I only play because it gives me a chance to see all my girls."

Bill shook his head. "Wonder where Teddy's gone off to this lovely night."

Charley looked up, stared out beyond the camp where dusk was deepening into night. "You reckon we should have us a fire going?"

"Why not?" Bill said. "It's going to get cold."

"I was thinking about what happened the other night, how that firelight might make us prime targets was there somebody out there with his rifle."

"You mean like that French fish feller?"

"Paris Bass," said Charley, letting the name sort of fall off his tongue rather than speak it aloud.

"Well, if it will make you feel better, let's go get us a cocktail."

"Harry Young's place?" Charley said hopefully.

"I'd just soon not go there and have to watch you make a spectacle of yourself with the doves."

"Alice already told me about you and her, Bill. And it don't bother me a smidge if it don't you. After all, I don't suppose you'd care one way or the other at this stage of the game, would you—you being married to Agnes and all?"

"It don't bother me who you want to fornicate with. But we're pards, Charley, and even though Alice and me have been quits three or four years now, I'd still like to think you honor the bonds of friendship and not fornicate with her knowing her and me had us a history together."

Charley started to present an argument to Bill he had rehearsed with himself just in case Bill played the friendship card, which Charley suspected he might, knowing how particular Bill was about certain matters—women he'd been intimate with most especially. But before he could get the opening statement out of his gullet a shot rang out, then another.

"Why's it always so goddamn dark a feller can't see to defend himself," Bill said, and cursed, backing farther into the shadows as he pulled both Navies free.

Chapter 28

—◆—

Jeff Carr got himself plenty drunk after the funeral. Some of his deputies came to Frenchy's to take him home. He refused them.

"I'm not bothering nobody," he claimed.

They expressed concern for his welfare when they saw he had his shotgun lying there atop the table. He told them to go to hell. Instead, they simply turned and left.

He sat alone. He drank alone. No one dared approach him.

The scent of wet earth caused him to ache. The thought of going home to an empty house was worse than anything imaginable. The silence of rooms where nobody moved about, of being in bed alone—all of it egged him on toward a mean drunk.

He was still there drinking when the Preacher went up the alley, across the vacant lots, and off toward the trees that overlooked the transient camp. He was there when the sky shaded from the dusty rose to the deeper purple that brought with it a sprinkling of stars.

* * *

Paris Bass settled himself down at the edge of the tree-line. The light was fading fast. In the distance he could see the encampment's fires in the same way he saw them back in the war. He would leave for the enemy's camps just at dusk, the way he'd left the town tonight. He would work his way behind the enemy's lines, hoping to pick off an officer. And if not an officer, than any man he saw. It made no difference to him, really. But his own commanders favored shooting officers, and so he shot them when he could. He'd made it a practice to do his sniping at night, something only he chose to do. The other sharpshooters stayed behind, waited until daylight. But he chose to go it alone, to make the darkness his ally, to come close to it and bring it close to him. The others saw night as a time of mourning, of licking their wounds, a time to feel safe, but not Paris Bass.

The jagged edges of the headache gnawed at him still, mangled his power to concentrate fully. He shucked the rifle from its scabbard. He'd missed his mark twice in a row. He would not miss it again.

Hickok was the one who wore the big pancake hat, the only one like it in all of camp. He would stand near the fire once it got dark and cold enough and hold his hands forth and warm them. For that was just naturally what men did—even the fair princes were not immune to certain comforts.

Paris Bass placed the barrel of his custom-made rifle with its long brass scope—the same one he'd used in the war—over the trunk of a fallen gum tree. Through the scope's eyepiece the campfire seemed hardly more than a few feet away, a dancing blaze in the soft blackness. Wind riffled through the upper branches of the pines. He shifted the rifle left to right to take in the scene. Saw two men, their backs to the campfire. One was shorter than the other. That would be Charley Utter. The taller man moved away from the campfire into the shadows. Hickok. Paris Bass waited, his breathing shallow, steady. He tasted the wind, adjusted for it. It was just a matter of waiting for the shot now.

Teddy moved quickly across the vacant lots once he saw Paris Bass enter the stand of trees. He knew if he got the chance, he would have to kill the man, perhaps without even a warning. His mind questioned whether he could do it. Was that how it had been with the man or men who had killed his brother? Without warning? But this was different, he told himself.

He went swiftly and silently like a shadow among shadows, the light all but gone now. The woods seemed to hold a deeper darkness still when he slipped into them. He guessed the direction of the camp and made his way as stealthily as possible.

Having raged all he could within, Jeff Carr rose from his table in Frenchy's, started to leave out of the bar, paused for a moment to look at the dark stain on the floor beneath the strategically placed table. Ned Loyal would always be part of Frenchy's until somebody tore it down, or until the last living witness was himself dead. Men would talk about how Jeff Carr blew a man in half with the double barrel, would tell about the gambler killed by the stray bullet and the dove shot through the leg and how she charged ten cents to look at the scar. The story would get distorted with each telling, and over time it might be ten men killed, a dozen doves shot in various places in their bodies. And the dove who was shot would grow old and still show her scar, only no man would pay to see it after a while.

In his mind, Ned Loyal was just part of the garbage needed to get rid of, and that's what he done—his job: human trash collector.

Well, there was some more trash needed gotten rid of, and he knew exactly where to find it.

He stormed out the swinging doors of Frenchy's and stalked off toward the tent city. If they wouldn't leave on their own, he'd by God see they left by his will. He had the shotgun swinging low in his right hand, liked the weight of it, hated the fact he had to carry it at all.

Teddy moved along at a careful crouch now, hoping to catch a glimpse of some movement or hear a sound there at the opposite end of the wood. The woods seemed a tomb of silence.

Down in camp, Bill was saying, "I oughter go make water."

Charley said, "I don't think you should walk up to them trees this time of night."

"Hell," Bill said. "When a man has to make water, he has to make water . . ."

*   *   *

The tall man came into view, the pancake hat unmistakable. All that long hair falling out from under it.

Paris Bass brought his finger against the cold curve of the trigger, took a deep breath, let half of it out, held the rest.

Teddy heard the sound of a hammer being cocked, slithered toward it.

Bill turned away from the light just as Charley stood from his game of cards.

"I don't think you oughter—"

There was a sharp crack. Teddy saw the muzzle flash of the rifle and fired his pistol into a space just behind. His own muzzle flash night-blinded him. For a long aching moment the world stopped turning.

Jeff Carr walked into camp ready to kill anyone who took umbrage with his presence. He near hoped somebody would. A shot rang out, then another, both at some distance. A stir went through the camp, curses, campers scurrying like rats. He figured somebody was killed. Then he saw Colorado Charley laid out, Bill kneeling next to him with a lamp near his bloody face. Jeff felt confused, deprived, leveled his shotgun at Bill, said, "Don't fucking move."

Bill looked at him with a calm countenance, said, "Somebody shot my pard. Was it you?"

Paris Bass felt the bullet bite in between his ribs. He tried to twist away from it, the rifle forgotten, left still there across the tree trunk. He smelled the wet earth, the places where men had gone to piss and drop their drawers. He clawed through his clothes to find the derringer. The pain in his side wasn't half as bad as the one in his brain that flared and exploded now like heat lightning.

"Who's there!" he cried.

He felt something in his pocket, tore it free. It was the small Bible, not the pistol, but it had a comfort to it the pistol did not have. He brought it to his face, pressed it against his eyes, prayed that the pain in his head would stop. It did not.

Then the shadow of a man loomed over him.

"Don't make me finish you," the man said.

"Go ahead, take away this cup from me."

Teddy struck a match. The light flared and he saw the face of Paris Bass, the Bible pressed to his forehead. He saw too the derringer there by his pocket and picked it up.

"It's over," he said.

The man began speaking strangely—a jumble of incoherent words tumbled from his mouth. Teddy had heard of such things, of reverent men speaking in "tongues." It was eerie and sad somehow; for it may as well been a madness, and not a religion at all, that the man was given to. Teddy felt through the man's clothes for more weapons, found the book instead and took it from him.

Charley revived on his own, opened his eyes, wiped blood from his face and said, "If I'm dead, why ain't I seeing angels instead of you two?"

Bill smiled, said, "Hell, how you know we ain't dead too?"

Jeff Carr, a little more sober now than he was when he walked into their camp, said, "I want you boys out of my town by tomorrow."

"I thought I told you once not to try and buffalo me," Bill said.

Charley raised a hand, said to Carr, "We'll be gone out of your prairie dog town tomorrow, Sheriff . . ." then passed out again.

Jeff Carr helped Bill get Charley to the doctor's office, where his scalp was washed free of blood and the doctor could see that the bullet had only plowed a neat furrow across Charley's scalp, missing by a good inch of blowing out his brains.

When the doctor announced that Charley was going to live, Charley promised God he would never again fornicate with doves and that he would spend the rest of his days doing good deeds and watching after his pard, Wild Bill. Amen.

"The good Lord has seen fit to spare me, boys. I'm turning over a new leaf. No more liquor or women or cards for me. Here, Doc, you can have these," Charley said, handing the doctor his deck of cards.

The doctor looked at the nude illustrations.

Charley quickly said, "I was thinking of becoming a medico myself once, thought those cards might help in my study of the human anatomy."

Jeff Carr was in his office nursing a bad head and bitter heart when the door opened.

The man in black wore a bloody shirt and held his side. The one behind him was the one Carr never did trust to be who he said he was, or more accurately, never said who he was.

"Lock this man up," Teddy said.

"For what? Looks like somebody shot him, and I'm guessing it would be you."

Teddy tossed the leather-bound book on Carr's desk—*Book of the Dead*.

"Read it and you'll know why you need to put him under arrest."

Later, Carr put the book down, his face twisted in anger, still red and blotchy from the liquor he'd drank earlier, but his mind clear now.

"Son of a bitch was the one who shot Molly," he said, rising, reaching for the shotgun.

"You going to shoot him in his cell, unarmed?" Teddy said.

"You goddamn right."

"Don't do it. Let the law hang him."

"She wasn't married to the law, she was married to me."

"Either way he'll get dead."

"It's my duty!"

"No, the law is your duty."

"What the hell would you know about it?"

Teddy thought of Horace, dying while upholding the law. Maybe it was a stupid thing to do. Why should he care whether Jeff Carr took his revenge out on Paris Bass?

"Fine, you want to shoot him like that, go ahead.

You think that's what your wife would want you to do, then do it. But I'll tell you this, if you kill him and there's a trial, I'll testify against you."

"Your word don't mean horse shit in this town."

Teddy took the Pinkerton's badge from inside his pocket and showed it to Jeff Carr.

"I came here to protect someone. I guess that's what you've spent your whole life trying to do, up until now. You kill that man back there, what makes you any different than him?"

Carr pushed past Teddy and stalked toward the cells. Teddy followed him.

Paris Bass looked up, his eyes bleary and rimmed red, the pain in his head crushing. He saw the sheriff shove the barrels of his shotgun through the bars.

"Get ready to die, you son of a bitch."

"Go ahead, do me that kindness."

Jeff Carr was caught off guard when Paris Bass fell to his knees, clasped his hands together and begged to be killed.

"Please, please, please . . . Kill me!"

He thumbed back the hammers.

"Please, dear Jesus, please, please shoot me!"

Carr's hands began to shake, the barrels of his shotgun clattering against the steel bars.

"Go ahead . . . Oh, damn you, go ahead!"

Carr felt a hand on his shoulder, a kindly hand.

"He's going to die either way," Teddy said, then turned and walked out.

Chapter 29

———— ◆◆◆ ————

Charley went to pick up his and Bill's mail the next day, a bandage wrapped around his head that made it hard to set his hat on straight. He was hoping he'd find a letter from his loving wife and daughters, and he did. But also there was a letter from Agnes to Bill, and Charley had a bad feeling over it.

The feeling was confirmed when Bill finished reading the letter back in camp. He held it between his graceful fingers like a butterfly's wing, the wind toying with it.

"You should have told me, Charley."

"Told you what, Bill?"

"About that Blue feller."

"What about him?"

Charley had that sinking feeling like he'd swallowed putrid meat.

"Who he was . . ." Bill said.

"Who is he?"

Bill shook his head, his hair falling about his face in such a sad, sad way, Charley thought. Bill looked a lot like what Charley imagined Jesus looked like, and it

was as if it *was* Jesus sitting across from him instead
of Bill—Bill/Jesus admonishing him with an accusing
look of betrayal in those sad, sad eyes.

Tapping a forefinger on Agnes's blue cursive, Bill
said, "Pinkerton's sent him to protect me. Alice hired
'em . . . Said you went along with her wishes. You
knew all this time, Charley. I'm sorely disappointed in
you . . ."

"Ah, Bill . . ."

"No. Don't try and wiggle out of it. Just admit you
knew and promise me you won't ever pull nothing
like this again."

"I was just—"

Bill cut him off with a wave of his hand.

"I don't doubt your intentions were well placed, as
were those of my darling wife. But it is a hell of a
thing for a man to learn that those he loves and trusts
conspired against him, that they think him incapable
of taking care of himself. It makes me feel old and
foolish, Charley, and I won't be made to feel such. Go
find that feller for me and bring him to camp."

Charley found Teddy eating breakfast in the American Café.

"I've got bad news," he said. "Bill wants to see you."

"He found out, didn't he?"

Charley nodded. For once he was all run out of
words.

Bill was bent low, his face near the paper on which he
was writing Agnes a letter. He seemed to Teddy a study
of a man who could have been almost anything—a

banker, lawyer, statesman. He was dressed in his usual fine attire and his hair was golden red under the morning sun.

Teddy and Charley stood there until Bill finished then looked up.

"Boys, you done me a wrongful thing trying to do me a rightful one. I'll forgive you this time because maybe you saved my sorry hide. I just wrote my Agnes a letter stating the same."

Charley coughed nervously and Bill rested his gaze on him for a moment before shifting it to Teddy. Teddy held his stare.

"You were a good pard, old son," Bill said, "as far as it went. But this is the end of the trail for you and me. Charley and me are going to Deadwood today and you'll be staying behind. Somebody wants to corral Wild Bill, they'll just have to try. I don't need a Pinkerton man changing my diaper. No offense, but I'd feel mighty put out if I was to see you strolling the streets of Deadwood."

Teddy thought to argue his case, or rather that of Bill's wife, Agnes. He had come to like Wild Bill. Like and admire him. He understood in that moment, as those sad eyes stared into his, that no man can alter another's destiny, no matter how hard they try or think they can.

If Bill were going to live, it would be through the grace of a greater power than his own, or that of his darling Agnes, or even Allan Pinkerton's detective agency. And if he was going to be assassinated, then such had been written in the stars a long time before any of them ever existed.

Teddy stepped forward and offered Bill his hand, and Bill shook it firmly, and the understanding between them was complete.

"What you going to do now, old son?" Charley said to Teddy as Bill went off toward the woods.

"Go back to Chicago, I guess. File my last report."

"After that?"

Teddy shrugged. "I was thinking about New Mexico."

"I'd sorta like to go there myself after Bill and me make our fortunes in Deadwood."

"I thought you wanted to go to Alaska?"

"Too cold, too far away from my wife and daughters."

Teddy watched Bill there in the distance, walking to the trees, proud and tall and seemingly unfazed by anything that had happened in the previous days.

"It would be a great shame if he doesn't live to be a very old man," Teddy said.

"I don't think he'd want it that way," Charley replied.

"Why not?"

"Bill could never stand not being what he once was."

Teddy saw Bill enter the trees, and then he was gone.

Chapter 30

———◆———

Agnes Darling, if fate decides we should never see each other again, if some greater hand should put me under, I will use my last breath to whisper your name. And whisper it still as I try and swim to the other shore.

> *Yr. Loving husband, J.B. Hickok*
> *— Wild Bill—*
> *August 1, 1876*

It was a hot day, even for the Gulch. Charley had commented on the weather: "It never got this hot in August in Colorado. This heat will make a man gamy as a badger."

Bill favored the warm weather because his rheumatism had gotten worse in the last few years and the heat made him feel generally better.

"I'm going to go down to play some cards," Bill said. "I feel lucky today."

Bill had purchased himself a new Prince Albert coat

and now shrugged it on and said, "How do I look, old son?"

"Like you was the prince that coat was made for."

"Prince of the Pistoleers," Bill said mockingly.

It was just past the noon hour when Bill entered the cool interior of Nutall and Mann's Number 10. Bill was glad to be out of the sun's bright glare, and removed his dark spectacles and slipped them into an inside pocket. Harry Young was behind the bar. Like everyone else, he saw his future in Deadwood, and Bill shook hands with him and ordered a cocktail.

"I feel lucky today," Bill said.

"That's a fine coat you have on, Bill." Harry examined the satin trim along the coat's lapels.

"It's like the one I got married in. Only I wore a hole in the sleeve of that one."

Carl Mann, one of the owners of the saloon, sat at a table playing poker with Charlie Rich and William Massie—an old riverboat captain. Bill knew all three. Carl waved Bill over to join them, which Bill was more than happy to do.

"Charlie, you wouldn't mind, I'd like to sit on that stool," Bill said. Charlie held the stool that kept his back to the wall, something Bill favored.

"Take the empty one," Charlie said. "Nobody's going to assassinate you in this place."

Bill didn't care for it much but took the seat because he had a good feeling in him that he'd win big at cards today. From where he sat, he had a good view of the front door; he could see whoever came and went, and so did not feel his usual caution.

"I feel lucky, boys," Bill said. "Deal them picture cards."

Several hands later, Bill was cleaned out.

Bill called to Harry Young behind the bar, "Bring me some pocket checks, Harry."

Harry brought Bill fifteen dollars worth of checks.

"Luck's gone cold on you as a whore's heart, Bill," Harry said teasingly.

"Like old love," Bill said, "gone but not forgotten and soon will return."

The front door opened and a smallish nondescript man entered and went to the far end of the bar just a few steps from the table. Bill took notice of him, then washed him out of his mind, because the first three cards Captain Massie dealt him were aces.

"You broke me on that last hand, old son . . ." Bill started to say to the Captain.

Perhaps a split second of recognition fell into Bill's consciousness—the shadow of someone suddenly behind him, the touch of cold metal brushing against his hair, the warm breath of another against his neck.

Death struck sudden as a lightning bolt is sudden— a flash, a crash, then silence.

Bill's head jerked forward, his limbs stiffened, his fingers locked. And for what seemed like long seconds nothing but the acrid smoke and the confused looks of the others permeated the room. A hole below Bill's right cheek leaked blood. It was as though they were observing a painting—*Still Life in Death*.

Then the Prince of Pistoleers fell back and toppled

sideways to the floor. No words of wisdom from his petulant lips did any of them hear; no grunt, nor groan, nor curse—not even his wife's name did he speak.

Bill was dead.

It was only later that Harry Young, mopping up the bloody floor, saw the cards spilled from Bill's fingers— a winning hand of aces and eights.

Bill's luck had changed again, from bad to good— too late, too late.

There was a knock at the front door, and Teddy laid aside his *Shakespeare* to answer it. All the furniture in the house stood under dust covers except for the bed where Teddy slept, the dining room table, and the sofa and chair in the parlor where he read. That was the way she'd left it—his libertine mother and her English poet lover—and that's the way it would remain as far as he was concerned.

He opened the door to find George Bangs standing there.

"May I come in?"

Teddy led him into the parlor. George looked around with either a look of amusement or bemusement on his face—it was hard to tell.

"I can see now why you chose not to take another case for us," he said. "Surrounded by luxury, why would you ever want to work for common wages?"

"This house is still my mother's," Teddy said. "I'm only living in it while she's off to Europe."

The windows were open and a gentle warm breeze came in from the lake.

Teddy led George into the parlor.

"Can I get you something to drink?"

George waved his hand. "Allan doesn't like for his employees to partake of hard spirits."

Teddy indicated the sofa, and George sat on it. Teddy sat in his chair by the window with its tall panes of leaded glass.

"Don't tell me you were just in the neighborhood and decided to drop in," Teddy said.

"No, actually, I didn't know if you'd seen this," George said, taking a copy of the *Inter-Ocean* newspaper from under his arm and handing it across to Teddy.

Teddy began reading the article at the newspaper's fold, but the words did not resonate until:

... in a handsome coffin covered with black cloth and richly mounted with silver ornaments, lay Wild Bill, a picture of perfect repose. His long chestnut hair, evenly parted over his marble brow, hung in waving ringlets over the broad shoulders; his face was cleanly shaved excepting the drooping moustache, which shaded a mouth in death that almost seemed to smile, but which in life was unusually grave; the arms were folded over the still breast, which enclosed a heart which had beat with regular pulsations amid the most startling scenes of blood and violence. The corpse was clad in a complete dress suit of black broadcloth, new underclothing and white linen shirt; beside him in the coffin lay his trusty rifle, which the deceased prized

above all other things, and which was to be
buried with him in compliance with an often expressed desire.

Teddy looked up.
"Some things can't be helped," George said.
"I think he knew."
"That he was going to be killed?"
"That it didn't matter any longer to him."
"Hell of a way to end such a glorified career."

Teddy shook his head, looked out at the bright, late
autumn day, at the chestnuts lining both sides of
Lakeshore Drive, at the children playing in the park
across the street. Life went on no matter what, the
world hardly paused to take a breath, and all men
were equal in death. He knew, like the days themselves, that all would soon come to an end, that
there'd be a change of seasons.

"Break the rules once and have a drink with me,
George, and let me tell you about Wild Bill and Colorado Charley Utter and all the rest . . ."

"There's something else I have to tell you, Teddy."

"Well, it's a days for news. What is it?"

"We found your brother's killer."

Teddy shook his head. It had been what he wanted.
It was why he became a Pinkerton. But now that the
information was so close, he felt that his ride wasn't
at its conclusion, but at its beginning.